Read On . . . Horror Fiction

Read On ... Horror Fiction

June Michele Pulliam and Anthony J. Fonseca

Read On Series

A Member of the Greenwood Publishing Group

Westport, Connecticut • London

Library of Congress Cataloging-in-Publication Data

Pulliam, June Michele.
  Read on—horror fiction / by June Michele Pulliam and Anthony J. Fonseca.
    p. cm. — (Read on series)
  Includes bibliographical references and indexes.
  ISBN 1-59158-176-1 (pbk. : alk. paper)
  1. Fiction in libraries—United States. 2. Horror fiction, American—Bibliography.
  3. Horror fiction—Bibliography. 4. Readers' advisory services—United States.
  5. Public libraries—United States—Book lists. I. Fonseca, Anthony J. II. Title.
  III. Series.
  Z711.5.P85 2006
  025.2′780883—dc22   2006012719

British Library Cataloguing in Publication Data is available.

Copyright © 2006 by Libraries Unlimited

All rights reserved. No portion of this book may be
reproduced, by any process or technique, without the
express written consent of the publisher. An exception
is made for nonprofit materials used for educational
purposes within the organization.

Library of Congress Catalog Card Number: 2006012719
ISBN: 1-59158-176-1

First published in 2006

Libraries Unlimited, 88 Post Road West, Westport, CT 06881
A Member of the Greenwood Publishing Group, Inc.
www.lu.com

Printed in the United States of America

The paper used in this book complies with the
Permanent Paper Standard issued by the National
Information Standards Organization (Z39.48–1984).

10 9 8 7 6 5 4 3 2 1

*To Eddie Puss (1986–2005),
who patiently loved us all.*

Contents

Acknowledgments xi
Introduction xiii

Chapter 1—Story 1
  Plot Types 2
    The Plot Thickens: Complex Plots 2
    Let's Twist Again: Plot Twists, Turnabouts, and Inversions 5
    I Myself Am Hell: The Monster in the Mirror 8
    He Said, She Said, It Said: Adaptations and Alternate Fictions . . . 10
    You Don't See *That* Every Day: Unique Storylines 13
  Endings 15
    The Big Bang: Stories with Intense Climactic Endings 16
    We're Doomed! Doooooomed!: Dark, Foreboding Endings 18
    Uh, What Just Happened?: Ambiguous Endings 20
    I Just Couldn't Put It Down: Sweet Dreams 22

Chapter 2—Mood and Atmosphere 27
  I'm in the Mood For 27
    Side-Splitting Maniacs and Demons That Like to Raise
      Hell: Comic Horror 27
    Ewww, That's Gross. Read It Again!: The Gory Story 30
    I'm Too Sexy for My Fangs: Erotic Horror 33
    Mind Benders: Intellectual Horror 36
  Fear Factors 38
    A Dark and Stormy Night: Haunting and Atmospheric 39
    I Think I Hear Something: Disturbing Reads 42
    Hey, Let's Poke It with a Stick: Morbidly Fascinating 44
    Bring out Your Dead: Gruesome and Disgusting 46
    What's the Matter? Scared of Something?: The Truly Terrifying 49
  Horror for All Occasions 51
    Is That Michael Myers at the Window?: Halloween Horror 52
    Death Takes a Holiday: Horror About Other Holidays 54
    Home Alone Meets *Scream*: He Knows When You're Alone 56
    Uh, It's Just the Wind, Right?: The Horror of Uncertainty 57
    Trains, Planes, and Automobiles: Travel Horror 59

Chapter 3—Setting 63
   Places, Everyone 63
      Home Is Where the Horror Is: Haunted Houses 63
      That's Probably Where They'll Bury Me: Small Town Horror 66
      Middle Class Mania: Suburban Scares 69
      Graffiti and Gore: Bright Lights, Big City 71
      The Woods Are Lovely, Dark, and Deep: Wilderness
         Adventures, Horror Style 72
      The Well-Traveled Victim: Horror in Exotic Locales 75
      Way, Way Out: Other Worlds, Alternate Universes 77
   Timing Is Everything 80
      The Way Back Machine: Historical Horror 80
      Coming Soon to a Nightmare Near You: Future Shocks 83

Chapter 4—Character 85
   Ah! The Humanity! 85
      Innocent—and Not-So-Innocent—Bystanders: Monster
         Makers and Unwilling Victims 86
      I Need a Hero: Psychic Detectives, Monster Killers, and
         Vampire Hunters 89
      Hey, You Look Much Smaller on TV: Historical and
         Famous Characters 90
   The Ghouls All Came from Their Humble Abodes: Monsters
      and Maniacs 92
      They're Creepy and They're Spooky: Our Favorite Monsters 92
      With Humans Like These, Who Needs the Supernatural?:
         Maniacs and Sociopaths 95

Chapter 5—Language 99
   Description 99
      You Can Almost Taste the Blood: Lush, Vivid Detail 99
      Say What You Mean to Say: Spare and Austere Language 102
      Think Before You Speak, and After: Reflective Horror 104
   Dialogue 107
      All You Do Is Talk Talk Talk: Lots of Interactive Dialogue 107
      Giving as Good as They Get: Witty Repartee 109
      Get This Down: First-Person Confessional 112
   Pacing 114
      Slam, Bam, Thank You Ma'am: Fast-Paced,
         Action-Packed Language 115
      Slow Agonies: Pensive, Plodding Stories 117

Appendix A: Horror on Film 121
    Books Made into Films 123
        Classics. 123
        Modern Classics. 125
        Remakes. 127
        Slasher Films 127
        Mainstream Horror. 128
        Cult Classics. 130
    Original (and Influential) Stories 131
        Classics. 131
        Modern Classics. 132
        Remakes. 135
        Slasher Films 135
        Mainstream Horror. 136
        Cult Classics. 138

Appendix B: Series Titles. 141

Appendix C: Genreblends 157
    Christian Fiction. 157
    Classics. 157
    Detective Fiction 158
    Fantasy 159
    Historical 160
    Mainstream/Literary. 161
    Medical Thriller 162
    Romance. 163
    Science Fiction 163
    Splatterpunk 164
    Young Adult. 165

    Index. 167

Acknowledgments

We would like to thank Clark at Highland Coffees, who never kicked us out for sitting with our laptops for hours in his best chairs. We would also like to thank our editor, Barbara Ittner, for her kind midwifery of this manuscript. And remember, they're coming to get you, Barbara . . .

Introduction

So You Like Being Scared?
The Popularity of Horror

In the last decades of the twentieth century, horror fiction has enjoyed a renaissance with readers. Stephen King, Dean Koontz, and Anne Rice on this side of the Atlantic, and Ramsey Campbell in England, as well as other horror fiction authors, have become household names. This is rightfully so, for these writers have beaten the odds again and again, turning out best seller after best seller.

However, this presents a problem for the horror reader. Most bookstores will stock novels by the aforementioned authors, and just about every library will stock multiple copies of the latest big money makers put out by these authors. But what does a reader do once he or she has read all the King, Koontz, Rice, and Campbell? A few Web sites exist solely to point horror fans in the right direction when they're looking for reading material by lesser known authors and smaller publishing houses, but these sites are not known to all readers of the horror genre. What this means is that readers often must rely on word of mouth or on the chance encounter with an Internet review to find something interesting to read.

This book is our humble attempt at helping to alleviate this problem, at aiding horror fans when they are looking for something good to read. Written by two people who read, write about, and review horror, it includes eclectic selections of horror for all tastes, moods, and occasions. When selecting material for this guide, we didn't stop at the few writers who are not embarrassed to be thought of as horror writers, or with the few publishers dedicated exclusively to horror. Instead, we included material from different genres and historical periods. The result is a guide that classifies and describes some of our favorite books in the hopes that readers can browse the categories and find something that interests them.

And there are a lot of horror readers out there, if statistics are any indication. According to *American Demographics Magazine* (July 1989), in 1987 there were approximately 1.2 million buyers of books about the supernatural and occult fiction. *American Demographics* predicted approximately the same number of buyers for the year 2010. Stephen King's sales figures alone are remarkable: He is the best-selling writer on Earth, and as of 1996 he had sold more than

100 million books. It is not uncommon for Stephen King to have two books on best-seller lists simultaneously, both the hardcover and paperback lists. He had top five books in both 2002 and 2003, according to *USA Today*. And according to *Book Publishing Report*, in 2005 one of his books was among amazon.com's top 500 sellers—six months before its release. In September 2005 *Books in Print* listed some 1,400 horror fiction titles published in the last year, while *Amazon* listed over 1,600 for the same time period. Many of these also fall under the broader categories of paranormal and speculative fiction, while some cross over into mainstream fiction.

And you may find it surprising to know who exactly is reading these books. In *Publishers Weekly* (September 20, 1993), Robert K. J. Killheffer noted that a 1988 Gallup organization study showed that there were at least two dominant segments in the horror audience: young males and older educated females. In his introduction to *Foundations of Fear* (1992), David G. Hartwell wrote that this same Gallup poll indicated that the teenaged readership for horror is almost exclusively male, but that much of the most popular horror is read by women. He noted that 60 percent of the adult audience is female, namely women in their thirties and forties. The fact is, horror fiction has been popular with all types of readers for centuries, and it will likely remain popular for centuries to come. Why? To describe the appeal of horror fiction in a few lines would be impossible and unfair. The features that readers enjoy about this genre are as varied as the readers themselves. However, it can be said with relative certainty that the appeals of tales of horror, although distinct, correspond to the appeals of all stories.

When the Haunted House Looks Like the Fun House: The Horror Fan

In his study of the horror genre, *Danse Macabre* (1980), Stephen King tells of sitting in an audience of young adults watching the sci-fi horror classic *Earth vs. The Flying Saucers*. During the film, the theater manager interrupted with an announcement that the Russians had launched *Sputnik*. This sudden terrifying intrusion of real world apocalyptic fears into the world of dark fantasy made a powerful impression on King—as it did on everyone in that theater audience (according to King). While it is an oversimplification to say that the overall purpose of horror fiction is to induce some level of fear in the reader, there is a good bit of truth to that statement. Horror fans generally want to be shocked, haunted, terrified, grossed out—or at least challenged. The subgenres of horror fiction—ghost stories, vampire tales, splatterpunk novels, dark fantasy crossovers—speak to those differing tastes and are a good way to give readers access to the qualities they enjoy in horror fiction. Our previous guide, *Hooked on Horror* (2d ed.), categorized horror into subgenres based on these diverse tastes, as have other guides to the genre. However, there are other literary elements that can help us gain insight into what readers enjoy about certain books. These are their "appeal features," as identified by Joyce Saricks, in *Readers' Advisory Service in the Public Library*, now in its third edition (2005), and elaborated upon and illustrated by Nancy Pearl in *Now Read This* and *Now Read This II* (1999 and 2002 respectively).

The idea behind this approach is that many readers prefer certain styles of storytelling over others or respond to different aspects of a story. Some readers relate to the characters of the story, some might respond to evocative settings, and some are stimulated by the voice of the writer or the language used to tell the story. Still others simply enjoy the way a plot unfolds. In addition to these appeal features, a reader's mood may affect reading choices as well as how much he or she enjoys a particular book. And there are all those subcategories based on quirky trends and interests that just don't fit any major genre schema—quick reads, books to travel with, confessionals—the list goes on.

This guide, then, is an attempt to apply categories, based on appeal features, to many popular horror titles published or reissued within the last decade, as well as some classics and benchmark titles. Four sections correspond to these features—story, setting, character, and language—and a fifth section focuses on mood. Because the evolution of the horror genre has been profoundly affected by the film industry, we offer Appendix A, which lists some of the benchmark horror films.

Series fiction, immensely popular with some readers, is included throughout, with complete lists of those series and their titles included in Appendix B. Titles that cross genres—for example, romance and horror—are included in Appendix C. The lists within each chapter are not of the usual ilk found in a literature reference. They do not use the common terms and phrases that can be found in the library catalog, or in indexes for that matter. Instead, they group titles together in other ways that correspond to what readers seek—stories with plot twists or dramatic endings, gory stories, comic horror, horror in the wilderness, novels with the scariest monsters, and fiction for such occasions as Halloween and Valentine's Day.

These lists are meant to provide readers and readers' advisors with some new ways to find enjoyable reading material, and they are meant to provide content for reading lists that libraries may wish to distribute or disseminate, whether in their newsletters, on Web sites, or in printed flyers. To that particular end, the guide can be consulted by readers' advisors as a quick reference. It can also be browsed by those who wish to familiarize themselves with the nuances of the genre, and it can be used as a reading checklist, or an idea guide for displays. Ultimately, in whatever way it is used, we hope that it contributes to the overall reading pleasure of those readers who, like us, really enjoy a good horror story.

Books that have received prizes are indicated by the following icons on the entries:

🎗 International Horror Guild winner

🎗 International Literary Guild winner

🎗 Bram Stoker winner

🎗 Pulitzer Prize winner

Young adult crossover books are indicated with the following icon: **YA**.

Each Reader His or Her Own Monster: Who This Book Is Aimed at, and What It Contains

We end on the following note: This guide is intended for *all* of horror's diverse adult readers, whether they are dedicated fans or occasional readers; and whether they read for the emotional, psychological, or intellectual content. We categorize a vast number of horror titles into lists based on various appeals, including timeliness. Because today's readers have a preference for all things new, our focus is on recent releases. For the most part, however, we exclude young adult horror, for practical reasons. Simply put, including YA horror would have doubled the size of this guide.

Despite limitations such as these, we feel we have provided a helpful guide for *all* fans of the genre. Our hope is that readers who enjoy atmospheric horror will be able to whittle their reading list down a bit by looking at our choices in the mood and atmosphere chapter, while fans of cool-as-a-cucumber maniacs like Hannibal Lecter will find much to their liking in the character chapter. Keep in mind that the intent of this guide is not to scientifically categorize titles but to provide guidance through various lists of books that share certain characteristics. Thus, the book is selective, not comprehensive, and the reading lists are selective and subjective, as any given novel or collection could rightfully be placed in any one of the chapters.

June Michele Pulliam
jpullia@lsu.edu
Anthony J. Fonseca
tony.fonseca@nicholls.edu

References

Fonseca, Anthony J., and June Michele Pulliam. 2002. *Hooked on Horror: A Guide to Reading Interests in Horror Fiction.* 2d ed. Libraries Unlimited.

Hartwell, David G. 1992. *Foundations of Fear.* Tom Doherty.

Killheffer, Robert K. J. 1993. "Rising from the Grave." *Publishers Weekly* 240, no. 38 (September 20): 43–47.

King, Stephen. 1983. *Stephen King's Danse Macabre.* Berkley.

Pearl, Nancy. 1999. *Now Read This: A Guide to Mainstream Fiction, 1978–1998.* Libraries Unlimited.

———. 2002. *Now Read This II: A Guide to Mainstream Fiction, 1990–2001.* Libraries Unlimited.

Piirto, Rebecca. 1989. "I Love a Good Story." *American Demographics* 11, no. 7 (July): 36–39, 54–55.

Saricks, Joyce. 2005. *Readers' Advisory Service in the Public Library.* 3d ed. ALA Editions.

"Stephen King." 1998. *Encyclopedia of World Biography.* 2d ed. Gale Research.

"Stephen King's Pulp Novel a Likely Windfall for Dorchester." 2005. *Book Publishing Report* 30, no. 10 (March 14): 4.

"Top Best Sellers." 2002. *USA Today,* March 27, D-1.

"Top Best Sellers." 2003. *USA Today,* March 26, D-1.

Chapter 1
Story

Readers often enjoy a particular type of storyline, whether it be the rescue by a handsome young man seen in so much romance fiction, or the scenario of the local boy making the final shot and winning the big game familiar to fans of sports fiction. Horror fans are no exception, so listed in this chapter are works in which the plot or storyline is central, to better help readers find just the right books that follow the patterns they enjoy. Some readers like convoluted sagas, complete with self-contained universes, while others prefer horror that comes from the inside and demonstrates that people can be their own worst enemies and even become the monsters they fear. Still others like the familiar—with a twist—those adaptations that retell an old, established story.

Readers more concerned with the journey's end than the journey itself will also find titles here categorized according to their endings. Some stories leave the reader with a sense of closure, while others leave lots of room for interpretation because of their ambiguous endings. Since this is a guide to horror fiction, keep in mind that most of these novels and stories won't end in a warm and fuzzy, life-affirming way. After all, each story must terminate in keeping with the basic laws of what happens when monsters are introduced into the everyday world. Therefore some novels culminate with intense, violent scenes (like those in action films) in which the monster is vanquished or subdued, while some finish in apocalyptic visions, with the world gravely changed, whether or not the monster is killed or subdued.

Plot Types

The Plot Thickens: Complex Plots

Few things are as engrossing as a novel with a huge cast of characters who wind their way through multiple, simultaneous storylines, their fates ultimately converging dramatically. Readers who enjoyed Stephen King's *The Stand*, an epic battle of good versus evil in the desert, will enjoy the titles here that are lengthy, filled with diverse characters, and sometimes epic in scope. And if you just *hate* it when you finally get to that last page and discover that you must now rejoin reality and leave the world created by the author, fear not. Many of these works are part of a series.

Barker, Clive.
Galilee: A Romance. New York: HarperCollins, 1998. 582pp.
>What? A romance? A family saga? Think in terms of the greatest of all gothic romances, *Wuthering Heights*. Galilee, the son of Cesaria (for whom Thomas Jefferson erected a monument), falls in love with a Caucasian woman, causing a rift between a wealthy, white, privileged family and an ancient black family that has literally been around since the time of Adam.

Bergstrom, Elaine.
Shattered Glass. The Austra Family series. New York: Jove, 1989 (reissued 1994). 372pp.
>This is the first volume in a complex series about an old European family with a little vampirism hidden in its closet (told from multiple points of view), which spans centuries but holds together well. The story begins when artist Helen Wells, stricken with polio, becomes infatuated with her handsome but strange new neighbor, Stephen, who is renovating stained glass in the local church. After Stephen takes Helen under his wing, bodies begin turning up in the city. As the series progresses, the reader meets various members of the Austra clan as they move from Austria to the United States and Canada. Finally the story reveals that the blood line runs back to one of the most infamous European nobles. Other titles in the series are *Blood Alone, Blood Rites, Daughter of the Night,* and *Nocturne*.

Borchardt, Alice.
The Silver Wolf. Legend of the Wolves series. New York: Ballantine, 1998. 451pp.
>This series is a veritable one-stop shop for fantasy, romance, horror, action-adventure, political intrigue, and history. It opens in this first volume in ancient Rome, where a young female werewolf is being forced into an arranged marriage. Enter a loner, a fellow lycanthrope, who will change her

life. The series then moves to Gaul and finally eighth-century Italy. If you like Anne Rice, you will enjoy Borchardt. Other titles in the series include *Night of the Wolf* and *The Wolf King*.

Boyd, Donna.
The Passion. The Devoncroix Dynasty series. New York: Avon Books, 1998. 387pp.

Alexander Devoncroix, a multi-millionaire werewolf and a pack leader, narrates this convoluted tale of lycanthrope history, ranging from nineteenth-century Siberia and France to twentieth-century America, where the pack becomes part of the market-driven economy and begins running billion-dollar corporations. When the family diary is found, the reader learns of the early history of lycanthropes in Europe and of their uneasy truce with humans. The second book in the series is *The Promise*.

Clark, Simon.
Vampyrrhic. London: New English Library, 1998. 441pp.

Some people truly are holier-than-thou. An influential family is blessed by the god Thor, who fathers a half-divine lineage. Now Thor wants payback, and he gives the family's patriarch an army of undead Viking warriors to defeat Christianity. Being human and none too keen about this battle of good versus evil stuff, the father flees to England, army in tow, and now he must control undead warriors living in the sewers and caves.

Due, Tananarive.
The Between. New York: HarperCollins, 1995. 274pp.

Hilton, a dedicated social worker, and his wife, the first African American judge in Dade County, are receiving threatening hate mail. This leads to weird dreams that convince Hilton he may not really be alive, and that in fact reality is not what it seems. This novel by the freshest new female voice in the genre is disturbing and highly original, with emphasis on character development.

Farren, Mick.
Underland. The Victor Renquist Novels. New York: Tor, 2002. 448pp.

Problems. Problems. That's all undead vampire clan leader Victor Renquist has. If it isn't controlling his brood every seven years during "the time of feasting," then it's dealing with challenges to his authority, or fighting off Cthulhu worshippers, or stopping an archeologist from turning himself into a powerful wizard. Victor's life is full of violence, sex, and melodrama, but all he wants is to retire. This is Farren's most recent title in the Renquist series. Other titles include *The Time of Feasting*, *Dark Lost*, and *More Than Mortal*.

King, Stephen.
The Stand. Garden City, NJ: Doubleday, 1978. 823pp.

    Whoops, shouldn't have pressed the "any" key! A nanosecond of computer error in a Defense Department laboratory ends the world as we know it, causing the demise of 99 percent of the earth's population. The survivors choose to be allied with either the good Mother Abigail, a frail 108-year-old woman, or the evil Randall Flagg, a man with a lethal smile and unspeakable powers.

Laidlaw, Marc.
🎗 *The 37th Mandala.* New York: St. Martin's, 1996. 352pp.

    Derek Crowe, a hack, writes the best-selling *The Mandala Rites*, a New Age book based on mandalas connected to Cambodia's killing fields. While Crowe believes the mandalas are comforting angels, they're really dangerous beings who feed on human suffering. Will Crowe's artistic license be revoked now that a reader has followed his directions and become possessed? A compelling, complex, and original novel that combines Lovecraftian horror with Eastern mysticism and New Age chicanery.

McCammon, Robert R.
🎗 *Swan Song.* New York: Pocket Books, 1996. 956pp.

    Scientists claim that Nuclear Winter is the most severe aftereffect of a nuclear war, but in this epic, the real threat is the spread of evil by "the man with the scarlet eye." The forces of good struggle to prevent his taking over the earth in this post-apocalyptic, nuclear holocaust novel. A ragtag bunch of survivors must protect the savior known as Swan, a young, vulnerable girl.

Scotch, Cheri.
The Werewolf's Kiss. Hunter's Moon series. New York: Berkley, 1992. 262pp.

    This is the first volume in a historical series in which Sylvie Marley leads a debutante's life on the bayous of Louisiana, until she meets Lucien Drago, a mysterious stranger from New Orleans. Drago is no ordinary tall, dark stranger. Like Sylvie, he is drawn to the moon, for he is a werewolf, and he knows the secrets of Sylvie's ancestry. Unfortunately, so does a local voodoo priest, who wants to use Sylvie. Other titles in the series are *Werewolf's Touch* and *The Werewolf's Sin*.

Simmons, Dan.
🎗 *Carrion Comfort.* New York: Warner, 1989. 884pp.

    In this convoluted, thought-provoking, and menacing story, elderly mind-control vampires dictate human history by feeding on and magnifying the violence inherent in humans. A Philadelphia police officer, a young African American woman who is the daughter of a recent victim, and a Jewish survivor of the Nazi concentration camps hold the key to stopping World War III.

Straub, Peter.
Floating Dragon. New York: Penguin, 1983. 515pp.

Think seeing dead people is scary? Try having visions of people who are soon to die—in the most stomach-churning ways possible. Nearly no element of horror is left out in this tour de force of reincarnation, occultism, techno-horror, and splatterpunk, in which a horrifying, gory accident in a chemical lab releases a flesh-eating cloud of gas and leads to the resurrection of an evil force that delights in mutilating an entire New England town.

Let's Twist Again:
Plot Twists, Turnabouts, and Inversions

Readers who enjoy the complex plots of the novels in the previous section will also like the selections here. They too feature complex storylines but differ significantly, as these tales are often difficult to predict for even the most dedicated reader of horror. In addition, these selections, while not exactly brief, are a bit shorter and offer the reader some surprises (and, no, we won't spoil the fun by telling you ahead of time).

Cook, Robin.
Coma. Boston: Little, Brown, 1977. 280pp.

A medical student suspects foul play when she investigates why young patients are in comas. Her investigation takes her into the hellish bowels of hospital administration, a place from which she herself may not escape to share her story. Cook, a physician, is credited with introducing the medical thriller genre with *Coma*, and readers particularly enjoy the way he makes medical terminology comprehensible and interesting to laypeople.

Ford, Steven.
Mortality. New York: Penguin-Berkley, 2003. 448pp.

Just can't find that vampire who will make you immortal? How about a fountain of youth? Dr. Paul Tobin, a cosmetic surgeon and recovering alcoholic, becomes the newest member of his ex brother-in-law's Florida Clinic, which possesses what it believes to be a fountain of youth cocktail. However, rather than finding a cure for aging there, Paul begins to suspect there is something wrong when patients start to die of old age.

Harwood, John.
The Ghost Writer. San Diego: Harcourt Trade, 2004. 384pp.

Ten-year-old Gerard Freeman sneaks into his mother's room and unlocks a secret drawer, finding a picture of a woman he has never seen before, along with a story of murder. Now an adult and a librarian, Gerard corresponds with an English pen pal, Alice Jessel, who lives in an institution. Her description of the grounds begins to sound eerily familiar, like something he had read as a ten-year-old . . . .

King, Stephen.
The Dead Zone. New York: Viking, 1979. 426pp.

If you knew someone was capable of great evil, would you terminate that person? A small-town schoolteacher falls into a lengthy coma after a car accident; after waking nearly a decade later, he has the ability to see briefly into a person's future. He sees a charismatic politician who will ultimately destroy the world as president. Follow his attempts to change history through various turns, arriving at a surprising, thought-provoking ending.

Koontz, Dean.
The House of Thunder. New York: Berkley, 1992. 252pp.

Some ghosts return for revenge, and some to finish off old business. Susan Thornton awakens from an accident-induced coma to find herself in the same hospital with the four men who murdered her boyfriend. The only problem is that these four men supposedly died violent deaths years before. Now it seems that they want to finish off the witness who got away the first time. Filled with plot twists and truly eerie moments.

Koontz, Dean.
Shadow Fires. New York: Berkley, 1990. 509pp.

When people are in a bad marriage, sometimes all they want is out. That's all Rachel Leben wanted, but she was thinking divorce, not widowhood. Her intentions don't matter, though, because her billionaire husband Eric is so embittered that he ultimately returns from the dead for revenge. And he's not the only one who wants Rachel dead. Suspenseful and action-oriented, with a myriad of plot twists. If you pick this one up, be prepared to finish it.

Lortz, Richard.
Lovers Living, Lovers Dead. New York: Putnam, 1977. 223pp.

Everyone has secrets, but when a literature professor suspects his young wife is hiding something dark, he takes an unconventional route to uncovering it. Teaming up with her psychologist, he uses deception to investigate his wife's relationship with her mysterious father. What he ultimately uncovers is millions in Swiss bank accounts and some unsavory activities that lead to the depths of darkness. This is ranked one of the top 40 horror novels of all time by the Horror Writers Association of America.

Priest, Jack.
Night Witch. Medford, OR: Bootleg Press, 2003. 340pp.

    This cat burglar better have nine lives. He breaks into a home containing many valuables and is overcome by the feeling that if he takes anything, a terrifying fate awaits him. He quickly leaves, but on his way out he foolishly pockets a locket for his daughter. The curio puts both their lives in danger, because it contains a powerful potion, and its secretive and mysterious owner wants it back.

Rice, Anne.
The Tale of the Body Thief. New York: Knopf, 1992. 430pp.

    Unimpressed with being undead, Lestat jumps at a chance to switch bodies with David Talbot. But David doesn't keep his word; he has no intention of this arrangement being temporary, as he had promised. Poor Lestat! While he is able to once again enjoy the pleasures of being mortal, he is also reminded that the flesh is indeed weak, for it can be damaged and destroyed. This is the fourth novel in Rice's <u>Vampire Chronicles</u>, after *Interview with the Vampire*, *The Vampire Lestat*, and *Queen of the Damned*.

Saul, John.
Black Lightning. New York: Fawcett Crest, 1996. 438pp.

    Meet journalist Anne Jeffers. A tough reporter with a nose for the truth, she was instrumental in having serial killer Richard Kraven executed. But has she sent an innocent man to death? It seems his execution has not stopped the killings and mutilations of victims. Worse yet, Anne's daughter is now on the killer's list.

Saul, John.
The God Project. New York: Bantam, 1982. 340pp.

    Everyone wants the perfect child, but how far is anyone willing to go to get one? In a small New England town, preteen boys are disappearing, while infant girls are suffering a mortality rate higher than anywhere else. After two mothers lose children, they begin to uncover a plot to reengineer human DNA and produce a race of superhuman, cold-blooded maniacs. This fast-paced read will keep readers guessing until the final page.

Wright, T. M.
Laughing Man. New York: Dorchester, 2003. 320pp.

    Jack Erthmun sees dead people, and he, uh well, talks with them. This can of course be useful for a police detective working homicide. Earthmun finds himself chasing three different—and very weird—serial killers in New York City. Throw into the mix a supernaturally strong and quick maniac known as "the loon," and the result is a wild ride filled with twists and surprises.

I Myself Am Hell: The Monster in the Mirror

Not all horror is supernatural or cosmic, stories based on monsters that actually exist "out there" and menace humanity. Sometimes people are their own worst enemies. Works here include ambiguous tales in which the main character or characters believe that they are haunted (and maybe they are) and tales in which characters themselves become monsters.

Broadstone, Christopher Alan.
Puzzleman. Philadelphia: Xlibris, 2004. 411pp.

> A young sculptor despondently searches for understanding after the tragic death of her infant son. A professor of history and a beautiful French vintner still long for the love they shared during World War II. A legless man seeks escape from a horror worse than death. These lives are woven together over time in a twisted vision of eternal life.

Campbell, Ramsey.
Obsession. New York: Macmillan, 1985. 247pp.

> Be wary of ghouls bearing gifts. Four teenagers receive an ad in the mail, which says simply, "Whatever you want most, I do." Of course, their wishes are fulfilled to disastrous ends when the four respond to the ad's come-on. And 25 years later the four suddenly find themselves being pursued by a power that wants payment. A subtle, erudite study of human psychology.

Clegg, Douglas.
Purity. Baltimore: Cemetery Dance, 2000. 118pp.

> People can't help who they fall in love with. Owen Crites, son of a gardener, pines for his debutante childhood sweetheart. Now both 18, the two meet again during a summer vacation on Outerbridge Island. The only problem is that she has a preppie tennis star boyfriend. But Owen has a few evil tricks up his sleeve, in this compelling study of the dark recesses of infatuation.

Fowler, Christopher.
Spanky. London: Warner Books, 1994. 338pp.

> Be careful what you wish for, lest it come true. This old adage applies in spades to furniture salesman Martyn Ross, a mediocre man who meets Spanky, his very own personal demon—and exact twin. Spanky promises Martyn that he will help him change his dull life, but will ask for a small favor in return. Of course, Spanky never mentions that what he needs most is a human host for his demonic spirit.

Koontz, Dean.
Mr. Murder. New York: Putnam, 1993. 376pp.

Marty Stillwater, well-known writer of murder mysteries, is being stalked by Alfie, his double, a genetically engineered hit man who, unknown to Marty, was cloned from his DNA. Alfie, psychically drawn to his original, believes that Stillwater has stolen his life, and he aims to get it back.

Korn, M. F.
Rachmaninoff's Ghost. Lansdowne, PA: Silver Lake Press, 2002. 146p.

A former engineering student transfers to a small school to study music, but although he is a talented piano player, he fails his first audition. Devastated, he goes to extreme measures to improve himself, including channeling a ghost. Suddenly he can play, but he hasn't channeled merely talent; he has invoked a spirit, and it needs a warm body to inhabit—permanently.

Sabastian, Stephen.
Solomon's Brood. Frederick, MD: PublishAmerica, 2004. 135pp.

Mark Anthony Wells, an ordinary guy in an ordinary world who is on a fishing expedition on his favorite lake, stumbles upon a new realm—a desolate battlefield where mortals fight immortals, a world beyond the rules of an earthly plane. Its inhabitants include a beautiful young female soldier out to conquer evil and take down anyone she can in the process, including Mark.

Stevenson, Robert Louis.
Doctor Jekyll and Mr.Hyde and Other Stories. Ann Arbor, MI: Ann Arbor Media Group, 2004 (1886). 208pp.

Nobody has a sweeter bedside manner than the highly respected London physician, Henry Jekyll. Or is he just a time bomb? After he creates a liquid solution that turns him into the ultra-violent Mr. Edward Hyde, readers see the purely evil side of the mild-mannered doc. Now this M.D. has become MAD. This is the classic alter ego tale.

Straub, Peter.
🎗*Koko.* The Blue Rose Trilogy. New York: Dutton, 1988. 562pp.

It seems bad luck and dead bodies follow Harry wherever he goes. In this follow-up to Straub's dysfunctional family/torture story "Blue Rose," members of Harry Beevers's Vietnam platoon are being systematically murdered by a crazed killer. Eventually PI Tim Underhill enlists the aid of a reclusive genius to clear a childhood friend of murder charges. Other titles in the trilogy are *Mystery* and *The Throat*.

Wooley, John.
Awash in Blood. Tulsa, OK: Hawk Publishing, 2001. 246pp.

    Televangelist Mo Johnston travels to Romania to help Christianize the locals. Instead he finds himself converted—into a blood-sucking reverend. In denial of his demonic powers, he returns to America and spreads stories about having fended off a devil. But he finds that his vampiric powers come in handy, even helping his floundering ratings skyrocket through the roof. Will he lose his soul in his attempts to save others?

He Said, She Said, It Said: Adaptations and Alternate Fictions

Readers who love not only the classics, but also retellings, modernizations, and adaptations of a classic story will love the titles listed here. They create new tales with old characters, either by retelling the story from a different point of view, by embellishing the original story itself to complete what was left unsaid, or by emphasizing a small detail—crafting it into a new tale in and of itself. The horror story most frequently retold is Bram Stoker's 1897 novel *Dracula*, and that trend is reflected in this section in novels and tales that emphasize the erotic nature of the vampire or supply histories of minor characters.

Cavelos, Jeanne, ed.
The Many Faces of Van Helsing. New York: Penguin-Ace, 2004. 400pp.

    He has been called fanatical, vengeful, genius, mad, and heroic. He has been portrayed on screen by some of the finest actors in history. He is the man known simply as Van Helsing. This unusual collection explores Bram Stoker's character, reinventing the man who fights all evil. Some tales speculate about his formative years, when he had his first supernatural encounter.

Elrod, P. N., ed.
Dracula in London. New York: Ace, 2001. 263pp.

    Count Dracula must have been up to more than just skirt chasing during his tenure at Carfax. This collection answers the question, "What *else* was Dracula doing in London?" That's easy: He was meeting the Prince of Wales and Alistair Crowley, or helping to make every vote count in his support of the Suffragettes in the early 1900s.

Jacobs, David.
The Devil's Brood. The Universal Monsters series. New York: Berkley Boulevard, 2000. 316pp.

    Can't get enough of those old-fashioned monsters who filled your black-and-white nightmares? In this volume, Dracula's daughter, the Countess Mary Zalenska, with help from the wolfman and Dracula, attempts to resurrect the Bride of Frankenstein while fighting off a two-bit gangster. In other books in the series, the wolfman visits LaMiranda, a small swamp town in Florida; a group of Satanic scientists kidnap Zalenska, the wolfman, and Dracula; and Dracula awakens to find himself in modern-day America. The other titles in the series are *The Devil's Night*, also by Jacobs; Jeff Rovin's *Return of the Wolf Man*, and Christopher Schildt's *Night of Dracula*.

Kalogridis, Jeanne.
Lord of the Vampires. Diaries of the Family Dracul series. New York: Delacorte, 1996. 347pp.

Arkady Tepesh, great nephew of Vlad Tepes, flees his undead uncle, only to become the creature he most abhors. Arkady enlists the aid of a young Van Helsing to overcome his own blood lust. This trilogy, of which this is the last volume, is highly erotic and told from multiple points of view—and this final novel is a clever retelling of *Dracula*. Other titles in the series are *Covenant with the Vampire* and *Children of the Vampire*.

Knight, Amarantha (pseudonym of Nancy Kilpatrick).
The Darker Passions: Carmilla. The Darker Passions series. Cambridge, MA: Circlet Press, 2004. 256pp.

Each volume in this series is a sensual and erotic, sometimes pornographic, retelling of a well-known story. *Carmilla* is a sexy tale about a beautiful young woman who is visited by a hungry, otherworldly female. In other books in the series, the original narrative of Dr. Jekyll and Mr. Hyde lends itself to a no-holds-barred, lustful narrative of debauchery; Frankenstein is updated to shock modern readers with unleashed scenes of desire and sexual violence; and Dracula, to put it bluntly, is rife with S & M.

Kupfer, Allen C.
The Journal of Professor Abraham Van Helsing. New York: Doherty, 2004. 204p.

Even Van Helsing was once a young man with sexual desires, and this diary format novel gives the reader a window into his early years. The journal and the comments of various other characters, as well as the marginal notes of Dr. Daniel Kupfer, Van Helsing's good friend and the author's grandfather, create a multilayered story about Malia, a female vampire who plagues the hapless, libidinous teenaged Van Helsing.

Lucas, Tim.
The Book of Renfield: The Gospel of Dracula. New York: Simon & Schuster, 2005. 403pp.

Hey look, Renny'll eat a bug if someone pays him enough! This adaptation focuses on how Bram Stoker's famous madman, Renfield, came to change so rapidly, from being fond of the nontraditional pets he keeps in his cell to being willing to consume these animals. It also genuinely fills in voids regarding other characters, particularly John Seward and Arthur Holmwood.

Monteleone, Thomas.
🩸 ***The Blood of the Lamb.*** <u>The Blood of the Lamb series</u>. New York: Tom Dougherty, 1992. 419pp.

    In 1968 the Catholic Church made a clone of Christ. Thirty years later, the clone lives as the charismatic Father Peter Carenza, who does good works in the inner city and is unaware of his genetic heritage. After discovering his true identity on the eve of the millennium, Carenza begins traveling across the United States in a Winnebago, performing terrifying and awesome miracles. But is he Christ, or the Antichrist? The second book in this series is *The Reckoning*.

Newman, Kim.
🩸 ***Anno Dracula.*** <u>The Anno Dracula series</u>. New York: Avon, 1992. 409pp.

    Newman's story begins with this volume, in Victorian London. In the course of the trilogy readers visit the trenches of World War I in *Bloody Red Baron* and end up in 1959 Rome with *Judgment of Tears*. Along the way, Newman incorporates every known vampire myth, along with historical characters such as Queen Victoria, Vlad Tepes, Archduke Ferdinand, Orson Welles, and Edgar Allan Poe. Based on the assumption that Dracula defeated Van Helsing and his vampire hunters, turning humans into the undead and leaving the rest to serve as cattle, Newman shows a history that is altered completely.

Reaves, Michael, and John Pelan, eds.
Shadows Over Baker Street. New York: Ballantine-Del Ray, 2003. 464pp.

    "But how did you know it was Cthulhu, Holmes?" This unusual anthology collects 18 original tales in which Sherlock Holmes and other Doyle characters confront the horror created by H. P. Lovecraft in his pulp stories. When faced with an unexpurgated copy of the *Necronomicon* and ancient and violent gods and monsters, what is one to do? Elementary, my dear Watson.

Ryan, Kevin.
Van Helsing. New York: Pocket Star, 2004. 272pp.

    The screenplay for Universal Pictures's blockbuster of the same name provides the story of this journey from industrialized Europe to the wild Carpathian Mountains, where Dracula, the Wolf Man, and Frankenstein's monster threaten to topple civilization. A secret society charges one man, Van Helsing, with defeating these monstrosities.

Saberhagen, Fred.
The Vlad Tapes. <u>Vlad Tepes series</u>. New York: Simon & Schuster, 2000. 537pp.

    Although the series (of which this is the last volume) is founded on Bram Stoker's *Dracula*, it also cleverly weaves well-known characters from other works of vampire fiction into the plot. Count Dracula sets the record straight about himself and those who would destroy him, later traveling through time to find his lost love. Stories in the series are told from the point of view of multiple characters, including Sherlock Holmes, Dracula, and his hunters. There are 10 titles in the series, including *The Dracula Tape*, *A Matter of Taste*, and *A Sharpness on the Neck*.

Yarbro, Chelsea Quinn.
The Angry Angel. Sisters of the Night series. New York: William Morrow, 1998. 368pp.

Just when Jonathan Harker thought he was safe from Dracula's three vampire wives, they are resurrected in Yarbro's trilogy-in-progress, beginning with the story of Kelene of Salonica. Kelene enters young womanhood, and Count Dracula comes to her—in the form of an angel—in her dreams. In the second book, *The Soul of an Angel*, Fenice Zucchar, Dracula's second concubine, escapes an arranged marriage and becomes Dracula's eternal concubine.

You Don't See *That* Every Day: Unique Storylines

Sometimes a writer produces a text that is either so original, or so strange, that it is difficult to classify it. These particular stories are wonderful for a change of pace if a reader is a little tired of the usual fare.

Bailey, Michael.
Palindrone Hannah. Bloomington, IN: Unlimited Publishing, 2005. 332pp.

This challenging read presents five wonderful tales in one novel: (1) An evil mirror connects two worlds decades apart, causing a man to lose his sanity; (2) a truly dysfunctional relationship between a purely egotistical man and a woman who holds a gruesome secret ends in blood and gore; (3) a psychologist treats a man who is God; (4) five children exact a hideous revenge on a bully; and (5) buried deep within them all is the story of Hannah, a mysterious little girl.

Braunbeck, Gary A., and Alan M. Clark.
Escaping Purgatory: Fables in Words and Pictures. Eugene, OR: IFD Publishing, 2001. 307pp.

Meet a distraught mother, who avenges a molester's murder of her daughter with a giant demon; an aging and reformed Jack the Ripper, who is a world renowned doctor but a failure as a father; and the newly dead in a small country graveyard, as they deal with a purgatorial existence. Poetic, descriptive, masterfully developed, and psychologically accurate tales of "personal hells," these stories are destined to be classics.

Campbell, Ramsey.
The Long Lost. New York: Tor, 1996. 384pp.

On a lark, the Owains, a happily married couple, explore a deserted island, where they find an ancient crone in an abandoned cottage. Upon discovering that she is actually a long lost relative of theirs, the Owains invite her to come live with them. Immediately she demonstrates an unsettling knowledge of their darkest secrets, which makes her grow more vigorous while shattering their lives. Eerie and wonderfully original.

Clark, Simon.
Blood Crazy. New York: Leisure, 2001. 394pp. **YA**

"This book might just save your life" is the line that begins this post-apocalyptic story. If nothing else, it will help the reader get through a long day. A teenager with nothing more than Big Macs and the local bully on his mind awakens one morning into a world where gangs of adults rip apart anyone under 20. The landscape is littered with the bodies of murdered children, their remains mutilated almost beyond recognition. After reading this, you may never trust anyone over 30.

Clark, Simon.
Darker. New York: Leisure, 2002. 410pp.

A disembodied voice offers starving nebbish Richard Young the chance to have ultimate power, the chance to control an invisible force that makes others willingly die for him; and when they won't, crushes whole houses like an invisible boot from heaven. And he's not going to use it? Richard's vacation in Greece turns into just that opportunity, but it comes at a price. Now he must find a virgin to help him control his power. Enter an unsuspecting British family.

Conley, Robert J.
Brass. New York: Leisure, 1999. 310pp.

Let's see FEMA clean up this mess! Millennia ago, according to the Cherokee legend, the sons of Thunder defeated Untsaiyi, or Brass, an evil spirit with metallic skin and a fatal love of gambling, by pinning him to the floor of the sea. In the late twentieth century, an unsuspecting Army Corps of Engineers frees Brass while cleaning up a beach. Brass emerges into a strange new world, determined to win a fortune—and mutilate anyone who stands in his way.

Gray, Muriel.
Furnace. New York: Doubleday, 1997. 360pp.

Scottish television personality Muriel Gray demonstrates impressive knowledge of life on the American road and of Canadian lore in her original novels. Here a descendent of Scottish alchemists relocated to Appalachia continues making gold from lead, while others pay a horrible price. Includes wonderful descriptions of life as a truck driver.

Kilpatrick, Nancy.
Dracul: An Eternal Love Story. San Diego: Lucard Publishing, 1998. 217pp.

The historical Vlad Tepes is imprisoned in Turkey with his brother, Radu. His wife, Helene, kills herself when his enemies falsely report his death, but she is reincarnated in Mina Harker, the intended bride of a London solicitor. Can Tepes, now a vampire, win back his love? As much a romance novel as a horror tale, this story is based on the musical of the same name and is accompanied by a music CD with 19 songs (DAT Records, 1996).

McCammon, Robert R.
🏆 *Mine.* New York: Pocket Books, 1990. 487pp.

What better name for an unforgettable villain than Mary Terror? This ex-freedom fighter from the 1960s carries a grudge and lots of weapons. She steals infants, brutally murdering them when they displease her. But when she kidnaps Laura Clayborne's child, Laura will stop at nothing to get her baby back. A nonstop thriller.

Mitchell, Mary Ann.
🏆 *Drawn to the Grave.* New York: Leisure, 1997. 313pp.

After learning that he's terminally ill, Carl is unable to face his own mortality, so he searches the world for a cure. He finds one in the Amazon rainforest, but it necessitates that he periodically become intimately acquainted with a victim before stealing his or her life. All goes well until he meets his match, a woman who can't be stopped by death.

Nicholson, Scott.
Thank You for the Flowers. Boone, NC: Parkway Publishers, 2000. 190pp.

A loving husband hears the same noise off and on almost nightly. A Little League coach ruminates over the loneliness of his star shortstop, a nice but friendless vampire. A burn victim and skin graft recipient is haunted by the ghosts of his donors. A radio talk show host gets call-ins from a woman who claims to have killed her husband. These highly original and haunting tales are reminiscent of Rod Serling's creations.

Endings

Endings, whether uplifting and reassuring or downbeat and ominous, can be very satisfying to readers. A novel's conclusion can also be intense and climactic —or dark and brooding (ending "not with a bang, but a whimper"). When it comes to horror, endings follow both the laws of reality as we understand it, and the laws of the supernatural, particularly in tales that contain threatening monsters; they either depict the monster as something that can be subdued for a while (but not destroyed, of course) or show how the monster continues to affect victims after it has been neutralized. Supernatural elements aside, these endings square with the real world: Good does not always triumph over evil, and bad things sometimes happen to good people.

The Big Bang: Stories with Intense Climactic Endings

Filled with suspense, the stories listed here will leave you on the edge of your seat, and their endings will astound you. The plots are action/adventure oriented, and most important, they feature dramatic and intense conclusions (both positive and foreboding).

Crichton, Michael.
Jurassic Park: A Novel. New York: Knopf, 1993. 399pp.
These scientists aren't singing "Hello Dolly" when they create creatures that are anything but sheepish in this techno-thriller. Using cloning techniques, scientists have re-created dinosaurs with recovered genetic material. Bad idea. Worse idea: open an amusement park featuring the beasts. When the animals prove to be difficult to control, terror ensues. This popular read was made into a movie by Stephen Spielberg in 1993.

Cisco, Michael.
The Tyrant. Canton, OH: Prime, 2004. 250pp.
Having "done" Europe, hoards of vampires decide to take a bite out of the Big Apple, New York City, and eventually to conquer the New World. The worm in their apple? Father Joe Cahill, an alcoholic priest who decides to redeem himself by fighting the undead. He joins forces with his activist niece and Carol Hanarty, a nun who makes explosives.

Coffey, Brian (pseudonym of Dean Koontz).
The Face of Fear. New York: Penguin-Berkley, 1977. 306pp.
Clairvoyant Graham Harris is an ex-mountain climber whose gift leads him to have visions of killings by "the butcher." In his latest vision, he sees his own death at the hands of this maniac, and this vision may come true if he cannot overcome his own fear—of heights. The final chase scene, involving the elevator shaft of an office building in the middle of the night, is sure to please action-oriented readers.

Gallagher, Diana G., and Constance Burge.
Mist and Stone: An Original Novel. New York: Simon & Schuster, 2003. 208pp. **YA**

Social worker Paige Matthews wants to make a difference for juvenile delinquent Todd Corman in this novelization of a *Charmed* episode. But Todd has been bounced from foster home to foster home for so long that he doesn't trust authority. Despite his protestations, Paige is determined to break through, even after Phoebe tells her that she has read the boy's future, and it may involve the darklighters. However, Phoebe's vision is shrouded in fog, which suggests that—maybe—something can be done to avert fate.

Gruber, Michael.
Tropic of Night. New York: William Morrow, 2003. 432pp.

A female anthropology graduate student travels to Africa with a male black poet, who turns out to be a powerful shaman. He allows her to commune with the spirits of Yoruba sorcerers, who almost destroy her. Fearing this power, she flees to Miami, but a series of murders of pregnant women convince her she will meet a gory end, in this page-turner.

Koontz, Dean.
Dark Rivers of the Heart. New York: Knopf, 1994. 487pp.

Spencer Grant is on the run from a nameless government agency, and he needs to remain hidden long enough to get to know the waitress who served him on the previous night. Unfortunately she is the real target of the agency's wrath. Both are caught up in a plot that involves computers, blackmail, and murder.

Koontz, Dean.
Darkfall. New York: Berkley, 1984. 371pp.

Two detectives, Jack Dawson and Rebecca Chandler, are called in to investigate a series of brutal gangland slayings. Dawson soon realizes that a practitioner of black magic named Lavelle is summoning creatures from the depths of hell to exact revenge. And now Lavelle threatens Dawson by promising to have his children brutally murdered if he does not back off the case. The last 70 pages are a masterpiece of suspense.

Strieber, Whitley.
Lilith's Dream: A Tale of the Vampire Life. New York: Simon & Schuster-Pocket Star, 2003. 400pp.

In this sequel to *The Hunger* and *The Last Vampire*, Lilith (Adam's first wife in the Bible, and creator of all vampires and humans) faces off in Manhattan against CIA-based vampire hunter Paul Ward. After fleeing her cave in Egypt after she learns of the destruction of virtually all the world's vampires, Lilith, with the aid of rock star Leo Patterson (one of her "children"), kidnaps Ward's child—and the body of Miriam Blaylock.

We're Doomed! Doooooomed!: Dark, Foreboding Endings

Stories here may offer a sense of relief and hope, but they are mainly about near-apocalyptic or post-apocalyptic worlds in which aliens have attacked, or science (sometimes with the help of vast government conspiracies) has gone horribly wrong, or various angry deities have returned to punish humanity for the sins of pride. Whether technology, nature, human nature, or otherwordly beings/supernatural forces have run amok, these novels will take readers to a place we all fear—the end of the world as we know it.

Alten, Steve.
Goliath. New York: Doherty-Forge, 2004. 512pp.
Covah, a Russian-born computer fanatic intent on ridding the world of nuclear weapons once and for all, has stolen the Goliath, a U.S. nuclear-powered "stealth submarine" with a biochemical computer "brain." He begins sinking ships and retrieving their nuclear weapons to use as leverage against nations that do not acknowledge his Declaration of Humanity; but when the sub's computer malfunctions, his mistake threatens to destroy Earth.

Grant, Charles.
Riders in the Sky. The Millennium Quartet. New York: Forge, 1999. 304pp.
This is the last title in the Millennium Quartet, in which four maniacs hitchhike across the country together, shedding blood along the way, looking for a small-town reverend whose murder will usher in the apocalypse. Worldwide famine and disease arrive when the killers have their final showdown with the Reverend Casey Chisholm, the only human who can defeat death. Grant's plot is so convoluted that it can only be told in four novels, yet each is suspenseful and stands on its own. The other titles are *Symphony*, *In the Mood*, and *Chariot*.

Herbert, James.
Portent. New York: HarperPrism, 1992. 319pp.
A scuba diver on the Great Barrier Reef sees a tiny light float pass him, then is ripped asunder moments later by the coral. In China's Taklimakan Desert, a mysterious light is spotted right before the sand engulfs those nearby. Near the Ganges, a boy sees a mysterious light and is then scalded to death by a geyser of boiling water. This series of unnatural disasters signifies the emergence of a new and terrifying force.

Koontz, Dean.
The Taking. New York: Bantam, 2004. 352pp.
One morning Molly and Neil Sloan awaken to a phosphorescent downpour that smells like semen. They lose power, but appliances come on without

a clear energy source, and the hands of all clocks run backward. Just before their telephone and Internet connections are gone for good, the couple learns that this is a global phenomenon. Earth is under attack by aliens who are introducing horrific new flora and fauna.

Sheehan, K.
Father Exorcist. Frederick, MD: PublishAmerica, 2004. 148pp.

A vampire working for the Vatican? And to save humanity? Father Michael, the mysterious, undead defender of the Vatican, answers his centuries-old call to action when an ancient evil has arisen and taken root in New York City. Cain, a malevolent wraith that feeds on fear and blood, has taken the form of the city's mayor and readies a demonic army.

Shirley, John.
Demons. New York: Ballantine, 2002. 372pp.

Grotesque demons terrorize and torture humans in a post-apocalyptic world. A young San Francisco artist joins up with a ragtag group of people who believe that because humans brought the mass slaughter of the demons upon themselves, self-awareness is the way to self-defense. This is a fast-paced, finely told horror tale about how people so often conspire in their own destruction.

Spellman, Cathy Cash.
Bless the Child. New York: Pocket, 2000. 608pp.

Most three-year-olds have a bit of heaven in them and can be quite impish at times, but Maggie O'Connell's grandson Cody is at the epicenter of a cosmic battle between good and evil. He is a messenger of the goddess Isis. But the yin to his yang is his crack-addicted mother's new husband, who just happens to be in control of The Stone of Sekhmet, which can usher utter evil into the world.

Stone, Del, Jr.
🏆 *Dead Heat.* Austin, TX: Mojo Press, 1996. 188pp.

Zombie see, zombie do, right? Not for loner and Harley rider extraordinaire Hitch, who finds himself joining the masses of the undead men walking through the Painted Desert in the Southwest after a biological apocalypse. The meat hook-swinging "hero" finds that he can control the other zombies, in this darkly humorous modern classic that won an award as "best first novel" for Stone.

Strieber, Whitley, Roland Emerick, and Jeffrey Nachmanoff.
The Day After Tomorrow. New York: Simon & Schuster-Pocket, 2004. 272pp.

During an intensely hot summer, the North Pole's record highest temperature is exceeded by 50 degrees. The rapid ice melt causes temperatures on Earth to drop radically, launching killer hurricanes and tornados, and culminating in a blizzard that will wipe out most life in the Northern Hemisphere. In the midst of the chaos, climatologist Jack Hall fights to save his son and a group of survivors in New York City.

Thorne, Tamara.
Thunder Road. New York: Kensington-Pinnacle, 2004. 352pp.

A young man fulfills his violent destiny, and the tiny town of Madelyn, in the California desert, begins to experience a rash of strange phenomena: unexplained lights in the sky, people vanishing, farm animals mutilated. Only a crazed millennialist cult leader seems to realize that the world is about to witness the Four Horsemen from the book of Revelations.

Uh, What Just Happened?: Ambiguous Endings

Endings in horror stories can be more realistic, in that just as in real life, they have ambiguous conclusions. In the following titles, the monster may or may not resurface, and readers are left to wonder what will happen. Even if the creature is killed, it's not made clear how those left behind will cope in the aftermath of their ordeals. Whether the monsters are flesh and blood or supernatural in origin, the end of the novel is not necessarily the end of the story.

Due, Tananarive.
The Good House: A Novel. New York: Atria, 2003. 482pp.

Angela brings her son Corey to her grandmother's rural home so they can spend the summer together and have a normal family life. But then Corey inexplicably kills himself, and Angela doesn't come back to her grandmother's house for three years. When she finally does return, strange things begin to happen, making Angela realize the house harbors powerful forces—and a terrible secret she must decipher in order to survive.

Due, Tananarive.
My Soul to Keep. The Living Blood series. New York: HarperPrism, 1997. 346pp.

What would have happened if a group of men had managed to get the body of Christ and actually drink his blood? The result is a cult of immortals, including a twentieth-century African American male who wishes to remain with his most recent human family. Unfortunately his action is in direct defiance of his fellow immortals, who discourage such relationships, by force if necessary, to protect the secrecy of their order. But how does one kill an immortal? This is the first entry in Due's Living Blood series. The sequel is *The Living Blood*.

King, Stephen.
🎖 *The Green Mile: A Novel in Six Parts*. New York: Plume, 1997. 465pp.
    Originally published as a serial novel, this story follows the last days of death row inmate John Coffey. Prison guard Paul Edgecombe is beginning to suspect that Coffey has almost godlike powers and can heal living creatures; and that a misunderstanding of his paranormal abilities is what ultimately landed Coffey on death row. But can he save the condemned man and the countless others Coffey may ultimately cure?

Little, Bentley.
The Ignored. New York: Signet Books, 1997. 429pp.
    Bob Jones is an average guy who likes hit movies, popular music, and chain restaurants. In fact, he's so average that he is Ignored: he has trouble getting served in restaurants, teachers never interacted with him in school, and even his parents don't remember him. Then one day Bob discovers that he isn't alone—a brotherhood of the Ignored has formed to gain recognition. But are acts of terrorism enough to make the Ignored visible?

Lumley, Brian.
Necroscope. The Necroscope series. New York: Doherty, 1986. 505pp.
    Meet Boris Dragonsani. He likes to play with dead people, literally, stealing their secrets in the process. Meet Harry Keough, the Necroscope. He sits in cemeteries all day so the dead can tell him their stories. Their fates, as well as the fates of an alien vampire race and (eventually) Harry's twin sons, collide. This is truly a series without end, in which each novel leaves enough wiggle room for its sequel to surprise and delight fans.

Rice, Anne.
Memnoch the Devil. The Vampire Chronicles. New York: Knopf, 1995. 353pp.
    Immortal Lestat continues to pursue his quest for the meaning of life, despite his doubts about the existence of God and Satan. After Satan shows him the world of the living and the dead, the aristocratic vampire revises his point of view. But Satan has an agenda: to make Lestat his second in command. How will this experience cause the atheist Lestat to experience himself as exotica in the savage garden? Other titles in the series include *Interview with the Vampire* and *The Vampire Lestat*.

Romkey, Michael.
American Gothic. New York: Del Ray, 2004. 304pp.
    The carnage of the American Civil war leads Nathanial Peregrine to despair, and to accept the embrace of the vampire. But immortality isn't all it's cracked up to be, and at the dawn of the twentieth century, Nathanial travels to Haiti and meets a woman who makes him long to be mortal again. Can Dr. Laville, an expert on diseases of the blood, help him redeem his soul? Can any vampire ever be redeemed?

Smith, James Russell.
Tulpa. Lincoln, NE: iUniverse, 2003. 76pp.

>Four kids at school have grown tired of being abused by the local crime family, so one decides to invoke a Tibetan Tulpa, or golem, created simply by imagining its existence. Eighteen months later, after they have forgotten about their experiment with mysticism, disturbing occurrences begin to plague the kids' community. Has the monster they created become their Frankenstein's creature, or has someone in the group snapped and become a Mr. Hyde?

Wyndham, John.
The Day of the Triffids. Garden City, NY: Doubleday, 1951. 222pp.

>After most humans have been blinded by a meteor shower, mobile carnivorous plants move in to topple civilization. The remaining people must figure out the best way to begin anew, but this endeavor requires cooperation among people with wildly different opinions about how to best organize the world. Can defenseless, newly blinded people survive this creeping kudzu with stingers? A Cold War–era classic that imagines the end of the world.

I Just Couldn't Put It Down: Sweet Dreams

Yup, we've all been there: 2:00 A.M., eyes red, yawning profusely. But we just have to finish that book. The texts in this section have in common the quality of being considered "unputdownable."

Cave, Hugh B.
The Evil Returns. New York: Leisure, 2001. 359pp.

>James Bond meets *Angel Heart* in this roller coaster ride of black magic. A Haitian bocur (evil shaman) devises an ingenious plan to take over the world. He procures clothing from the 10-year-old granddaughter of one of the president's most trusted advisors, and takes over her mind. Through her he takes over her father, and ultimately the grandfather, who can then steal a few items that will allow the bocur to possess the president.

Couch, J. D.
One Dark Night. Frederick, MD: PublishAmerica, 2004. 140pp.

>Everyone knows what damage dogs can do to a well-kept lawn. In Drexel, a small town where nothing extraordinary happens, Count Vladimir has arrived to change the town's dogs—into his instruments of destruction. Retiree Jason Donner and his friend John Morel realize that they cannot stop this evil animal army by themselves, so the two decide to recruit the expertise of a mysterious rabbi. Now if they can only survive one night.

Golden, Christopher.
Strangewood. New York: Signet, 1999. 304pp.

What happens when imaginary friends start taking on lives of their own? A writer of an extremely popular children's fantasy series finds himself being stalked, but not by a crazed fan. Rather, disgruntled characters from his Strangewood books are seeking revenge by kidnapping his son. Now he must go into a coma so he can battle these dark characters. This is a highly original tale of horror and parental love.

Koontz, Dean.
Midnight. New York: Putnam, 1989. 383pp.

Shaddack is not your average computer hacker. Rather than change a hard drive or take over a program or two, he aims to take over someone's body. A jogger is attacked and mutilated by animalistic humanoids, werewolf-like beings that are the creation of a childlike computer genius who is attempting to replace humans with his improved "new people." This is a real page-turner, full of cliff-hangers, the perfect diversion at bedtime.

Koontz, Dean.
Night Chills. New York: Atheneum, 1976. 334pp.

The government is using the inhabitants of Black River in an experiment, without their knowledge, when they are plagued with "night chills." Mistaken for a virus, this genetically engineered condition causes the afflicted to become violent. Filled with action, suspense, and erotic language, this novel is a good read for those nights when you're alone and want to pass the time.

Koontz, Dean.
Twilight Eyes. New York: Berkley, 1985. 451pp.

Slim Makenzie has "twilight eyes," an extraordinary psychic gift allowing him to discern whether someone is a mere mortal or an evil being disguised as a human. And although Slim is currently wanted for murder, he might actually be humanity's best defense against the "others," genetically engineered demons belonging to an ancient civilization. This suspenseful work is an easy read, perfect for downtime.

Laws, Stephen.
The Wyrm. New York: Leisure, 1987. 342pp.

Michael Lambton, a lonely author suffering from writer's block, moves from the big city to a small border village called Shillingham to hide from the world. When highway construction workers nearby unearth an old gallows destined for a museum, grotesque and brutal killings begin to occur. Can a man who is more about keyboards than killing stop a mysterious, shapeshifting entity from decimating an entire town of 650 innocent bystanders in just one outing?

Masters, Paul.
Meca and the Black Oracle. New York: Leisure, 1999. 327pp.

All people need to hear is the term "human sacrifice" to make their skin crawl and the hair stand up on the back of their necks. For Police Lieutenant Steve Tanner, the term means that he must race against time to stop a mysterious cult from serially kidnapping, murdering, dissecting, and disinterring young women. But to stop the cult, he will have to infiltrate their ranks. A page-turner that will keep anyone awake.

Masterton, Graham.
The Manitou. New York: Pinnacle, 1976. 216pp.

Dr. Hughes, a specialist in tumors, examines an unfortunate young woman who has a strange growth on her neck. Later she "gives birth" to Misquamacus, an ancient and evil Native American shaman. Only a fake psychic and a Sioux shaman can help her now. Readers who like borderline splatterpunk imagery and highly disturbing visuals, masterfully handled, and a brilliant cast of characters rather than swaggering action figure types will enjoy this modern classic.

Palahniuk, Chuck.
Lullaby. New York: Doubleday, 2002. 260pp.

Talk about being sung to sleep! Only in this punky novel full of bantering and witty exchanges between jaded characters, the dreamer NEVER wakes up. An African culling song meant to euthanize the very young and the enfeebled during times of famine is reproduced in a book of children's poems. Now parents, innocently reading the ancient lullaby to their children at bedtime, induce the big sleep in their offspring.

Palmer, Michael.
The Society. New York: Bantam, 2004. 351pp.

Robin Cook may be responsible for getting medical thrillers on the charts, but no one makes them more engaging, thrilling, and scary than Michael Palmer. His novels are perfect reading for those long waits to see the doctor—for the brave and fearless. They make it frighteningly clear how greatly we are at the mercy of those in the medical profession we entrust with our lives, and they are hard to put down. In this, Palmer's eleventh medical thriller, Dr. Will Grant and rookie cop Patty Moriarity take on the managed care industry.

Saul, John.
Midnight Voices. New York: Ballantine, 2001. 384pp. **YA**

A recently widowed mother marries a widower who seems too good to be true. Unfortunately for her children, Laurie and Ryan, he is. He lives in a haunted building, and he absolutely refuses to allow anyone to enter his private study. When the children start having nightmares and creepy elderly neighbors begin visiting, even their mother is afraid. This novel begs to be enjoyed in one sitting, in the dark, huddled in the corner of the couch.

Tryon, Thomas.
Harvest Home. New York: Knopf, 1973. 403pp.

Howling skulls in trees, people getting their tongues cut out, and human sacrifices make this small town anything but peaceful—that is, at least for Theodore's family, which exchanges its city life for a supposedly simpler and more meaningful existence based on ancient folkways. But Theodore soon discovers that his wife and daughter's newfound devotion to rural domesticity conceals deadly secrets, particularly for the men of the village.

Chapter 2
Mood and Atmosphere

Mood and atmosphere are integral to the horror genre, and that means there are horror books for virtually any taste. In this chapter are titles to fit every mood—whether the reader enjoys chuckling or laughing out loud, or has read so much in the genre that he or she has been desensitized to the normal level of violence and therefore prefers works that would make others gasp in disgust, or is someone who does not mind being discomforted or disquieted by fiction that challenges accepted understandings of reality, psychology, and religion. Then again, maybe a reader is a horror purist—one who just likes having the beejeezus scared out of him or her. What's *your* reading pleasure?

I'm in the Mood For . . .

Side-Splitting Maniacs and Demons That Like to Raise Hell: Comic Horror

In the 2004 horror comedy film *Shaun of the Dead* there is a wonderfully funny scene in which a young female zombie attacks the main character (a clueless 29-year-old electronics salesman named Shaun), ostensibly to take bites out of his flesh. Since Shaun and his drinking buddy Ed assume she is drunk, Ed runs off to get a camera so he can take a snapshot of the girl trying to kiss his best friend. Our hero fights off the zombie and shoves the girl away onto a spike, from which she promptly removes herself, showing a huge hole in her abdomen.

Shaun and Ed stand dumbfounded, and in perhaps the funniest audio joke of the film, the audience hears Ed advancing the film on the camera, until Shaun smacks his arm in a "stop that" gesture.

This contemporary movie is not an exception, but a rule. Horror is not, and has never been, without its comic side. Some writers in the genre, like newcomer Andrew Fox and the well-seasoned Christopher Moore, arguably the best comedian in horror, make a living out of being funny. Others, like Ray Bradbury, William Browning Spencer, and Laurell K. Hamilton, write tongue-in-cheek tales of the macabre. These authors understand that demons and zombies can be hell raisers once they are raised, and that for every good fright, there are at least several false starts, whereby the hapless hero realizes that he has prepared to fight for his life against a cat that has been locked in the closet, or the heroine discovers that the mysterious stranger attempting to get into her chamber is nothing more than a loose branch scraping against the window. Keep in mind that a genre founded on the articulation of our deepest fears can't take itself seriously all the time and will ultimately lapse into parody. Hence the titles in this section, beginning with the classic *Northanger Abbey*, which argues that it probably *is* all in our heads, reflect the more humorous side of the genre.

Austen, Jane.
Northanger Abbey. Philadelphia: Pavilion, 2004 (1818). 384pp.
   When Catherine Morland comes to Northanger Abbey, she imagines the worst. Fortunately she has at hand her own fundamental good sense and the irresistible but unsentimental Henry Tilney. Disaster does eventually strike, but without spoiling for too long the gay, good-humored atmosphere of this most delightful of books. Austen's classic novel is a parody of the gothic novels of its time, which today's readers still enjoy.

Bradbury, Ray.
From the Dust Returned. New York: Avon, 2001. 204pp.
   A Victorian mansion in a small Midwestern town is the site of the riotous reunion of a family of immortals reminiscent of the Addams family or the Munsters. Grand Mere, a 4,000-year-old mummy and pharaoh's daughter, lives in the attic. Uncle Einars plays with the neighborhood kids—by sporting enormous wings and allowing them to use him as a kite. Other relatives include vampires and ghosts, and one very normal mortal foundling.

Davidson, Mary Janice.
Undead and Unwed. Undead series. New York: Berkley Sensation, 2004. 277pp.
   One day Betsy Taylor is an unemployed and unmarried former model and lover of fine shoes. Then she's killed by an SUV. She awakens as a vampire; worse still, she has been dressed in a hideous pink suit and cheap shoes by her evil stepmother. After reclaiming her designer shoe collection from

her stepmother, Betsy sets out to right other wrongs. Unfortunately she is abducted by an aged vampire, who believes her to be his prophesied queen. This title launched the Undead and . . . series. Others series titles are *Undead and Unemployed* and *Undead and Unappreciated*.

Johnson, Adam.
Parasites Like Us. New York: Viking, 2003. 368pp.

Anthropology professor Hank Hannah and his graduate students unleash a deadly, prehistoric contagion when they dig up the remains of an ancient Clovis man. While Hannah is busy dealing with legal problems, two graduate students use a Clovis arrowhead to kill a pig, unwittingly unleashing a deadly prehistoric contagion on the Midwest.

Kemske, Floyd.
Lifetime Employment. Corporate Nightmares series. Highland Park, NJ: Catbird Press, 1992. 236pp.

We all may think our bosses are part blood-sucker, but imagine that your boss hired a "turn-around specialist" who just happened to be a real vampire. Or that the company is slowly being taken over—by a computer named CHUCK, which controls what you do at work and wants to control your personal life. Or perhaps you may find yourself working somewhere where the only way to move up is to assassinate your supervisor.

Koontz, Dean.
Ticktock. New York: Ballantine, 1997. 335pp.

Some families will do anything to get straying members back in the fold. One night a young estranged Vietnamese American man finds on his doorstep a cursed rag doll. After he brings it inside, it turns into a reptilian demon and pursues him, growing bigger and bigger as it chases him back to his family's house. While escaping, he meets a young woman. Could it be love at first fright? Perhaps Koontz's only true comic horror novel.

Lansdale, Joe R.
Bumper Crop. Urbana, IL: Golden Gryphon Press, 2004. 275pp.

Ever hear of a deity that inspires serial killers? A set of possessed false teeth? They're both here, in 26 over-the-top stories written by Joe R. Lansdale. This volume contains "God of the Razor," "Chompers," "On a Dark October," "Bar Talk," "The Companion" and "Bestsellers Guaranteed." Lansdale has also written a short introduction for each of the tales in this volume.

Moore, Christopher.
Bloodsucking Fiends: A Love Story. New York: Simon & Schuster, 1995. 300pp.

Mild-mannered secretary Jody wakes up under a dumpster with an aching neck, superhuman strength, and the realization that she will never drink—wine—again. C. Thomas Flood moves from Indiana to become a night clerk and frozen-turkey bowling aficionado in a San Francisco Safeway. That is, until the night a beautiful redhead named Jody walks into his life. Too bad she's undead.

Moore, Christopher.
The Lust Lizard of Melancholy Cove. New York: Spike, 1999. 304pp.
    As if Pine Cove hasn't had enough problems, now it is home to a gigantic prehistoric lizard. The strange folk who grace this tour de force include a psychiatrist who yanks everyone's zanax, an elderly blues singer named Catfish, a former B-movie starlet, a pot-head town constable, a crooked sheriff, and a pharmacist with a bizarre sexual fixation on sea mammals.

Moore, Christopher.
Practical Demonkeeping. New York: St. Martin's, 1992. 243pp.
    One-hundred-year-old ex-seminarian and scholar Travis O'Hearn is looking for a way to rid himself of Catch, a demon with a nasty habit of eating most of the people he meets. He travels to Pine Cove, California, looking for an incantation that will return the demon to Hell. On Travis's side are the King of the Djinns and August Brine, Pine Grove's purveyor of bait, tackle, and fine wines.

Spencer, William Browning.
🏵 *Resume with Monsters*. Sag Harbor, NY: The Permanent Press, 1995. 212pp.
    Philip Kenan bounces from one menial job to the next with no ability to advance, until he finally realizes that his previous bosses are in league with Lovecraftian monsters, whose goal is to enslave all of humanity through an entity called "the system." Can Kenan save himself and his lover, or will he be branded an insane stalker?

Wilde, Oscar.
The Canterville Ghost. Mineola, NY: Dover, 2001 (1887). 80pp.
    A classic tale about an American family that moves into a haunted English manor, then refuses to believe in its resident ghost, who just happens to be a celebrated and feared apparition—and proud of it. The teenaged daughter begins to witness strange occurrences, but can she convince her parents that the supernatural is at work in their new domicile?

Ewww, That's Gross. Read It Again!: The Gory Story

Those who read a lot of horror may find that they have become desensitized, immune to representations of death, mayhem, and gore. Maybe they like their horror kicked up a notch, or want horror that doesn't pull any punches and embodies the punk ethos, challenging conventional morality. Novels, collections, and anthologies in this section often break taboos about sex and violence. And if a reader's taste runs to the gory side of horror, he or she should consult the index at the back of this guide to find other titles under "splatterpunk" (a subgenre of horror). On the other hand, if someone is easily offended, or feint of heart, that reader should move quickly to the next section . . . .

Arnzen, Michael.
Grave Markings. New York: Dell, 1994. 400pp.

An insane, egomaniacal tattoo artist named Kilpatrick becomes obsessed with the mad images in his mind and the need for recognition, so he seeks new flesh to fulfill his ambitions. Nothing, not even death, will stop him in his art. Kilpatrick's sick world becomes more and more vivid, and Arnzen forces readers to see the world through Kilpatrick's eyes.

Cacek, P. D.
The Wind Caller. New York: Dorchester, 2004. 355pp.

In Arizona, the wind can be not only chilling, but biting as well, and a cold wind could appear seemingly out of nowhere, dropping the temperature by some 15 degrees. Against the backdrop of craggy mountains, lonely deserts, dark caves, and resort hotel projects of the Painted Desert, windcaller Gideon Berlander turns unpredictable nature into a vicious killing machine, ripping buildings, animals, and people to shreds right before the reader's very eyes.

Gonzales, J. F., and Mark Williams.
Clickers. Grandview, MO: Dark Tales, 2000. 238pp.

Seafood lovers get their comeuppance in the small town of Phillisport, Maine. Giant crablike creatures with voracious appetites, foot-long claws, and poisonous stingers that turn human flesh into rotting meat wake after centuries of hibernation. They are ready to strike again, and aided by a semi-intelligent race of reptilian humanoids that coexisted with primitive homo sapiens, they threaten to eat every person in town—and they like their food fresh.

Gustainis, Justin.
The Hades Project. Sidney, NY: Wahmpreneur-Brighid's Fire Books, 2003. 433pp.

A special operative has been called in to investigate the grisly killing of 12 scientists who were working on a top secret project in a laboratory in Fairfax, Virginia. Many of the scientists, both male and female, have been raped, and most of them have been seriously mutilated. Is it the work of a psychopath? Or are these heinous crimes the handiwork of a familiar demon?

Harper, Andrew.
Red Angel. New York: Dorchester-Leisure, 2003. 368pp.

    An asylum technician/corrections officer with a troubled past has less than 24 hours to catch a vicious serial killer of children, who leaves the bodies behind, decorated with bird's wings and made to look like angels. To do so, he enlists the help of an equally vicious, insane genius currently being held in the maximum security ward, and at stake is a friend's child.

Houarner, Gerard.
Painfreak. Orlando, FL: Necro Publications, 1996. 116pp.

    Take a rabid dog, give it a human body, a bad attitude, and a license to kill, and you have Max, a man whose only pensive moments are when he has to decide whether to kill or "sex up" a woman. A government assassin, Max is a "loose cannon" who spouts Eastern philosophy. But he'll need all his skills when ghosts of his victims trap his son. Readers who like max-imum pain and max-imum gore should check out this series! Other "Max" titles include *The Beast That Was Max* and *Road to Hell.*

Lee, Edward.
Flesh Gothic. New York: Leisure, 2005. 404pp.

    Reginald Hildrith, a decadent billionaire, purchases a porn production company, then holds a bloody orgy with the company's actors in his mansion, where all, including himself, perish. But his wife is convinced that Reginald is undead, somewhere, in some other dimension, and she hires a team of psychics and investigative reporters to search for him in the mansion, where guests are molested and sometimes killed by unseen forces.

Shirley, John.
Crawlers. New York: Ballantine-Del Rey, 2003. 400pp.

    The hapless residents of Quiebra, California, assume that a mysterious capsule that falls from the sky is from outer space, and that they are besieged by aliens, because the nano-bacteria within the craft transform everything into a fusion of biological material and machine. Strangely, it seems that only the teenagers of the small town are resistant to the invasion.

Slade, Michael.
Bed of Nails. New York: Penguin-Onyx, 2003. 448 pp.

    The Ripper, a man who believes he was the notorious Whitechapel murderer once known as Jack the Ripper, is one of the prisoners in the Riverside Insane Asylum. In the darkness of his heart he still craves the thrill of the kill, if only he could escape. Unfortunately for Riverside, he manages to do so. Royal Canadian Mountie Robert DeClercq chases this serial murderer, who leaves a trail of grotesquely mutilated bodies behind. *Death's Door* is another title by Slade that features DeClercq.

I'm Too Sexy for My Fangs: Erotic Horror

There is a great deal of romance horror, or horror romance, if you will. Anyone who has seen Francis Ford Coppola's *Bram Stoker's Dracula*, or read Stoker's original *Dracula* for that matter, can attest to the attractiveness—and sometimes downright sex appeal—of various "monsters" (especially vampires). Ghosts, as well as vampires, are particularly popular subjects of romantic and erotic horror. Gothic fiction, which often lacks a supernatural element, can often be an equally popular type of romantic horror, particularly when it comes to tales of star-crossed lovers. However, don't expect all titles here to be misty reads about romantic heroines beset by supernatural lovers, and vice versa. Some selections feature particularly graphic, and often disturbing, representations of sexuality (which are not always heterosexual). And those who enjoy the love and horror combination should check out Appendix C, "Genreblends," for more romance/horror titles.

Armstrong, Kelley.
Bitten. Women of the Otherworld series. New York: Plume, 2002. 382pp.

In Armstrong's loosely affiliated series, female werewolves and witches make their way in a man's world, using their extraordinary powers either for good or just for the fun of it, and always attracting the attention of men, mortal and otherwise, who would take these powers for themselves. The series begins in this volume with Elena Michaels, who grew up as an orphan, being turned by a charming vampire named Clayton. Other titles in the series are *Stolen, Dime Store Magic, Industrial Magic,* and *Haunted*.

Brass, Perry.
Warlock: A Novel of Possession. Bronx, NY: Belhue Press, 2001. 224pp.

Alwyn Barrow is not quite a lunatic, but he raves in this first-person narrative. Barrow goes from being a cog in the banking system to finding himself in the fanciest restaurants and sleaziest dives of New York, and finally at an exclusive lodge in the Swiss Alps. But all is not fun and games for him, as a mysterious stranger named Destry Powars seems to be taking possession of him—and draining his blood.

Brite, Poppy Z., ed.
Love in Vein: Twenty Original Tales of Vampire Erotica. London: HarperCollins, 1995. 432pp.

This is the anthology that put erotic horror on the map. Brite has brought together this genre's most powerful and seductive authors in an original and award-winning collection of vampire erotica, including authors well known in the genre (such as Christopher Fowler, David J. Schow, and Richard Laymon) and lesser-known newcomers of merit. These stories blur the lines between pleasure and pain, between love and obsession, and are not for the timid. A second volume was released two years later: *Love in Vein Two: More Original Tales of Vampire Erotica*.

Campbell, Ramsey.
Scared Stiff: Tales of Sex and Death. Los Angeles: Scream Press, 1987. 173pp.

Campbell, a typically proper British stylist whose strength is subtlety and atmosphere, shows he can shock with the best of them in these seven stories. Characters visit the darkest recesses of the human mind, discovering the connection between death and sex. A real challenge for readers who can appreciate tales without tidy or happy endings, this is perhaps the finest collection of erotic horror stories published to date.

Gelb, Jeff, and Michael Garrett, eds.
Hotter Blood. New York: Pocket, 1991. 336pp.
Hottest Blood. New York: Pocket, 1993. 256pp.

Nocturnal submission, degenerate vices, and erotic nightmares: A geek yearns for a hideous revenge, while a devil's deal is gruesomely updated when a rock star sells his soul for success, and a woman has additional sex organs transplanted into her body in order to be able to be the only woman at a multi-male orgy. Ever hear the horror version of the classic farmer's daughter joke? It's all here, written by masters of horror.

Harbaugh, Karen.
Night Fires. New York: Dell, 2003. 384pp.

Simone, a Frenchwoman, is pledged to preserving life, while Corday, an Englishman, is dedicated to taking it. They find themselves joined on a dangerous mission in which both may rediscover their lost souls. In a very loosely connected sequel, *Dark Enchantment*, the ravishing fugitive Catherine de la Fer is driven into the deadly night by a shattering act of violence, which turns her into a hunted criminal.

Jefferson, Jemiah.
Wounds. New York: Leisure, 2002. 361pp.

A German vampire flees the Nazi occupation. Now in Hollywood, he becomes a cross-dressing bisexual, and he is entranced with a zaftig, long-suffering artist stripper—a "dancer"—who is a sadist and a masochist, and a murderer to boot. Jefferson's vampires not only can engage in sexual activity, but they can do IT rather well, and they dine in style at four-star establishments in this gothic, stylish novel.

Lewis, Matthew ("Monk") G.
The Monk. Mineola, NY: Dover, 2004 (1796). 320pp.

Ambrosio, a well-respected clergyman, discovers that one of the novice monks in his monastery is actually a beautiful young woman, Matilda. Matilda seduces Ambrosio in the monastery and eventually works with him to arrange the rape of a young virgin, which leads to a murder and grotesque acts of necrophilia. This is a classic tale of Satan tempting a clergyman.

Mitchell, Mary Ann.
Sips of Blood. Marquis de Sade series. New York: Leisure, 1999. 358pp.

The Marquis de Sade is alive and well—sort of—and he is still introducing young women to the pleasures of his vices. Now a vampire, de Sade and his dominatrix mother-in-law are accidentally creating too many vampires, leaving these former innocents to figure out how to feed themselves without drawing too much attention to their existence. Their only hope is to find their mysterious maker. Other titles in the series include *Quenched*, *Cathedral of Vampires*, *Tainted Blood*, and *The Vampire de Sade*.

Mitchell, Mary Ann.
Siren's Call. Palm Beach, FL: Medallion, 2004. 305pp.

Sirena is a beautiful young stripper living in small-town Florida. When a local detective visits, it turns out to be strictly a business call. A local businessman has gone missing, and he was last seen at Silky Femmes, the strip club. Gradually the detective discovers that Sirena has a deadly hobby, and he suspects that she has been handpicking men for private meetings. But can he resist her charms?

Moore, Elaine.
Dark Desire (Originally published as *Madonna of the Dark*). The Dark Madonna Trilogy. New York: iBooks, 1999. 269pp.

In sixteenth-century Scotland, Victoria MacKay is seduced by the vampire Johann Nikolai. The clash of her vampire nature and the unbridled gifts of her Celtic bloodline make Victoria more than human, but more bound to the living than the undead. For centuries she is pursued across Europe, Africa, and America by Nikolai, eventually awakening from a deep vampire's sleep to find a world filled with violent drug- and sex-addicted monsters. Other titles in the series include *Retribution* and *Eternal Embrace*.

Taylor, Karen E.
Blood Secrets. The Vampire Legacy. New York: Kensington, 1993. 303pp.

Follow the sexy exploits of Deidre, made into a vampire when she was pregnant; Mitch, the detective whom Deidre loves; and Lily, Deidre's supposedly stillborn child, who inherited her mother's blood curse, starting with this first book in the series. In various novels in the series, Deidre and Mitch walk the nights in New York City trying to trap renegade vampires, who go on killing sprees and must be stopped, and fighting off Lily as she attempts to exact revenge on the mother who abandoned her. Other titles in the series include *Bitter Blood*, *Blood Ties*, *Blood of My Blood*, *The Vampire Vivienne*, *Resurrection*, and *Blood Red Dawn*.

Mind Benders: Intellectual Horror

Many authors in the horror genre, including the most highly praised of them all, Ramsey Campbell, lean toward the intellectual side of horror and Gothicism, with mind-bending tales that haunt readers. Readers who prefer these cerebral tales, including more traditional horror stories, can sink their intellectual teeth into these tales, including classics by Sir Arthur Conan Doyle, Algernon Blackwood, and H. P. Lovecraft, just to name a few. The premise of these titles is that terror is 99.9 percent mental.

Bierce, Ambrose.
The Moonlit Road and Other Ghost and Horror Stories. Mineola, NY: Dover, 1998. 91pp.

If Poe is the precursor to writers like Stephen King and Anne Rice, then Bierce is the original Rod Serling. These 12 tales, selected from the 1909 collection of America's other "master of the macabre," are thoughtful, often mind-boggling, and told from various points of view. And Bierce is just as at home with the traditional ghost story as he is with tales that delve into the darkest recesses of the human mind.

Boyd, Donna.
The Awakening. New York: Ballantine, 2003. 208pp.

Mary wakes up in a sanitarium, barely remembering an accident that killed her husband and daughter. Her therapist convinces her to return to what he says is her family home. The catch is that the people who live there are not new tenants; they are supposedly her nearest and dearest—and they are far from deceased—or so it seems. But why can't they see her, and what of her nightly torment of seeing a blood-spattered kitchen in her dreams?

Campbell, Ramsey.
The Overnight. New York: Tor, 2005. 400pp.

When Woody takes over the management of a bookstore, the neatly arranged shelves seem to disorganize themselves overnight, and the employees are ready to come to blows with one another. He must finally order his staff to do an overnight inventory to put things to rights, but employees disappear into the basement one by one, leaving a shimmering trail of slime behind them. Campbell excels at creating challenging reads that flesh out the horror of everyday work life.

Ligotti, Thomas.
🏆 *The Nightmare Factory.* New York: Carroll and Graf, 1996. 551pp.

My Work Is Not Yet Done: Three Tales of Corporate Horror. Poplar Bluff, MO: Mythos Books, 2002. 200pp.

If there is anyone who typifies the term intellectual horror more than Ligotti, we haven't read him. Who else could have imagined a cursed pair of pants that makes its owner's legs decay? Who else could have created Frank Dominio, a bitter and frustrated longtime cog-in-the-machine at a nameless, faceless company, who eventually undertakes the murdering of co-workers by exercising his powers of transforming atoms?

Little, Bentley.
The Return. New York: New American Library, 2002. 354pp.

In Arizona, archeologists discover shards of pottery bearing pictures of themselves and their homes. Indian artifacts in museums get up and leave. Overnight, the populations of entire desert towns disappear without a trace. Could there be a connection between these strange events and the mysterious fate of the Anasazi Indians, a once sophisticated culture whose inhabitants inexplicably began to practice cannibalism, then disappeared?

Monahan, Brent.
Book of Common Dread. The Book of Common Dread series. New York : St. Martin's, 1993. 328pp.

Any rare book collector's mouth would water if upon finding a 3,000-year-old manuscript that accurately described DNA, the particles of an atom, and the heliocentric theory of the universe. But what if this manuscript also told the secrets of vampires, and an ancient bloodsucker skilled in torture was sent to destroy the evidence, and anyone who has seen it? Simon Penn, rare book curator, unfortunately finds himself in this position. The second book in the series is *The Blood of the Covenant*.

Morrison, Toni.
Beloved. New York: Knopf, 1987. 275pp.

Voices whisper. Furniture flies. Dreams turn into nightmares. The house called 124 is haunted, and an ex-slave named Sethe knows why. Sethe and her children tried to escape to freedom in the 1840s, but a bounty hunter tracked them down. There were screams, there was blood, and there was a murder. What happened in this small Ohio town will haunt Sethe forever, unless she can rid herself of a mysterious young female visitor.

Naylor, Gloria.
Linden Hills. New York: Ticknor and Fields, 1985. 304pp.

Linden Hills, an upper-middle-class black suburb, and its creator, Luther Nedeed, are known far and wide. Once a patch of rocky soil and home to people respectable society had disowned, it's now a place that African Americans will literally sell their souls to live in. During the last days of the year, though, a son of a Hills' resident and an intimate of the nearby slum discover the private horrors in Luther's basement.

Vizenore, Gerald.
Chancers. Norman: University of Oklahoma Press, 2000. 159pp.

This is a challenging read, unique in its approach, that is based on oral narrative structure and content. A group of Native American solar dancers begin sacrificing the faculty of a small university. Their goal: to resurrect a mythological figure and once again empower their tribe. Characterization and story are more important than action and gore here. Will appeal to fans of gentle reads.

Weinberg, Robert.
Dial Your Dreams. Kansas City, MO: Dark Tales, 2001. 199pp.

Anyone who dials this 1-900 number will find out that revenge is only sweet when one is on the right end. Or maybe the caller will find himself in the dark—literally—trying to escape a crazed killer. Or maybe she'll end up registering voters, both alive and dead. Better call psychic detective Sidney Taine to see if he can figure out how to escape from this collection of nightmares and phobias.

Wheeler, Robert E.
Travel Many Roads. Miami, FL: Minerva, 2001. 191pp.

A libertine liberal arts professor with few scruples gets involved with one of his star pupils, and it doesn't take long for him to realize that she is obsessed with him. After they break up, she begins stalking him. As his acquaintances and friends disappear, their bodies later found mutilated, it becomes apparent that the pressure of the teacher–student relationship is pushing both over the edge. One of them may even be a murderer.

Wooley, John, and Ron Wolfe.
Death's Door. New York: Dell, 1992. 386pp.

In this intelligent, philosophical novel, Security Guard Case Hamilton is literally given a second chance at life. While a cop, he was fatally wounded, but he was resuscitated after 10 minutes of death. He becomes a guard at a famous surgeon's lab, where he discovers that he is one of the "experiments." A second brush with death leads to visitations by The Grey Man, Death itself, who now wants more than one life.

Fear Factors

Horror fans agree on quite a few things (besides the fact that most of us do not want to eat insects): that a work of horror fiction should have as its purpose the intention to either scare, or at least cause disquiet for, the reader; that horror fiction should include either a monster of some sort or at least the threat of one; and that atmosphere is an integral part of the horror experience. Yet within those parameters, the horror genre contains great diversity. The truth is that fans of the genre are diverse, and while some enjoy the exaggerated violence and gratuitous gore that characterize the splatterpunk subgenre, others prefer the subtleties of what is often called traditional horror. Or, to extend our *Fear Factor* analogy, whether they prefer the terrifying (bungee jumping), horrifying (being dropped suddenly from a skyscraper window), disturbing (being covered with scorpions), or disgusting (eating a centipede), all will find something here to their liking. The categories that follow progress in intensity from haunting to terrifying. For works toward the more genteel end of the spectrum, peruse the first subsection, about haunting and atmospheric horror; for a more intense read, check out the titles listed in the last, "terrifying" subsection. Of course, some of us enjoy it all.

A Dark and Stormy Night: Haunting and Atmospheric

Most people associate haunting and atmospheric horror (what is sometimes called Gothic) with older classics in the genre by benchmark writers like Horace Walpole, Bram Stoker, Joseph Sheridan LeFanu, Ambrose Bierce, M. R. James, and H. P. Lovecraft. Certainly some of those names appear in this section. However, not all atmospheric works of horror were written prior to the Stephen King era. Some titles in this section are recent, as contemporary authors revisit the idea of creating fright without body counts and eviscerations. Although there isn't any graphic violence here, the works in this section are no less compelling. Some of the texts tend to rely on the psychological more than the supernatural to create an eerie atmosphere. Indeed, in these stories and novels, a mind is very often a terrible thing.

Andrews, V. C.
Flowers in the Attic. The Dolanganger Children series. New York: Pocket, 1979. 412pp. **YA**

In this first book in the series, the sudden death of the Dolanganger family patriarch leaves their mother dependent on the benevolence of her parents, who never approved of her marriage or the children it produced. The price of her parents' support is keeping her children in the attic in order to undo their existence. This extremely popular dark, gothic series features characters who are modern versions of those found in fairy tales and gothic novels. Other series titles include *Petals on the Wind* and *If There Be Thorns*.

Arensberg, Ann.
Incubus. New York: Knopf, 1999. 218pp.

    It's just another ordinary year in the life of Dry Falls, Maine, a small community known for its spirituality and its neighborliness. But then comes the weird summer. Crops die, animals give birth to mutations, married couples cease to have sex, and six young girls are found sleeping naked, with no idea how they got that way. The wife of the town's pastor narrates this atmospheric tale of disturbances.

Bailey, Dale.
House of Bones. New York: Penguin-Signet, 2003. 384pp.

    Eccentric billionaire Ramsey Lomax bribes the city to halt the demolition of the notorious Dreamland housing project so he can reside there for two weeks and investigate alleged ghostly activity. He advertises for people to accompany him, and four respond, including a medium, a journalist who was formerly a resident, a doctor who is losing her career, and a veteran with a shady past.

Campbell, Ramsey.
Ancient Images. New York: Tor, 1989. 311pp.

    It's a filmmakers' dream: A colleague has just located a rare movie starring Bela Lugosi and Boris Karloff. Film editor Sandy Allan is on cloud nine at first, but then her colleague dies mysteriously, and others who come anywhere near the movie—or the short story on which it is based—meet tragic fates. To keep herself from being found on the cutting room floor, Allan must figure out the curse.

James, M. R.
Casting the Runes, and Other Ghost Stories. New York: Oxford University Press, 1987. 352pp.

    Fellow traveler of the dark, herein are the marvelous tales of a vicious crank whose occult-oriented revenge is turned against him so that he meets a gory end, and of a dying man who is hunted by giant spiders. James's strength is his subtle way of incorporating horror into a tale, calling attention to what readers do not fully see, or what they think they hear. Another collection of haunting tales by James is *Ghost Stories of an Antiquary* (Mineola, NY: Dover, 1988 [1911]. 168pp.).

Le Fanu, Joseph Sheridan.
Green Tea and Other Ghost Stories. Mineola, NY: Dover, 1993. 96pp.

    Sometimes it's what we see in our mind's eye that scares us the most, as is the case in these four classic short stories by one of the nineteenth century's masters of the genre, who appeals to the more sophisticated reader and fans of gentle reads. Works collected here include a classic story written from the point of view of an apprentice occultist, who is haunted by a strange, animalistic apparition that no one else can see.

Le Fanu, Joseph Sheridan.
In a Glass Darkly. New York: Oxford University Press, 1999 (1872). 347pp.

Stories collected by the character Dr. Hesselius, a "metaphysical doctor," include the vampire novella *Carmilla,* in which a young girl befriends a woman, seemingly of noble birth, who is actually a vampire. This nineteenth-century classic is characterized by its highly descriptive prose, indirect style, and use of first-person narration in journal form, as well as the inclusion of traditional vampire and banshee folklore.

Masterton, Graham.
Prey. New York: Leisure, 1999. 352pp.

The government's raising and lowering of interest rates is the least of David Williams's worries when he takes on the job of restoring Fortyfoot House, an abandoned orphanage on The Isle of Wight. In this eerie, disturbing read, David Williams has agreed to restore this habitat that houses many ghosts, but he soon discovers that he may have placed himself and his son in danger.

Onions, Oliver.
The Beckoning Fair One. Mineola, NY: Dover, 2004 (1911). 96pp.

So you've just noticed that the faucet in your new apartment drips to the tune of a song you cannot quite place? Join the club. In one of the most famous horror novellas of all time, a young man who moves into a haunted house finds himself becoming the target of the affections of a female ghost. At first the presence is subtle, but as it becomes more and more insistent, he is in danger of losing his grip on reality.

Rice, Anne.
Violin. New York: Ballantine, 1997. 336pp.

Following the death of her lover, Triana Becker seems to be losing her mind. A mysterious violinist on the streets of New Orleans forces her back into her painful past through his music, and his playing is relentless. It turns out the violinist is a ghost, dammed by his hatred and guilt to wander aimlessly, and he wants Triana to be his companion—forever.

Stoker, Bram.
The Jewel of Seven Stars. Halicong, PA: Wildside Press, 2001 (1903). 304pp.

An Egyptologist accidentally finds a fabulous gem, then is stricken by an unknown force. He awakens the soul of Tera, an ancient Egyptian queen. Through eerie and unsettling, atmospheric scenes, Tera quickly possesses his daughter's body. He can save his child only by reanimating the body of the mummy, which may then endanger all of society.

I Think I Hear Something: Disturbing Reads

Similar to those in the previous category, works here differ in degree of intensity. Some may be slightly more disturbing, reminiscent of surrealistic nightmares. Still, readers who enjoyed the gentle reads in the previous section will find the tales in this section to their liking.

Bear, Greg.
Dead Lines. New York: Ballantine, 2004. 256pp.

Deeply grieving, Peter Russell longs to connect with his murdered daughter and his dead best friend. He thinks his prayers are answered when he finds Trans, a sleek, handheld interpersonal communication device capable of flawless operation anywhere in the world. But he soon finds he has been transported to the edge of an eerie world where apparitions reach out in torment.

Campbell, Ramsey.
The Darkest Part of the Woods. New York: Tor, 2002. 364pp.

Dr. Lennox Price and his family move to the isolated locale of Goodmanswood, in England. Soon Lennox loses his mind and is committed to Mercy Hill, a local asylum, where he becomes a cult leader. Meanwhile, his archivist daughter Heather begins to investigate the eeriness of the place, which is haunted by the presence of something local children call the sticky man.

Cisco, Michael.
The Divinity Student. Tallahassee, FL: Buzzcity Press, 1999. 149pp.

A young seminary student is beset by strange dreams after a near-death experience when he is struck by lightning (and his organs are replaced by pages from a book). Now he is known only as the Divinity Student, a "word finder" extraordinaire. He is doomed to travel through a nightmarish world of the dead to find the secret meanings of "lost words."

Chambers, Robert W.
Out of the Dark: Origins. Ashcroft, B.C.: Ash-Tree Press, 1998. 170pp.
Out of the Dark: Diversions. Ashcroft, B. C.: Ash-Tree Press, 1999. 206pp.

A play that, if read, causes certain madness and murderous tendencies? The play is *The King in Yellow*, and the people in these stories did not heed the government warning label. Now they must suffer the consequences. Any fan of the truly weird will not want to miss these tales, including the over-the-top grotesquerie, "The Repairer of Reputations" and the surreal "The Yellow Sign," two of Chambers's signature pieces.

Machen, Arthur.
The Three Imposters and Other Stories. Oakland, CA: Chaosium, 2001. 234pp.
The White People and Other Tales. Best Weird Tales series. Oakland, CA: Chaosium, 2003. 234pp.
The Terror and Other Stories. Best Weird Tales series. Oakland, CA: Chaosium, 2005. 234pp.

Anyone who has read *The Ring* or Peter Straub's *Ghost Story* is familiar with the idea of being "frightened to death." But readers may not know that these two stories owe their existence to pulp writer Arthur Machen's "The Great God Pan," a classic set in London, in which a mysterious female is killing off royalty. Here also is "The White People," considered by some to be one of the greatest horror stories ever.

Matheson, Richard.
Offbeat: Uncollected Stories. San Francisco: Subterranean Press, 2002. 240pp.

This mix of 13 stories includes four previously unpublished works and a fragment of a novel. Science fiction master and editor Nolan chooses tales such as "And in Sorrow," about future reproductive technologies. In another story, a death row inmate attempts to convince his executioners that they've got the wrong man. Then there is the ever-popular deal with the devil, and more.

Piccirilli, Tom.
The Night Class. New York: Leisure, 2002. 278pp.

If you think that the most evil presence in college is a strict professor who grades hard, think again. Caleb (Cal) Prentiss attends a downright evil university, and he is assigned a haunted dorm room. A pensive and intelligent student, Cal becomes obsessed with the girl who was assigned to the room before him: She was brutally murdered, and her spirit seems to still haunt the place.

Rubie, Peter.
Werewolf. Stamford, CT: Longmeadow Press, 1991. 272pp.

His temper has ended his marriage and put his daughter into a coma, but in this dark psychological thriller set in World War II London, policeman George Llewellyn must find a serial killer of children, whose corpses are found torn as if eaten by wild animals. But first he must deal with a belligerent gypsy community and with the people on the streets, who are talking about werewolves and curses.

Straub, Peter.
Mr. X. New York: Ballantine, 2000. 544pp.

Ned Dunstan returns to his small hometown of Edgerton, Illinois, to attend his mother's funeral, only to find himself implicated in several murders. To exonerate himself, Ned begins digging into local history, discovering that he was fathered by the scion of a wealthy local family and might have a sibling who is more of an evil doppelganger than a twin. Disturbing, complex, and truly original.

Hey, Let's Poke It with a Stick: Morbidly Fascinating

A decadent fascination with the darkest secrets of the human heart leads the reader into more gruesome territory. Stories here allow readers to rubberneck at the scene of the accident, as it were, without actually staying focused on the bodies strewn along the ground.

Baker, Trisha.
Crimson Kiss. New York: Pinnacle, 2001. 432pp.
   Simon is a vampire who really believes that sometimes it is necessary to be "cruel to be kind." Meghann is happy, that is until she meets Simon. She does an undead version of "the burning bed" when she stakes him and leaves him on a rooftop at sunrise, but he escapes. And nothing is more dangerous than an angry, sadistic vampire, who will torture and kill friends to get revenge.

Brust, Steven.
Agyar. New York: Tor, 1993. 254pp.
   Okay, so you've been turned into a vampire. If that in itself doesn't make your life suck, then imagine how you'll feel when the vampire who turned you further attempts to ruin your life by framing you for a murder. John Agyar, a vibrant young man who has taken up residence in a haunted house in Philadelphia, is suffering this exact fate.

Clark, Simon.
Darkness Demands. New York: Leisure, 2001. 395pp.
   If the dead started leaving you notes, asking for food, drink, and other comforts, would you comply? A novelist trying to finish his newest project is constantly interrupted by mysterious letters wrapped around bits of gravestone. At first he believes them to be a practical joke, but he soon finds out that terrible things have happened to people who ignored such notes. His investigation leads him to a huge Victorian cemetery of some 80,000 graves.

Cullen, Mitch.
Tideland. Chester Springs, PA: Dufour, 2000. 192p.
   Focusing on a poor, developmentally challenged girl named Jeliza-Rose, this morbid version of *Alice in Wonderland* pulls no punches. Jeliza keeps her dead father around for days, and places Barbie heads on her

fingertips so she will have friends to talk to while braving grotesque adventures no child should face alone. Will she survive, with only an eccentric female taxidermist and a 33- year-old, mentally retarded man as neighbors?

Fowler, Christopher.
Demonized. London: Serpent's Tale, 2004. 256pp.

    Here is an exploration of the uncanny in the innermost recesses of the human heart. A journalist wrangles an invitation to the Führer's chalet in hopes of persuading a former girlfriend, now a devoted Fascist, to escape with him; a tailor seeks revenge on a sultan who takes pleasure in manipulating and executing others; and the reader learns what is necessary for a woman to truly succeed in a man's world.

Kimball, Michael.
The Way the Family Got Away. New York: Four Walls, Eight Windows, 2000. 143pp.

    Children shouldn't play with dead things. Through the eyes of a brother and sister, ages five and three, the reader learns the story of a cross-country trek by a down-on-its-luck family—with a dead baby in the family trunk. In the small town of Mineola, Texas, an infant dies of yellow fever. Distraught, the mother and father dig up the coffin and pack all of their belongings to head north, where the extended family resides.

Little, Bentley.
The Mailman. New York: Penguin, 1991. 320pp.

    The mailman in a small, lazy town commits suicide, and his replacement is pure evil. At first people receive only good news in the mail, but later everyone gets threatening letters, bad news, and gory photographs of mutilated bodies. Can the mailman be stopped before he drives everyone to the brink of insanity? An original and clever look into people's fascination with "dirty laundry." Also a hard book to put down.

Matheson, Richard.
Come Fygures, Come Shadowes. Colorado Springs, CO: Gauntlet Press, 2003. 144pp.

    What? Not interested in going into the family business? Then meet a spirit medium named Morna, who wishes her daughter Claire to follow in her footsteps. Unfortunately Claire has no desire to be clairvoyant, and when she's forced to sit for séances and be the conduit for ectoplasmic manifestations, she becomes violently ill and feels as if she's been sexually violated.

Palahniuk, Chuck.
Haunted. New York: Doubleday, 2005. 416pp.

    Attempting to re-create the Villa Diadoti scenario that spawned Mary Shelley's *Frankenstein*, a group of aspiring authors lock themselves in an abandoned theater for three months. The results are several disturbing stories, framed by the narrative of their "retreat," during which they deny themselves access to phones, electricity, and ultimately food to demonstrate their dedication to art. Both the stories and the frame tale are gory and disturbing.

Poe, Edgar Allan.
The Fall of the House of Usher and Other Writings: Poems, Tales, Essays and Reviews. New York: Penguin, 1986. 539pp.

A private look at a brother–sister pair that shares the family insanity, a tale of inescapable death, a study in the intricacies of torture, a detective tale that seemingly has no "elementary" solution, stories of obsession and murderous revenge, and the ever-popular murderer-with-a-conscience story, among others, fill this volume of the best works of an early master of horror.

Siodmak, Curt.
Donovan's Brain. New York: Triangle Books, 1942. 234pp.

He should have settled for a hot air balloon ride around the world. Millionaire scientist Dr. Patrick Cory allows mogul Warren Donovan to die, so he can keep his brain alive in his laboratory. This is all well and good, until the brain develops telepathic powers, and Cory finds out that the lack of arms and legs is no big deal. This raw and uncompromising classic is not for the faint of heart.

Bring out Your Dead: Gruesome and Disgusting

These stories are perhaps the most disquieting (and sometimes the most disgusting) of all, with authors pulling out all the stops to frighten and discomfort the reader. The two texts that epitomize this style of writing are Nancy Holder's *Dead in the Water*, which unsettles the reader with its nightmarish descriptions and surreal characters, and John Shirley's *Black Butterflies*, which shocks the reader with its sado-masochistic sexual escapades (just what the metal thing is that these guys shock themselves with to achieve sexual gratification is beyond us) and torturous killings. Those who enjoy these tales should have a look at the listings under "Ewww, that's gross. Read it again!", the "gory story" subsection in the "I'm in the Mood for" section of this chapter.

Heck, Victor.
A Darkness Inbred. Kansas City, MO: Dark Tales Publications, 2000. 155pp.

Old Ezekiel had a farm. And on this farm he had a demon. An unfortunate couple has an accident on a remote country road and is dragged off to meet Ezekiel, his family, and a creature that the family found in a coffin. It seems the creature needs a female human host to impregnate with its "piggies." In addition, the family practices sadism and sexual mischief, which is described in raw detail using visceral prose.

Holder, Nancy.
🎀 *Dead in the Water.* New York: Dell, 1994. 432pp.
    The cruise aboard the *Pandora* begins with a message from the ship's captain: "This is how it will be when you drown." The situation only gets stranger as crew members and passengers alike begin to fall into and out of nightmarish, violent alternative realities. If only they can stop the unstoppable Captain Reade, the demonic puppeteer of their nightmares, they may survive.

Jacob, Charlee.
Haunter. New York: Leisure, 2003. 374pp.
    To put it bluntly, you don't want to know what the main character here does on a bet when he sees a dead animal. This is splatterpunk and gore at its best, by the only writer who can rival John Shirley. This gruesome, loose sequel to *This Symbiotic Fascination* (see next entry) picks up one of the minor characters and tells his Vietnam story, complete with vivid details of the life of a 10-year-old prostitute, torture sequences, and immolations.

Jacob, Charlee.
This Symbiotic Fascination. New York: Leisure, 2002. 394pp.
    An overweight, unattractive female and a werewolf-like shapeshifter strike up a protective friendship. However, she is unaware of his being possessed by beasts; when these beasts take over his body, he becomes a serial rapist and mutilator. Meanwhile, a grotesque Nosferatu is prowling the streets, literally tearing women limb from limb, and a cursed videotape turns a female officer into a killing machine. Worse yet, the heroine is turned into a murderous vampire.

Johnstone, William W.
The Devil's Kiss. The Devil series. New York: Kensington, 1980. 400pp.
    Sam Balon dies and finds himself in a personal hell, but he is resurrected so that he may protect his wife and son from Satan. He has lots of undead company; people have been turned into zombies and vampires, and many are bent on raping and torturing the living. Lots of action-packed, visceral horror and graphic sexuality inform this series, in which the devil uses sexual desire to take over a small community.

Koontz, Dean.
Odd Thomas. New York: Bantam, 2003. 399pp.
    Clairvoyant cook Odd Thomas takes pride in his work, so his fame has spread, bringing strangers to the restaurant in Pico Mundo. But then one day a mysterious stranger enters, and Odd senses that this is a man with an appetite for terror and extreme violence; for what makes Thomas truly odd is that he communicates with the restless dead.

Shirley, John.
🏅 ***Black Butterflies*** (Originally published as *Black Butterflies: A Flock on the Wild Side*, 1998). New York: Leisure, 2001. 350pp.
🅑

Those looking for a gentle read should pass on this one. It's a no-holds-barred collection, in which carjackers become victims of a woman with hypnotic powers and an axe to grind, police officers defile the bodies of murder victims, every type of sexual perversion imaginable results in a party with a body count, and a slasher film director is drawn into his own world of horror and mayhem.

Shirley, John.
Wetbones. Shingletown, CA: Ziesling, 1991. 273pp.

Ephram Pixie is a psychic vampire, a human being who lives on the life force of others while forcing them to do his bidding—until he uses them up completely. Working on his twenty-seventh victim, he is turning a teenaged girl into a murderous slave. Her father cannot save her alone, so he enlists the help of a Hollywood writer, whose wife was the most recent victim, left as a husk for anyone to find.

Skipp, John, and Craig Spector.
The Light at the End. New York: Bantam, 1986. 385pp.

Some people wouldn't be caught dead taking the New York City subway at night. This is not the case on the night that Rudy rides, and unfortunately for the passengers, a sadistic vampire makes sure they don't arrive alive. Rudy is left with vague memories of blood-splattered seats and windows, a pain in his neck, and an insatiable thirst for blood. Now his girlfriend and best friend must team up—to kill him.

Slade, Michael.
Headhunter. Special X series. New York: Onyx Books, 1984. 422pp.

CSI fans will thoroughly enjoy this police procedural/horror series set mainly in Canada. In the first novel in this series, Royal Canadian Mountie Robert DeClerq is receiving Kodak moments from hell. A serial killer called The Headhunter randomly murders and then beheads women and sends DeClerq pics. The gore continues, with a killer obsessed with H. P. Lovecraft's Cthulhu Mythos, militant feminist Satanists, and an amateur archeologist who considers himself a reincarnated Highland warrior. Other titles in the series include *Ghoul, Cut Throat, Ripper, Evil Eye, Primal Scream*, and *Burnt Bones*. Slade is the pen name adopted by the original writing team of Jay Clarke, John Banks, and Lee Clarke, kept as the pen name for the series by subsequent writing teams.

Taylor, Lucy.
The Safety of Unknown Cities. Woodstock, GA: Overlook Connection Press-Infinity Fiction, 1999. 225pp.

Val and Breen have a desperate need for human connection. Val attempts to achieve this connection by frequently changing sexual partners. Breen, on the other hand, achieves the same ends by burglarizing people's houses and rifling through their possessions, and later, by perusing the actual contents of their bodies, in this graphic and disturbing novel.

What's the Matter? Scared of Something?: The Truly Terrifying

Kick up the fear factor another notch, with descriptions a bit more graphic, and fear levels a bit more intense. Works in this section are by no means over-the-top, yet in many instances they are able to inspire intense fear. Some are fast-paced, leaving the reader breathless after a roller coaster ride of fear. They're rather like a good Halloween haunted house, where new surprises jump out at every turn.

Blatty, William Peter.
The Exorcist. New York: Harper & Row, 1971. 340pp.

Newsflash to parents—teenagers sometimes act as if they're possessed. In this terror classic, 12-year-old Regan McNeil begins acting strangely, and her mother, a lapsed Catholic, begins to suspect that her daughter may actually be possessed by demons. She reluctantly calls in Fathers Merrin and Kerris. The experiences suffered in this haunted household, especially in Regan's bedroom, end up solidifying both the faith of the mother and of Kerris, who is himself questioning his beliefs.

Campbell, Ramsey.
Nazareth Hill. New York: Doherty-Forge, 1997. 384pp.

The first few chapters here will send chills up the reader's spine, and the ending will leave that reader slack-jawed. This is a one-of-a-kind, truly terrifying, yet realistic novel. When her father holds up eight-year-old Amy so she can see inside one of the windows of Nazarill, a decrepit building, she sees something spidery and ghostlike moving in a corner. Eight years later, Nazarill is a renovated hostelry, and Amy's father is the caretaker.

Card, Orson Scott.
Lost Boys. New York: HarperCollins, 1992. 582pp.

In a tale that is heavy on atmosphere and slow-developing threat, a devout Mormon family moves to the small town of Steuben, North Carolina. Step Fletcher and his wife soon discover that their new Southern home is not another Mayberry; rather, it is the site of a great evil—and it has their son Steven in its grip. Card successfully interweaves the mundane details of everyday Mormon life with a subtle use of supernatural horror.

Clegg, Douglas.
The Nightmare Chronicles. New York: Leisure, 1999. 360pp.

Imagine O. Henry's "The Ransom of Red Chief" with slashers, demons, and gore; that's this double award-winning collection of 13 tales that cross every line when it comes to the taboo and push the envelope as far as possible for violence and pure terror. A young boy is kidnapped by a motley crew, but he turns the tables on them by forcing them to listen to stories that challenge their sanity.

Harris, Thomas.
Red Dragon. The Hannibal Lecter Novels. Toronto: Academic Press, 1981. 348pp.

Someone is slaughtering families, elaborately arranging the bodies, putting mirrors in their eyes, then filming the carnage. FBI agent Will Graham must catch the killer, using his ability to predict serial murders by thinking like the killer, but this leads him to a disturbing realization about how victims are chosen. A truly scary, graphic read that was made into the TV movie *Manhunter* and later remade as a feature film with the original novel's title. Other novels in the series include *The Silence of the Lambs*, *Hannibal*, and *Behind the Mask*.

King, Stephen.
Bag of Bones. New York: Scribner, 1998. 529pp.

Those refrigerator magnets spelling out weird messages again? A writer who returns to his lake home in Maine to investigate his wife's death, opening himself to a visitation from her spirit. And she's not the only ghost on the premises. In a community that has a lot of skeletons in its closet that it would like to keep hidden, all ghosts may not be friendly and helpful.

King, Stephen.
It. New York: Viking, 1986. 1138pp.

He's the monster in the sewer. He's the scary thing in the dark cave. He's Pennywise the Clown, personification of all that is scary and dangerous and evil, and he has returned to a small New England town to claim the souls of a handful of adults whom he terrorized as children. This wonderfully frightening read, which was made into a television miniseries, will give readers another reason to think clowns are just a bit creepy.

Little, Bentley, et al.
Four Dark Nights. New York: Dorchester, 2002. 336pp.

    The four stories here occur in the space of one terrifying evening. Little's "The Circle" is particularly horrifying and gory and will have readers wincing in sympathy for the hapless citizens of a doomed neighborhood. Douglas Clegg's "The Words" tells of two alienated teens who are led into the "world of Nowhere," and a supernatural experience allows a woman some closure with her deceased father in Christopher Golden's "Pyre." Tom Piccirilli also contributes.

Nassie, Joseph M.
Riverwatch. St. Petersburg, FL: Barclay Books, 2001. 370pp.

    Anyone who thinks that demons look like Elizabeth Hurley and want nothing more than to trick people into selling their souls is in for a nasty surprise. The demon Moloch, accidentally set free when a construction crew in Vermont finds a tomb hidden beneath a lake, wants nothing more than to tear people limb from limb. And it REALLY likes killing. Only a descendant of a warlock can stop it—if he can remember how.

Simmons, Dan.
Summer of Night. New York: Putnam, 1991. 555pp. **YA**

    Think your first grade teachers were scary? Well, sickeningly grotesque ghosts walk the halls of Old Central in this frightening, nightmarish novel about the escapades of six teens who discover that death reigns supreme at the oldest elementary school in Elm Haven, Illinois. What chance do they have against The Rendering Man when even their parents don't believe the horrors they've witnessed? One of Simmons's best, this story introduces characters who appear in his later novels.

Straub, Peter.
Ghost Story. New York: Simon & Schuster, 1979. 567pp.

    Although the title of this modern classic is misleading, it is one novel you will not want to read while you're alone. Full of ritualistic animal slayings, extremely gory "accidents," and lurking evil presences, it tells of five elderly men who share a dark secret. Now their pasts are coming back to haunt them—literally. And unfortunately for the townspeople, the evil that is stalking the men does not discriminate when it metes out vengeance.

Horror for All Occasions

    Around Halloween, readers may find themselves picking up novels centered on that holiday or perhaps simply grabbing something that stars witches and goblins, or texts that appeal to childhood fears. Realizing that a demented mind is a terrible thing to waste, they may enjoy merry horror near Christmas or romantic horror near St. Valentine's Day. Certainly if there is a time for every purpose under Heaven, there is a time for readers to let the words on a page turn their hearts a little more fearful. Sometimes an occasion can be something as simple as a dark and stormy night: the lone reader, in a bedroom filled with antique, dark-stained wood furniture, or in a large study or library, with candles providing the only light to read by—that is until lightning illuminates a window and makes clear the shadows of swaying tree branches outside. This reader sits in serious concentration, hunkered over a terrifying tome of murder or mayhem, or worse yet, of supernatural evil invading the world of humanity. Then again, many of us travel, and the horror fan may want books that fit that occasion, or texts that simply can be read in almost one sitting. And then there are those who read right before bedtime, to encourage "sweet" dreams.

Is That Michael Myers at the Window?: Halloween Horror

No event could be more fitting for horror than the celebration of all things ghostly, Halloween. It should come as no surprise that many horror texts are set around All Hallow's Eve. Another type of book that might be appropriate for the holiday is the anthology or collection. These present shorter horror fiction, perfect for the time spent waiting between trick-or-treaters.

Braunbeck, Gary A.
In Silent Graves (Originally published as *The Indifference of Heaven*, 2000). New York: Leisure-Dorchester, 2004. 378pp.
> The subjects of death and deformity—not merely in their philosophical sense, but in their most raw, grotesque, physical manifestations—provide the impetus for this fairy tale for adults. An egocentric newscaster loses both his wife and their unborn child on Halloween, the same night he meets "split face," an indescribably deformed young man who shows him that reality is like a carnival fun house, only more disturbing, and that life is not what it seems.

Clegg, Douglas.
The Halloween Man. New York: Leisure, 1998. 360pp.
> Stony Crawford returns to his small hometown after a 12-year absence to dispose of an evil presence he unwittingly helped create when he was just 15. Will the teenaged boy he has in tow, kidnapped from a strange religious compound, help him destroy this presence? Or will he have to destroy the boy? This is an action-oriented page-turner with a complex plot.

Clegg, Douglas.
Mischief. Harrow Academy series. New York: Leisure, 2000. 359pp.

Think only people have histories? Be prepared to take a century-long trek through Harrow House, in its various incarnations. The tale begins in 1926, when the cursed Hudson River Estate is left to Ethan Gravesend. Eventually the mansion becomes part of a boy's prep school and home to the aptly named Cadaver Society, as well as a well-known haunted house studied by students and an occult professor. Other titles in the series include *The Infinite*, *The Nightmare House*, and *The Abandoned*.

Clegg, Douglas.
The Necromancer. Forest Hills, MD: Cemetery Dance Publications, 2004. 140pp.

This novella borrows from Clegg's own Harrow House mythology, supplying the prequel to the events of the series by giving readers the story of the early years of Justin Gravesend's life. When Gravesend leaves his hometown and moves in with his uncle in the 1920s, he enters college. During a trip to London, he is made aware of a part of himself he never knew existed when he meets his master, the Necromancer.

Golden, Christopher.
Wildwood Road. New York: Bantam, 2005. 305pp.

On Halloween, Michael nearly hits a girl while driving home. Anxious to help her get to safety, he brings her to the run-down house she says is her home. Afterward he finds himself being haunted by her image—and a group of wraiths that steal his wife's essence. When he tries to find the girl to ask for an explanation, it's as if she, or the house, never existed.

Greenberg, Martin H., and Al Sarrantonio, eds.
100 Hair-Raising Little Horror Stories. New York: Sterling, 2003. 512pp.

So you need something to do between visits from little Frankensteins, Draculas, and Samaras? Master editor Greenberg and scary-as-hell author Sarrantonio showcase the best of the best. These short works by the likes of Edgar Allan Poe, H. P. Lovecraft, Fritz Leiber, Nathaniel Hawthorne, Stephen Crane, Charles Dickens, Robert Barr, and Washington Irving will keep the shivers running down your spine while you sneak pieces of candy.

Hand, Stephen, Damian Shannon, and Mark Swift.
Freddy vs. Jason. New York: Simon & Schuster, 2004. 254pp. **YA**

Freddy Krueger, now in Hell, gets a little restless when he finds out that the townspeople of Springwood are learning to control their dreams enough to keep him from living through them. So he manages to release Jason Voorhies to Elm Street, to remind its citizens what fear is. Jason, however, gets carried away, so Freddy is faced with the task of returning himself, to stop Jason's rampage.

Laymon, Richard.
Once Upon a Halloween. Baltimore: Cemetery Dance, 2000. 252pp.

Laymon blends over-the-top horror and tongue-in-cheek humor in this tale about a boy who returns from a night of trick-or-treating with fear in his eyes, screaming that monsters are after him and have followed him home. The problem is, neither his parents nor his friends are of help, because they do not believe him.

McBean, Brett.
The Last Motel. Duluth, GA: Biting Dog, 2004. 258pp.

What could be a better place for a serial killer to flourish than a remote motel, located far off on a hilly road, on a Halloween night? And this killer revels in slow-motion torture, related in a cut-by-cut, detailed description of the most heinous acts imaginable. Caught in his trap are a police officer's widow, a middle-aged homeowner who accidentally shot a teenager, his hysterical wife, two bungling car thieves, and a hapless teen.

Rice, Anne.
The Witching Hour. The Mayfair Witches series. New York: Ballantine, 1990. 965pp.

What could be more appropriate at Halloween than a witch? A family of witches, of course. Rowan Mayfair returns to New Orleans to learn about the legacy of the Mayfair witches and the demonic spirit Lasher, which has allowed the family to prosper. But the bargain struck long ago with the first of Rowan's line demands that the thirteenth-generation witch—and that would be Rowan—pay Lasher his due, which means certain madness and an early death. Other titles in the series are *Lasher* and *Taltos: Lives of the Mayfair Witches.*

Sarrantonio, Al.
Hallows Eve. Forest Hills, MD: Cemetery Dance, 2004. 270pp.

After his career is suddenly ruined and he loses his lover, 30-year-old photographer Corrie Phaeder finds himself on a train to his hometown, Orangefield. He is met not with parades, but with a horrifying, surreal messenger who has the body of a scarecrow and the face of a living pumpkin. It seems that the epitome of evil, Samhain, is about to take over the town on Halloween, and only Corrie can stop him.

Death Takes a Holiday: Horror About Other Holidays

Okay, so Michael Myers wasn't a good boy, and got a lump of coal in his stocking. But does that mean he shouldn't be allowed to celebrate Christmas? Or that he shouldn't send Samara a box of candy on Valentine's Day? These writers apparently think not, and those who enjoy holiday horror appreciate them all the more.

Devereaux, Robert.
Santa Steps Out: A Fairy Tale for Grown-ups. New York: Leisure, 2000. 360pp.

    Just because Halloween is over doesn't mean readers can't enjoy a good scare. Here St. Nicholas is not the jolly fat man from malls and street corners. He's a satyr, left over from earlier pagan times. One fateful night in 1969, God stops paying attention and Santa Claus and the Tooth Fairy (a former nymph) cross paths. Christmas will never be the same after reading this gory and transgressive, but fun, novel.

Dokey, Cameron.
Truth and Consequences. New York: Simon & Schuster-Simon Pulse, 2003. 208pp.

    Ah, the perfect love triangle story for Valentine's Day—just me, you, and a demon from hell. Phoebe accepts a friendly dinner date with a handsome stranger but gets caught when her boyfriend, Cole, returns from work early. His mistrust of her comes to the fore, and a rift is created between the two that also threatens to destroy The Power of Three, in this *Charmed* novelization.

Koontz, Dean.
The Vision. New York: Putnam, 1977. 224pp.

    Twas' the night before Christmas, and all through the house, not a creature was stirring—thanks to a vicious serial killer on a rampage. A young woman has visions of grisly murders that are taking place during the Christmas holidays. Can these visions be connected to her traumatic childhood and her intense fear of sex?

Moore, Christopher.
The Stupidest Angel: A Heartwarming Tale of Christmas Terror. New York: William Morrow, 2004. 288pp.

    Cookies and milk just won't cut it when these newly animated zombies come down the chimney, and through the windows, and through the walls . . . . In fact, Pine Cove, California, will never be a typical small, sleepy town again, since Lena Marquez killed her cheating husband on his way home from playing Santa Claus. Enter the Archangel Raziel, who saves the holiday by bringing Santa—and various other fresh corpses—back to life.

Newman, Kim.
The Quorum. New York: Carroll and Graf, 1994. 311pp.

    In this erudite cross between Wall Street and *American Psycho*, three young British college students become involved with Derek Leech, a Mephistopheles-like multimedia mogul, who delivers fame and money in the form of phenomenal success—for 15 years. All that is necessary is that their friend Neil be constantly in pain. But when Valentine's Day rolls around, it is time for the extremely successful young men to face their damnation.

Home Alone Meets *Scream*: He Knows When You're Alone

This section of books needs no introduction. You're alone. He's out there. Enough said.

Brooks, Susan M.
Collecting Candace. Seal Beach, CA: Small Dog Press, 2005. 193pp.

Love hurts—literally—in this imagistic stalker story, told in vivid language that evokes the smothering stillness of a Florida summer with no air conditioning. The nameless narrator falls in love at first sight with Candace on a stiflingly hot summer night, thinking that, "he didn't know if she had a husband, but he imagined that if she did, he would like very much at [that] moment to kill him."

Campbell, Ramsey.
Silent Children. New York: Tor, 2000. 384pp.

Contractor Hector Woollie, a self-described "angel," brings peace in his own special way to young children whom he feels have been abused by their parents: a pillow over the face, a knife across the throat. Then Hector calmly disposes of the bodies in the foundations of houses he's working on.

Hooper, Kay.
Touching Evil. New York: Bantam Books, 2001. 358pp.

Maggie Barnes is a woman who literally feels the pain of others. She walks into homes where kidnappings have occurred and feels the violence that occurred there. She senses emotions when interviewing victims, and both she and her twin brother can sculpt and paint images of the future. Mutilations, killings, past lives, and familial connections hint back as far the earliest American literary serial killer in this detective thriller.

Koontz, Dean.
Demon Seed. New York: Bantam, 1973. 182pp.

In this case, IT knows you're alone. Dr. Susan Harris is guarded round the clock by a computer that runs every aspect of her home. When this artificial intelligence decides it wants to better understand the ways of the flesh, it turns against her, imprisons her in her home, and impregnates her with a cyborg-like fetus. This is perhaps Koontz's best work.

Koontz, Dean.
Intensity. New York: Ballantine, 1995. 436pp.

> While on a college break, Chyna Shepherd witnesses the brutal murders of her best friend and her entire family and decides to follow the killer to his isolated home to exact revenge. There's only one problem: The killer, the sadistic Edgler Vess, knows he's being followed. This cat-and-mouse tale of suspense and courage is a fan favorite.

Koontz, Dean.
Whispers. New York: Putnam, 1980. 444pp.

> According to the old saying, "What doesn't kill you makes you stronger." Unfortunately for Hollywood writer Hillary Thomas, who returns home to discover a male acquaintance hiding in her closet in order to rape and kill her, this may be all too true. Hillary chases him away with a gun, but he never gives up, returning again and again—even after she fatally stabs him during an attack.

Prescott, Michael.
In Dark Places. New York: Penguin-Onyx, 2004. 384pp.

> Psychiatrist Robin Cameron is perfecting an experimental treatment to alter the brain structure of serial killers whose crimes stem from anger. She seems to be on the verge of success with Justin Gray, a killer of high school girls who didn't rape or torture his victims and now seems nearly rehabilitated. But then Gray escapes.

Tem, Melanie.
Slain in the Spirit. New York: Leisure, 2002. 317pp.

> Former teacher Lelia Blackwell is legally blind: She can only make out dim shapes, watch films, and read with some assistance. She is kidnapped by Russell Gavin, a former student now professing a particularly twisted version of evangelical Christianity. He wishes to repay her—his favorite teacher—by reversing their earlier roles.

Uh, It's Just the Wind, Right?: The Horror of Uncertainty

These texts are known for the authors' use of atmosphere, for their eerie quality. There isn't a lot of slice 'em and dice 'em horror here, nor any over-the-top apocalyptic visions—just books that make readers shiver, and jump every time they hear a noise.

Campbell, Ramsey.
Ghosts and Grisly Things. New York: Tor, 1998. 300pp.

What could be a better accompaniment to forked lightning, howling wind, and driving rain than the traditional ghost story, in which every creaking noise and gentle draft can mean an otherwordly visitation? In this collection are tales of haunted houses, vengeful ghosts, Cthulhian creatures, and things that go bump in the night. Watch for "Mackintosh Willy," one of the most anthologized modern ghost stories. Other ghostly collections by Campbell include *Cold Print* (New York: Tor, 1987. 331pp.) and *Dark Companions* (New York: Tor, 1992. 318pp.).

Clegg, Douglas.
You Come When I Call You. New York: Leisure, 1996. 394pp.

This complex but atmospheric, haunting tale mixes past and present. Twenty years before the action takes place, a California desert town was completely destroyed. Now, tapes and diary entries tell how inhabitants unwittingly struck a deal with a female demon. What will researchers uncover? Was the town a victim of a bargain with evil? Is that evil still present and waiting to pounce again?

Doyle, Arthur Conan.
The Captain of the "Pole-Star": Weird and Imaginative Fiction. Ashcroft, BC: Ash-Tree Press, 2004. 460pp.

Although Conan Doyle is rightly acknowledged as a fine writer of detective stories, he was also an accomplished teller of tales featuring the weird, the supernatural, and the horrific, with "The Haunted Grange of Goresthorpe" written when he was only 18. This collection showcases 37 stories of ghosts and mummies, psychic vampires and psychological terror, and horrors of the earth.

Goingback, Owl.
Darker Than Night. New York: Penguin, 1999. 342pp.

A novelist inherits his grandmother's house, a portal for shadowy creatures from a netherworld. These creatures, called "boogers" because of the childhood name they were given, threaten to destroy the world as we know it, beginning with his family. This novel is based on a real-life incident in Spain in 1971, when mysterious faces appeared on the floor of a small cottage. It is heavy on atmosphere and eerie-ness.

Gursick, Sara.
One Against the World: A Ghost Story. Philadelphia: XLibris, 2004. 264pp.

In 1984, Samantha Hunt leaves St. Louis for a simpler life, causing friction in her marriage. Shortly after moving into her country dream home with her two daughters, she is plagued by eerie dreams and visions, and she comes to believe there is a ghost in the house. Meanwhile, her vivid nightmares threaten to expose a centuries-old secret that the community would prefer be left buried.

Hawthorne, Nathaniel.
The House of Seven Gables. New York: Oxford University Press, 1991 (1851). 328pp.

    Phoebe, scion of a dwindling New England family, comes to the House of Seven Gables to help her impoverished Aunt Hepzibah earn a living. But they cannot escape a family curse somehow linked to a grotesque daguerreotype of the family patriarch, who was accused of witchcraft two centuries before. This nineteenth-century novel is written in prose characteristic of the time and emphasizes atmosphere and characterization over action.

Hodgson, William Hope.
Boats of the "Glen Carrig" and Other Nautical Adventures. Newberg, OR: Nightshade Books, 2003. 400pp.

    A diary found in an ancient stone house in Ireland leads to subterranean monsters. The *Mortzestus,* an unlucky ship, is haunted by "too many shadows." From his chilling *Ghost Pirates* to the strange and haunting *House on the Borderland* and *The Night Land*, Hodgson is recognized as one of the benchmark authors in the literature of the weird and fantastic. Included is the classic occult detective tale, "Carnacki the Ghost Finder." Two additional volumes follow.

Straub, Peter.
Shadowland. New York: Berkley, 1981. 468pp.

    Apparently the boys at a Northeastern boys' school didn't read *Carrie*, or they would have known better than to pick on Tom Flannagan and Del Nightingale. These two teenaged misfits spent their summer as apprentices to a magician so they could polish their amateur act. Now horrible "accidents" begin happening to the school bullies. Could it be black magic?

Wright, T. M.
The House on Orchid Street. New York: Dorchester-Leisure, 2003. 322pp.

    This slow-paced and thoughtful spine-tingler begins when Katherine Nichols purchases a Victorian mansion out in the country—not realizing that it was the only house to survive a fire that decimated a poor urban neighborhood. Soon she discovers that she is plagued by a grotesquely fat woman she saw in a painting, various whispering voices, and other ghostly visitors.

Trains, Planes, and Automobiles: Travel Horror

We all like to read while we're traveling by plane or train, and some of us even manage to read while riding shotgun. The stories in this section may appeal to those who do like to read while traveling, as they either follow unwary protagonists as they trek across America or are short and sweet, just right to finish in one sitting.

Bacon-Smith, Camille.
Daemons, Inc. (Omnibus). New York: Science Fiction Book Club, 1998. 478pp.

First there was Perry Mason. Then Columbo. Then Jessica Fletcher. But with criminals becoming more "sophisticated," it takes a superhuman sleuth like Kevin Bradley to match wits with otherworldly fiends. When the crystals of the Dowager Empress of China begin disappearing into thin air, he and a group of American detectives are called in to find a supernatural thief. An omnibus edition of *Eye of the Daemon* and *Eyes of the Empress*.

Darrah, Royal C.
The Hotel California. Victoria, BC: Trafford Publishing, 2004. 300pp.

"You can check out any time you like, but you can never leave" the Hotel California. This mystery, based not on a classic text but on a classic rock song, invites the reader to visit an undisclosed location between the sand and sagebrush of the unforgiving desert. Cliff and Sara Bower are making a last attempt to salvage what's left of their marriage, and they are lost—and out of gas.

Koontz, Dean.
Shattered. New York: Berkley, 1985. 289pp.

Alex Doyle and his nephew are traveling by road from Philadelphia to San Francisco, but to their horror, they're being followed by a white Automover van whose owner has murderous intentions. This is a good potboiler for those who enjoy reading material that might prevent them from nodding off on the bus and missing their stop.

Koontz, Dean.
Strangers. New York: Putnam, 1986. 526pp.

Across the country, a handful of people who don't know one another have similar nightmares and share a sense of paranoia. They all travel to the Nevada desert and congregate at an out-of-the-way hotel. Little do they know that they are being watched and are part of an experiment that has infected each of them with a mysterious malady.

Laymon, Richard.
The Lake. New York: Dorchester, 2004. 352pp. **YA**

When she was a young, rebellious girl, Leigh longed for a summer of excitement by the lake. She met a handsome boy who was willing to row her out to an abandoned beach house, but what she found was fear. Now that her daughter is going through the same restless emotions, Leigh realizes that the terror she found out in that cottage is coming back to haunt her and her family. Soon both mother and daughter will be plunged into a nightmare from which there seems to be no escape.

Powers, Tim.
Declare. New York: William Morrow, 2001. 517pp.

Move over, Indiana Jones! Oxford lecturer Andrew Hale, a secret member of Her Majesty's Secret Service, is headed to Mount Ararat—but not to find the Holy Grail. He has been recalled to finish a job he began during World War II. It's 1963, and the Soviet government has enlisted dark forces to harness the power of the sacred site in order to end the Cold War once and for all.

Chapter 3

Setting

Setting plays an important role in all fiction. It creates a world for characters to inhabit and for readers to experience. In horror, setting is crucial because it creates an atmosphere of suspense and foreboding. The famous cliché, "it was a dark and stormy night," demonstrates the primary importance of setting for drawing readers into the plot of a tale of terror. Whether it is a specific location, such as the Puritan town with a crisp veneer and a seething, dark underside in Stephen King's *Needful Things,* or the big city (St. Louis, in this case) of Robert J. Randisi's Joe Keough Novels, setting prepares the stage for the story. In some novels, setting is such a powerful force that it takes on the role of a character, directing the plotline. In any case, setting provides the fertile soil in which terror grows.

Places, Everyone

Home Is Where the Horror Is: Haunted Houses

Your house may be your castle, but unless it is surrounded by some kind of psychic moat, the supernatural can always cross the threshold, make itself at home, and destroy your peace of mind. In this section are stories set in various houses, sometimes even in the family "home," where the safety of the family unit, or the protection that Mom and Dad represent, is shattered.

Clark, Simon.
In This Skin. New York: Dorchester, 2004. 384pp.

Welcome to the dance palace from Hell. Chicago's condemned, decaying Luxor dance hall, which resembles an Egyptian temple, possesses a strange magnetism, and several people begin to believe that it is their home. But the spirits there are not just found in a bottle; mysterious forces lurk beneath its cushioned floors and want to keep these hapless humans for eternity.

Gates, R. Patrick.
The Prison. New York: Kensington-Pinnacle, 2004. 384pp.

Even the big house can be haunted. Tim Stage, fresh from the correctional officers' training facility, feels he is ready to walk the walls of The Hill; but he's been there before in disturbing dreams that have him wandering through the building's eerie hallways, dealing with the increasing madness of the inmates and the desires of deceased prisoners.

Giron, Sephera.
House of Pain. New York: Leisure, 2001. 360pp.

Do you know the entire history of your home? What if some unspeakable crime had been committed in your very basement? Lydia thinks she has found security at last when she marries Tony, an up-and-coming executive who has just built their dream house. But why can't she bring herself to unpack all her belongings once she moves in? Is it cold feet? Or is it the nightmares that frighten both her and her dog?

Haining, Peter, ed.
The Mammoth Book of Haunted House Stories. New York: Carroll and Graf, 2000. 576pp.

Horror scholar S. T. Joshi sums up the selections in this wonderful anthology as fusing "intellectual substance with a clutching horrific atmosphere [through] nightmarish, hallucinatory prose" that both establishes characterization and will keep readers on the edge of their seats. In other words, creepy shadows will slowly emerge to become horrifying apparitions. This has been called the best and only widely published anthology of haunted house stories.

Harper, M. A.
The Year of Past Things: A New Orleans Ghost Story. Athens, GA: Hill Street Press, 2004. 256pp.

The spirit of an ex-husband and legendary Cajun musician appears at will and inhabits everyday objects in a couple's New Orleans home. The couple tries various remedies to rid themselves of the annoying presence—exorcists, psychics, even a well-known novelist—but to no avail. This ghost wants something, and it isn't a new accordion.

Jackson, Shirley.
The Haunting of Hill House. New York: Penguin, 1984 (1949). 256pp.

    Sometimes a person doesn't choose a house; sometimes, a house chooses a person. In spare, haunting style, Jackson tells us the story of Hill House, which has stood untenanted for the past 80 years, since a series of "unfortunate accidents" and a feeling of malaise drove away the last of its occupants. When a professor of the paranormal comes to document the disturbances and recruits others to join him, Hill House comes to life to claim a companion for all eternity.

Johnson, Scott A.
An American Haunting. Martinez, GA: Harbor House, 2004. 300pp.

    An old house in Texas seems like the ideal place for a young couple to live: It's close to town and surrounded by a large yard and gardens. But it's the house that every child in the neighborhood whispers about, and where visitors always feel as if they are being watched. It's the house that will enslave family members in a cycle of pain that has lasted for nearly a century.

Kahn, James.
Poltergeist. Poltergeist and Poltergeist, The Legacy series. New York: Warner, 1982. 301pp.

    In this book, based on the famous movie by the same name, Kahn tells the story of a family trapped in a haunted suburban home. In the series' spin-off titles, written by various authors, ancient Egyptian deities contest The Legacy members and all of Christianity in a race for a lost manuscript at the bottom of a mysterious sea. Two Legacy members who visit Plymouth Rock on Thanksgiving witness a deadly terrorist attack that kills one member's son. The son comes back as a ghost to help hunt down the responsible terror cell. Other titles in the series include Kahn's *Poltergeist II*, Rick Hautala's *Poltergeist, The Legacy: The Hidden Saint,* and Matthew J. Costello's *Poltergeist, The Legacy: Maelstrom.*

Lee, Edward.
The Chosen. New York: Kensington, 1993. 379pp.

    If things seem too good to be true, they probably are. Just ask Vera. Her professional and personal lives are quite satisfactory, but when she's offered a job managing an expensive resort at three times the salary she's currently making, she can't resist. Things just get creepier from there. The resort, located in an old sanitarium rumored to be haunted, is now a place where many guests are raped and killed.

Matheson, Richard.
Hell House. New York: Tor, 1999. 301pp.

    Words to the wise: If you are invited to stay someplace with the word "hell" in its name, politely refuse. A professor of the occult and his students stay in The Belasco House, also known as Hell House, rumored to be the most haunted place on Earth. It is a site of unimaginable decadence and cruelty, and it has driven its inhabitants mad, often leading them to suicide.

Matthews, A. J. (pseudonym of Rick Hautala).
Looking Glass. New York: Penguin-Berkley, 2004. 352pp.

Mirror, mirror on the wall, who's the scariest of them all? Ask the Irelands. After they move to the country for peace and quiet, they discover that their new abode has drawbacks beyond the everyday strains of living in a new home. A hideously scarred woman begins appearing in all the house's mirrors. Now the family must discover the meaning behind her presence or continue suffering from the frightful appearances.

Nicholson, Scott.
The Manor. New York: Kensington-Pinnacle, 2004. 384pp.

What's that scraping noise in the walls? Rats? Maybe. Ghosts? A sculptor and terminally ill parapsychologist Anna Galloway meet at Korban Manor. Neither realizes that the original owner is neither dead nor alive, but lives in the walls and the glass of the home he loved so much. This is a traditional ghost story by one of the best up-and-coming writers in the genre, perfect for those who love classic horror.

That's Probably Where They'll Bury Me: Small Town Horror

Having too much space to yourself may mean that when the time comes, nobody will be able to hear you scream. Or if they can, it is just as likely that whatever is about to get you will get your local sheriff, well before the FBI or the National Guard can locate the only state highway in or out of town on their maps. Remember, sometimes the safest looking locales—even Mayberry—may be haunted.

Franz, Darren.
Ghost Train. Frederick, MD: PublishAmerica, 2004. 227pp.

All aboard! Next stop Barron, a sleepy Midwestern railroad town just like the kind in 1950s movies. And unfortunately, one that is cursed. Every so often the Ghost Train rides through. People turn up missing or dead. Eddie Drake knows all about it; it killed most of his family. But can Eddie use his knowledge to stop the train?

Goingback, Owl.
🎖 *Crota.* New York: D. I. Fine, 1996. 292pp.

Most people stay away from thoroughfares named Cemetery Lane or Graveyard Road, but not Buddy. He foolishly takes Graveyard Road, and promptly runs out of gas. Soon he is a statistic. Details of the forensic investigation lead Skip Hastings, the sheriff of a sleepy Midwestern town where people normally feel safe, to suspect something terrifying. Can he get anyone to believe that a demonic beast possesses an insatiable hunger for "local cuisine?"

Hand, Elizabeth.
Black Light. New York: HarperPrism, 2000. 380pp.

    A Christmas card village nestled in the hills of upstate New York is a town with a troubled and mysterious past. Teenagers commit suicide, and adults show no remorse. Everything revolves around Axel Kern, a mysterious figure who owns Bolerium, a mansion made of ancient Cornish stones that serve as a portal to the Underworld. In the midst of this, three teens are making plans for college—if they live that long.

Karamesines, P. G.
The Pictograph Murders. Salt Lake City, UT: Signature Books, 2004. 352pp.

    There couldn't be a more perfect locale on the planet for a loner who feels connected to the earth than the Utah desert, where an amateur archeologist can pack up her Siberian husky and go off to enjoy the beauty of the landscape. But Alex McKelvey's presence causes the disappearance of the site's owner and the appearance of a dangerous mythological creature: the Coyote trickster.

King, Stephen.
Needful Things. New York: Viking, 1991. 690pp.

    Castle Rock is a peaceful, small town where inhabitants agree to disagree in matters of religion and politics. Then Leland Gaunt arrives and opens Needful Things, a curio shop that carries everyone's heart's desire. And while Leland's curios are not to be resisted, each comes at a terrible price that could ultimately shatter the peace of Castle Rock.

King, Stephen.
'Salem's Lot. Garden City, NJ: Doubleday, 1975. 439pp.

    Not much happens in Jerusalem's, or 'Salem's, Lot, a small town on the verge of death. Then a mysterious stranger comes to town and buys the mysterious Marston, an old cursed mansion that has stood vacant many years. Soon townspeople disappear, and those who remain have radically altered personalities. Could the events have something to do with the new inhabitant of Marston House?

Koontz, Dean.
Winter Moon. New York: Ballantine, 1994. 472pp.

    Pulsing sounds. A glowing light. These appear on the far end of an isolated Montana property. Eduardo Fernandez documents his experiences with what he calls "the door." Then he disappears without a trace. Now Officer Jack McGarvey and his family have inherited the idyllic country home, knowing nothing of what happened to the previous owner.

LeBlanc, Deborah.
Family Inheritance. New York: Leisure, 2004. 357pp.

Deep in the Louisiana swamps, a healer lives surrounded by gators and snakes. He knows that he must leave when he heals a patient and sees Maikana, a death's head with a vertical mouth, the spirit of insanity and destruction. Thirty years later a Cajun woman in Memphis with a special gift for healing is called back to her Louisiana roots when her younger brother starts to hear voices and suddenly becomes violent.

Massey, Brandon.
Dark Corner. New York: Kensington, 2004. 256pp.

Mason Corner, Mississippi, is a down home place that houses a great many secrets, including Diallo, a vampire who has resided there since antebellum times. When his father dies unexpectedly, David finds himself on the next plane to Mason Corner, thinking he will take over the family business. Little does he know that part of that business was pest control of sorts: His pop was a vampire hunter.

Rickman, Phil.
The Wine of Angels. London: Pan Books, 1998. 629pp.

Reverend Merrily Watkins comes to Lewardine expecting a dreary existence in a village of black-and-white houses. But she's drawn into a fight about how to represent Lewardine's history when the natives want to downplay their ancestors' participation in a seventeenth-century martyrizing. Soon a townie's teenaged daughter goes missing, and villagers begin to meet gruesome ends. Rickman is particularly adept at re-creating life in a modern English village.

Saul, John.
Punish the Sinners. New York: Dell, 1978. 415pp.

Ah, the first day of work at a new job—a day full of potential and promises. Or perhaps it will be a day full of evil. A young professional fresh from seminary school gets his first job in a small, desert town school, where students are inexplicably driven to murder and suicide. Is this some sort of mass hysteria, or is this an evil that can be traced back to the Inquisition?

Saul, John.
Sleep Walk. New York: Bantam, 1991. 449pp.

Think that the worst part of high school was dealing with bullies and cliques? Think again. In the sleepy small town of Borrego, New Mexico, a teenager jumps to her death in a canyon, while a high school teacher goes insane in the middle of class. As other instances of irrational behavior occur, Judith Sheffield, hometown girl who returned to teach high school, begins to suspect more than a coincidence.

Middle Class Mania: Suburban Scares

Many horror tales imply that there is always strength in numbers, and that monsters can get us only when we are alone, as in one of the small towns in the previous section. However, as these "suburban scare" titles show us, we are never safe from the supernatural, no matter how close our neighbors live. Even gated communities, where a certain amount of neighborhood control is exercised and people know one another and therefore presume total safety, can become nothing more than convenient boxes full of human bodies, which vampires, succubi, werewolves, and demons find as appetizing as takeout.

Anson, Jay.
The Amityville Horror. Englewood Cliffs, NJ: Prentice-Hall, 1977. 207pp.
> When it comes to learning the ABCs of suburban horror, just remember, "A is for Amityville." A dream house on Long Island turns out to be a nightmare even Bob Villa couldn't fix, as inexplicable events occur. But what should one expect when buying a suburban home that was once the site of mass murder? This easy-to-read novel put haunted houses back on the map.

Dobyns, Stephen.
The Church of Dead Girls. New York: Henry Holt, 1997. 388pp.
> One by one, teenaged girls with long hair are disappearing without a trace in the normally quiet town of Aurelius, New York. As the narrator, a deeply closeted homosexual, relates the story of their disappearance and the ultimate discovery, the reader becomes acquainted with the secret longings of all in this ostensibly placid and bland suburban enclave. What is more horrifying, the killer or the neighborhood's dirty little secrets? Or how easily people turn on one another?

Epperson, S. K.
The Neighborhood. New York: Leisure, 1996. 304pp.
> We think we all know our neighbors: the quiet guy who lives alone, the woman with all the cats, the couple that never comes out during the day . . . . A nurse moves into a new neighborhood to help take care of an AIDS patient. Little does she know that her neighbors include a Peeping Tom, a burglar, and a sadistic serial killer. So much for the safety of suburbia. Quirky and original.

Garton, Ray.
The New Neighbor. Lynbrook, NY: Charnel House, 1991. 280pp.

> The inhabitants of a normal suburban neighborhood find themselves entranced by their beautiful new neighbor, Lorelle Dupree. As the entire block gets to know her, families that normally live in harmony and watch out for each other's children begin arguing—and everyone starts to look a little more pale than usual. Lorelle has come to suburbia to steal souls.

Little, Bentley.
The Association. New York: Signet, 2001, 436pp.

> Even if you read the fine print when purchasing a home, you may end up in suburban hell. Bonita Vista's neighborhood association isn't like any other. After Barry and Maureen Welch receive their first citation for failing to abide by a relatively trifling rule, they discover that The Association's vocal opponents "accidentally" fall from balconies or suddenly disappear. They try to sell their home, but escaping just isn't that easy.

Moran, Tom.
Acquired Taste$. Frederick, MD: PublishAmerica, 2004. 230pp.

> After writing a best-selling novel that earns him a fortune, small-town English teacher John Smith finds himself living the American dream. With his new wealth, he purchases a home in an *exclusive* neighborhood and befriends his elitist neighbors. John is initially fascinated by this materialistic culture, but soon his friends begin to disappear, and bodies start to pile up.

Neiderman, Andrew.
Neighborhood Watch. New York: Pocket Books, 2001. 326pp.

> Move to picturesque Emerald Lakes, where Stepford meets Alcatraz. The houses are similar in every minute detail, and residents dare not move the furniture that comes with the homes. The Morris family innocently purchases a home in this exclusive subdivision, finding themselves surrounded by luxury at a surprisingly affordable price. Too bad they signed the paperwork before reading the fine print, for "subversives" find themselves victims of robberies or "decide" to commit suicide.

Searcy, David.
🏆 *Ordinary Horror.* New York: Viking-Penguin, 2001. 230pp.

> The scenes of tract housing and suburban ennui in this novel will unsettle as much as the story itself. A retired teacher who loves gardening decides to try to stop gophers from ruining his roses. Afraid of chemical insecticides, he orders an exotic South American plant that will not harm pets (he is considerate of his neighbors) from a mysterious newspaper. Unfortunately, these plants have the potential to bring about the end of the world.

Graffiti and Gore: Bright Lights, Big City

Dark, dreary inner cities are known for being conducive to crime, vermin, and depravity, and they have long held a place of fear in our collective unconscious. Urban horror reveals that cities are vast, impersonal, and filled with nooks and crannies where anything can happen. And salvation is nowhere to be found.

Banks, L[eslie]. A.
The Minion. Vampire Huntress Legend series. New York: St. Martin's, 2003. 320pp.

    Yo yo yo! Hip-hopper Damali Richards is keeping it real and bringing music to the people. She balances her day job as singer and spoken word artist for Warriors of Light Records with her night job—hunting vampires and demons. She and her Guardian team battle rogue vampires that have been knocking off hip-hop and rap artists, both at Warriors and its rival record company. Other titles in the series include *The Awakening*, *The Hunted*, *The Bitten*, and *The Forbidden*.

Brite, Poppy Z.
The Devil You Know. Burton, MI: Subterranean Press, 2003. 198pp.

    In this case the devil we know is The Big Easy, as seen through the eyes of Dr. Brite and other locals. Stories paint gothic portraits of the city, including the New Orleans Carnival (Mardi Gras), local restaurants and colorful chefs who murder for their art, area swamps haunted by mythical creatures, and the night life rock music scene.

Levin, Ira.
Sliver. New York: Bantam, 1991. 190pp.

    When Kay Norris moves into a Manhattan high rise, she discovers that the whole building is under video and audio surveillance. But what she doesn't expect is the allure of voyeurism—or how far the building's owner will go for his scopophilliac pleasure. This story is truly disturbing and is very popular with fans, so much so that it was made into a film of the same name in 1993.

Lonardo, Paul.
The Apostate. St. Petersburg: Barclay Books, 2001. 254pp.

    The modern secular world has made it possible for Satan himself to take the elevator up once again, this time to open a bakery chain in the growing metropolis of Caldera, New Mexico. There, the devil sets up shop, keeping the human masses ignorant of his plans by getting them addicted to his baked goods and inverting the communion ceremony as he tricks humans into ingesting his essence.

Marffin, Kyle.
Gothique: A Vampire Novel. Dairen, IL: The Design Image Group, 2000. 431pp.

What could be cooler than working in the magazine industry in a big city like Chicago? But what if a romp through the Chicago night life and Goth scene turns into a modern version of stories from classic vampire folklore? *Gothique* is the tale of an old palace theater that once stood decrepit and empty, until vampires decided there can be no better way to run a posh Goth club than to recruit new blood (pun intended).

Randisi, Robert J.
In the Shadow of the Arch. Joe Keough Novels. New York: St. Martin's, 1998. 355pp.

Joe Keough, a man with more machismo than emotion, spent years in Brooklyn on the NYPD but was forced to resign. In this series packed with local diners, nightclubs, expressways, and side streets, he returns to St. Louis, where he just wants the chance to be a detective again. On Keough's first day as a St. Louis detective, three-year-old Brady Sanders wanders into the precinct house, his pajamas soaked in blood and his parents missing. Other titles in the series are *Alone with the Dead*, *Blood on the Arch*, *East of the Arch*, and *Arch Angels*.

Reutter, R.
Lycanthropes and Leeches. Lincoln, NE: iUniverse, 2004. 248pp.

Table for one? May we recommend the blood pudding? It is quite delectable tonight. In San Francisco, a young woman feels unfulfilled and yearns to break free from her duty of running the family restaurant. Fleeing home to escape domestic violence, she finds herself living on the dirty boulevards, where danger lurks at every corner—and where werewolves and vampires wait to pounce.

Skipp, John, and Craig Spector.
The Cleanup. New York: Bantam, 1987. 379pp.

The reader can almost picture Billy Rowe looking into a mirror and repeatedly asking, "You talkin' to me?" in this thriller about a loser in New York City who decides to take an "angel" up on its offer to help him clean up the riff-raff of the streets. Christopher, a celestial being, gives Billy the power to control everything in his surroundings. But absolute power corrupts absolutely—and justice too easily becomes vengeance.

The Woods Are Lovely, Dark, and Deep: Wilderness Adventures, Horror Style

Landscapes have a powerful impact on the atmosphere of a story. Faced with images of isolated, mysterious stone circles, high ragged cliffs, wild vegetation, and fog-covered lakes, readers get a sense of the otherworldly. Like those areas of industrial decay mentioned in the previous section, the wilds have been hot spots for the occult and paranormal, starting with many of the early masters in the genre: Nathaniel Hawthorne, Algernon Blackwood, and H. P. Lovecraft.

Benchley, Peter.
Jaws. New York: Ballantine, 1974. 311pp.
    A reader who thinks that the wilderness begins and ends with vegetation cannot see the forest for the trees. Perhaps the most dangerous frontier is the ocean. A gigantic shark terrorizes a small town beach community, and now all fear to enter the water. Who can stop this killing machine from decimating the tourists? *Jaws* was made into a blockbuster film in 1975 and spawned popular interest in shark attacks.

Freeman, Brian.
Blue November Storms. Forest Hills: MD: Cemetery Dance, 2004. 352pp.
    The Lightning Five reunites for a weekend of hunting and fishing at a summer cottage, but after a mysterious meteor shower awakens the forest creatures from their quiet slumber, the five high school pals find themselves trapped on the roof of the cottage. Even there they are not safe.

Kiernan, Caitlin R.
Threshold: A Novel of Deep Time. New York: Onyx, 2001. 272pp.
    Deep in the Alabama mountains, a young female paleontologist explores hidden tunnels and finds something evil. Now she is cursed with the death of her grandfather and with abandonment by everyone she has ever cared for. She meets a girl who claims she battles monsters and talks to angels and an alcoholic psychometrist with clairvoyant gifts; together the three battle against the forces of evil lurking beneath the Alabama soil.

King, Stephen.
Gerald's Game. New York: Viking, 1992. 332pp.
    To spice up their dull marriage, Jessie Burlingame and her husband vacation at a secluded cottage in the wilderness, where she reluctantly agrees to engage in one of Gerald's sex games. But when Gerald suffers a fatal heart attack, Jessie finds herself handcuffed to a bed with no one around to save her—and nothing but wild animals as company. King's novel is an excellent example of psychological horror and a study of dysfunctional families.

Laimo, Michael.
Deep in the Darkness. New York: Dorchester, 2004. 384pp.
    It's not nice to foolishly deprive Mother Nature of what she asks. Dr. Michael Cayle moves his wife and daughter to the small town of Ashborough, set deep in the woods. The surrounding wilderness may be picturesque, but it

is home to a mysterious force, and the heads of each of the town's families are expected to make sacrifices to Nature—or else.

Laymon, Richard.
Darkness, Tell Us. London: Headline, 1991. 312pp. **YA**

Talk about having to earn those college credits the hard way! Six female students take a camping trip to an isolated California mining area called Calamity Peak. Their professor, along with a fellow student, follows them to keep them safe. However, the eight end up being hunted by a mysterious, maniacal killer armed with a machete.

Laymon, Richard.
No Sanctuary. London: Headline Feature, 2001. 352pp.

Four young hikers, three female, go into the California woods. Recipe for disaster? Well, stir in a menacing madman, wildcats, and Gillian O'Neill, a bored millionaire who steals into vacated homes to "vacation" in them to create the perfect fare for horror hunger pangs. But wait! It gets worse. O'Neill has just broken into an isolated cabin where he finds S&M videos and clippings about missing young women.

Massie, Elizabeth.
Sineater. New York: Leisure, 1998. 396pp. **YA**

In the Appalachian woods, the pious still need the Sineater to cleanse the dead of sin. Traditionally, he lives as a recluse in the woods, approaching humanity only to partake of food left on the chests of the departed. But the current Sineater breaks with tradition by having a wife and family, and this change causes a spate of grisly murders in a small mountain town.

Matheson, Richard.
Hunted Past Reason. New York: Tor, 2002. 335pp.

Bob's career as a screenwriter is going great. To research a current project, he needs the help of his friend Doug, an experienced outdoorsman who can show him the woods. What Bob does not know is that Doug has been bitten by the green-eyed monster named Envy and is a bitter man, driven to desperate acts. If Doug has his way, only one will leave the woods alive.

Saul, John.
The Presence. New York: Fawcett, 1997. 338pp.

Aloha means both hello and goodbye in Hawaiian—and good-bye to any sense of security and safety in this thriller. A city-weary New Yorker takes her ailing son to Hawaii so they can live in a more natural, life-affirming environment. But alas, the mean streets of New York have their counterpart in killer marine life forms caused by volcanic activity.

The Well-Traveled Victim: Horror in Exotic Locales

Don't we all want to see the world and travel to exotic lands? In horror, characters who appease their wanderlust often find their reception quite chilly, as the seeming paradises of far-off lands and cultures hide unspeakable terrors for those who venture there.

Bergantino, David.
Hamlet II: Ophelia's Revenge. New York: Simon and Schuster-Pocket Star, 2003. 256pp.

Globe University Football star Cameron Dean's father is murdered, and he inherits a Danish mansion—well, a castle, actually. He decides to share his fortune with his best friends, so he takes them on a tour. However, he comes to realize that a man's house may be his haunted castle when the ghost of a drowning victim recognizes in him a kindred soul.

Campbell, Ramsey.
The One Safe Place. London: Headline, 1995. 373pp.

The Travises immigrate to England in search of a peaceful life, only to be stalked by the Fancys, a family of petty criminals, after Don runs afoul of their patriarch during a traffic scuffle. The Travises go to the authorities for help, but the police can't protect them in this supposedly nonviolent society that bans guns and violent films. Campbell does an excellent job of representing his country through American eyes.

de Lint, Charles.
Mulengro. New York: Berkley, 1985. 357pp.

A gypsy community in modern-day Ottawa, Canada, finds itself at the center of a series of bizarre murders that seem to be connected to it, but the Romany know that one of their own isn't the killer. A man, dubbed "Mulengro" because of his relationship with dead spirits, believes he's on a mission from God to eliminate them. And a local detective gets dragged into the action when he inherits the case.

Due, Tananarive.
The Living Blood. The Living Blood series. New York: Washington Square Press, 2001. 511pp.

In a poor African country, a small clinic uses Western medical technology. Carefully guarded stories about a healer who cures all illnesses with doses of her own blood emerge, and wealthy men the world over seek to obtain this "miracle drug." Meanwhile, a child with incredible powers is learning to make hurricanes and to fly. This is the sequel to *My Soul to Keep*, the first novel in The Living Blood series.

Hardy, Robin, and Anthony Shaffer.
The Wicker Man. New York: Pocket Books, 1978. 239pp.

Summerisle, Scotland, is not a charming, remote island community with quaint folkways. Instead, it is place with sinister pagan fertility rituals and deadly secrets, as Officer Howie will discover when he comes from the mainland to investigate a local girl's disappearance. Adapted from the film of the same name, this is a masterpiece exploring cultural and religious clashes.

Ketchum, Jack.
She Wakes. New York: Berkley, 1989. 260pp.

A writer and a group of fellow travelers find more than heavenly topless beaches, friendly local waitresses, and colorful street barkers selling flowers in the Grecian Islands. The awakening of an evil goddess summons Jordon Thayer Chase, who hears the voices of ancient gods and feels the power of sacred places, and knows he must fulfill his destiny, even if it means his death.

Klavan, Andrew.
The Uncanny. New York: Crown, 1998. 343pp.

If you're reading this, you probably love horror movies, but do you ever stop to wonder where writers and directors get their ideas? Well, Hollywood producer Richard Storm did, so he traveled to England to find the real ghosts that inspire so many of the flicks he had funded. He should have checked his itinerary; he ends up in an alternate reality that follows one of his horror storylines.

Simmons, Dan.
Children of the Night. New York: Putnam, 1992. 382pp.

Suppose Vlad Tepes, better known as "Vlad the Impaler," actually was a vampire. Would it not stand to reason that his progeny, even distant relatives, might also be bloodsuckers? Kate Neuman, an American hematologist, is called to post-Ceaucescu Romania to treat an abandoned infant with a rare blood condition: The baby is able to digest blood to cure hemophilia. A kidnapping and multiple murders lead her to discover the horror behind the infant's "gift".

Simmons, Dan.
The Fires of Eden. New York: Putnam, 1994. 399pp.

Progress is always for the good of everyone, right? But what if beauty is destroyed in the name of progress? The construction of a posh condo in Hawaii has awakened the Hawaiian gods of the underworld, and now they want revenge. Although this story begins as a straightforward tale of horror, the masterful, subtle comedy soon becomes apparent. A fun read. Simmons portrays the beauty of Hawaii, even of its volcanoes, exceptionally well.

Simmons, Dan.
Song of Kali. New York: Doherty, 1985. 311pp.

According to journalist Robert Z. Luczak, "some places are too evil to be allowed to exist.... Calcutta is such a place." Amid homeless beggars and violent thugs, Luczak discovers an evil that is beyond human comprehension: a cult of killers so unmerciful that skinning people alive is within their realm. And now it's just possible that these killers, worshippers of the goddess Kali, are scheming to infect the world with their sadism.

Radyshevsky, Dmitrv.
The Mantra. New York: Jove, 2002. 473pp.

Set mainly in the exotic mountain ranges of the Himalayas, this rock-till-you-drop-dead tale deals with DJ Tune Ra's release of an urban, industrial song embedded with a powerful Buddhist mantra. It becomes an overnight success and is suddenly heard in major cities worldwide as well as remote areas of the globe, where it has sinister, deadly effects on its listeners and ultimately has the power to transform the world.

Rickman, Phil.
Candlenight. New York: Berkley, 1995. 463pp.

Unlike other parts of Wales, the ancient village of Y Groes has resisted outsiders and outside influences and stuck to its traditions. Outsiders foolish enough to make a home here are killed, while the descendants of villagers are lured back to the village and kept there—by force if necessary. *Candlenight* is so steeped in Welsh tradition that it comes with its own glossary of Welsh words.

Yarbro, Chelsea Quinn.
Hotel Transylvania: A Novel of Forbidden Love. The Saint-Germain Chronicles. New York: St. Martin's, 1978. 279pp.

The Court of Louis XIV? Been there; met him. The Spanish Civil War? Been there; fought that. The eruption of Krakatoa? Been there; seen it. Yarbro's popular series, now including 18 titles, covers the globe and the span of history. After all, for an immortal the possibilities are endless. Visit with the immensely popular Count St. Germain, a more human-friendly version of Anne Rice's Lestat, an erotic vampire who is more human than bloodsucker. Travel to 1743 Paris, a Renaissance monastery, Nero's Rome, and medieval China, among other places.

Way, Way Out: Other Worlds, Alternate Universes

Dark fantasy is a term that could arguably be applied to most horror (and sometimes is), but generally it refers to a fantasy text containing threatening monsters. Likewise, many science fiction titles that are set in outer space, or on other planets, contain aliens bent on destroying the invading human population, even if those humans have innocently stumbled on the aliens' abode. Because these fantasy and science fiction worlds are ruled by laws not necessarily akin to those of the everyday world, these monsters can be more dangerous and more deadly, and even their habitats can, in and of themselves, be extremely dangerous.

Barker, Clive.
Abarat. New York: Harper Collins, 2004. 496pp.
    Abarat is an archipelago of 25 islands, one for each hour of the day and an extra one for things that occur out of space and time, and it is ruled by the Lord of Midnight. When a 16-year-old girl from Minnesota accidentally stumbles into this parallel universe, she discovers that not only has she been here before, but she has also managed to make many enemies who want her dead.

Bedwell-Grime, Stephanie.
Guardian Angel. Surrey, England: Telos, 2003. 220pp.
    In this dark fantasy, Heaven, Inc. has a corporate address (so does Hell, for that matter). Porsche, a guardian angel, can only keep her job if she saves her current charge, whose soul is in grave danger, but she also suspects that Hell may be planning a hostile takeover. When Porsche is demoted to the Dreams Department, all hell threatens to break loose.

Bishop, K. J.
The Etched City. New York: Bantam-Spectra, 2004. 400pp.
    Two citizens of Copper County are forced to flee and make a new life in the city of Ashamoil, a place of dark miracles where artists occasionally turn into sphinxes, flowers routinely spring from the newly dead, and children are born part crocodile. A mercenary slave trader and an altruistic physician must survive this strange and dangerous land.

Clegg, Douglas.
Naomi. 2000. New York: Leisure, 2001. 344pp.
    In this intricate story, a newly divorced man searches for his childhood sweetheart, Naomi, who mysteriously disappeared in the New York City subway system. She comes to him in prophetic dreams, which he decides to follow. His search leads him to The Below, where a centuries-old creature waits for its chance to return to the world of humans.

Gaiman, Neil.
Coraline. New York: HarperTrophy, 2002. 162pp. **YA**
    With no playmates who live nearby, school out, and nasty weather, Coraline wanders lonely through her family home. She soon discovers a door to another dimension—an Oz-like land where Other Mother lives. Other Mother seems very nice at first, but something is not quite right. Other

Mother keeps Other Father locked in the cellar, and her children become unsubstantial wraiths.

Koontz, Dean.
Lightning. New York: Berkley, 1989. 355pp.

Imagine choosing between two suitors—one evil incarnate, the other a guardian angel—both claiming to come from another reality. Two men show up during life-and-death events in Laura Shane's life—a blond stranger who often saves her from peril, and a dark-haired man with a facial scar, bent on killing her.

Lee, Edward.
City Infernal. City Infernal series. New York: Leisure, 2001. 366pp.

Goth chick Cassie Heydon is an "Etheress," looking for her twin sister (a suicide). Aided by an angel and by a dorky student and "Etherean," she invades Lucifer's capital, Mephistopolis, a cybergoth, bleak and horrible mirror of New York City. Here terror, pain, sex, and drugs prevail, while the King of Fallen Angels has created a time-traveling device and a "Hex-Clone" of Jesus. Follow this with the next title in the series, *Infernal Angel.*

Lee, Tanith.
Faces Under Water. Secret Books of Venus. Woodstock, NY: Overlook Press, 1999. 335pp.

In a world ruled by alchemical magic and the four elements lies the city of Venus (similar to sixteenth-century Venice). Here, magic is possible within a landscape comprised mostly of canals, and two powerful families feud over a patch of earth to use as a graveyard. Meanwhile, a slave with fiery hair conjures flame, making people believe she is touched, either by God or Satan. Other titles in the series include *Saint Fire*, *A Bed of Earth (The Gravedigger's Tale)*, and *Venus Preserved.*

Masterton, Graham.
The Doorkeepers. Sutton: Severn House, 2001. 313pp.

After Josh's sister Julia is brutally murdered and Scotland Yard has no leads, Josh and his psychic girlfriend decide to investigate. It appears Julia ceased to exist in this world nearly a year before her murder. Josh discovers the doors to an alternative universe, another more sinister London, a theocracy where the Puritans continued to rule after Cromwell's death.

Masterton, Graham.
The Hidden World. New York: Severn House, 2003. 192pp.

Orphaned in an accident and bullied in school, Jessica becomes introspective and studies faeries. A household accident later causes her to suffer head trauma, and she begins to hear voices coming from the wallpaper. She and a few friends venture into this strange, new world, finding terror and a host of frightened children.

Pike, Christopher.
Alosha. New York: Tor, 2004. 304pp.
After her mother died in a car accident, Ali Warner clings to fantasies that she is secretly a princess from a far-off land. When logging threatens the Southern California forest that has always been her refuge, Ali discovers her true powers in a dark fantasy world that will appeal to the Harry Potter crowd.

Waggoner, Tim.
Necropolis. Farmington Hills, MI: Gale Group-Five Star, 2004. 238pp.
Detective Matt Adrian accidentally follows a killer into another dimension, where he discovers the city of Necropolis, which is inhabited by vampires, werewolves, witches, ghosts, and zombies. Unfortunately for Adrian, he is killed while in Necropolis, becoming a zombie. He has only two days to find an antidote for his condition.

Timing Is Everything

In a world where time and space are fluid, it is theoretically possible to visit bygone eras and jump ahead into the future to find out just how much that technology stock you've been eyeing increased in value. Readers who appreciate those writers who allow them to vicariously travel back and forth in time will enjoy these period pieces, in which the temporal aspect of the setting, or the time in which the tale is set, is both setting and main character.

The Way Back Machine: Historical Horror

Horror set in the past allows the luxury of reading about a known era (the history of a place and time) while enjoying newly created fictional characters and stories that take place within it. Some of the most imaginative of all horror texts are included here, and they add new dimension to places like ancient Egypt, the Roman Empire, and Victorian England. Sometimes historical figures make cameo appearances in these stories, often creating the monster that threatens the entire world.

Bleys, Olivier.
The Ghost in the Eiffel Tower. New York: Marion Boyars, 2003. 356pp.
In 1888 France, two apprentice architects, Armand and Odilon, are working with Gustave Eiffel to build the Eiffel tower. For them the tower is the symbol of an age of scientific marvels, but in the gaslit streets of Paris,

strange beliefs, dark desires, and mysterious forces persist. The two become involved with spiritualists and hold meetings in the morgue, while an American draftsman works to destroy the project.

Bloch, Robert.
American Gothic. New York: Simon & Schuster, 1974. 222pp.

Loosely based on nineteenth-century serial killer Herman Mudgett, Bloch's novel tells the tale of Dr. Gordon Gregg, who lured victims at the Chicago World's Fair with the promise of inexpensive lodging in his apartment building. This edifice was also outfitted so the doctor could more easily kill his victims and dispose of them. A female reporter discovers his identity, but will she become one of his victims?

Bray, Libba.
A Great and Terrible Beauty. A Great and Terrible Beauty series. New York: Delacorte, 2003. 403pp. **YA**

Stuck at a nineteenth-century finishing school for proper young ladies, Gemma discovers she has access to magical powers, which she uses to help her friends avoid the stultifying lives their parents have planned for them. But what happened to two girls from the class of 1871, who were also dabbling in this variety of magic? More answers to this question are provided in *Rebel Angels*, the second novel in the series. An erudite and compelling dark fantasy, written in a convincing Victorian style.

Earhart, Rose.
Dorcas Good: The Diary of a Salem Witch. New York: Pendleton, 2000. 376pp. **YA**

Sarah Good, four-year-old daughter of a Salem witch hunt victim, relates the story of the very real horrors of the period and brings to life the murders of innocent women. A victim of physical and sexual abuse at the hands of her father and her jailers, she is eventually forced to become the town whore and is tried and imprisoned for witchcraft.

Elrod, P. N.
Jonathan Barrett: Gentleman Vampire (Omnibus). Jonathan Barrett series. New York: Doubleday, 1996. 960pp.

In 1773, just three years before the Revolutionary War, 17-year-old Jonathan Barrett is sent from his colonial American home to Cambridge University, where he is made into a vampire. He returns to America to save his family and estate from a scheming relative, while talk of revolution brews, only to flee to England with his sister, in this marriage of horror, action, and historical (revised and often expanded) drama. This omnibus includes all four series titles: *Red Death, Death and the Maiden, Death Masque,* and *Dance of Death.*

Gresham, Stephen.
Fraternity. New York: Kensington-Pinnacle, 2004. 384pp.

At Mantis College in Sweet River, Alabama, during the 1930s, the Alpha and Omega houses compete for pledges. However, their prospective members have to suffer through more than the usual time-honored pranks and hazing rituals; they must choose between remaining human and embracing the everlasting life of the undead, and must survive a battle between two rival vampire clans.

Lumley, Brian.
Khai of Ancient Khem. New York: Berkley, 1980. 306pp.

Khai begins life in ancient Egypt as the son of Pharaoh Khasathut's chief architect, but when he dares to challenge the pharaoh, he is condemned to be a slave. Escaping, he flees to neighboring Kush, where he earns the rank of general in the army of Queen Ashtarta. Later, in twentieth-century England, Khai searches for his reincarnated love, Ashtarta.

Martin, George R. R.
Fevre Dream. New York: Poseidon Press, 1982. 350pp.

It's the Golden Age of riverboats, and the *Fevre Dream,* one of the fanciest steamboats ever made, is completed by mysterious Captain Abner Marsh and his partner, Joshua York. Joshua eats only at midnight, and only in the company of his friends, none of whom is ever seen in the Louisiana daylight, prompting wild rumors on the Mississippi.

McCammon, Robert.
Speaks the Nightbird: Judgement of the Witch* and *Evil Unveiled (2 novels, omnibus edition). Speaks the Nightbird series. Montgomery, AL: River City Publishing, 2002. 726pp.

In a struggling Carolina settlement in 1690, Matthew Corbett, a magistrate's squire, finds his life touched and changed by witchcraft trials, which involve religious fervor, deceit, and a mysterious pirate treasure. In eighteenth-century colonial America, a young widow is accused of witchcraft, in this dark fantasy with more than its share of grisly moments.

Rice, Anne.
Pandora. New Tales of the Vampires series. New York: Ballantine, 1998. 368pp.

A female vampire named Pandora narrates this tale that takes us from the Rome of Augustus Caesar into modern-day Paris. In the next series title, *Vittorio, the Vampire*, the rich and powerful son of a local merchant in the Medici Court of Renaissance Italy, Vittorio (now a 500-year-old ancient), flees to the creepy town of Santa Maddalana, which has made a pact to sacrifice its young to a vampire horde.

Rice, Anne.
Servant of the Bones. New York: Knopf, 1989. 387pp.

    In ancient Babylon, Azriel is painted in gold and sacrificed to become the immortal Servant of the Bones, to permit his people to return to Jerusalem. Now Azriel tells of his life around the world and through history: in ancient Babylon, in Europe during the time of the Black Plague, in ancient Greece, in Paris, and finally in New York.

Coming Soon to a Nightmare Near You: Future Shocks

Mary Shelley's 1887 classic *Frankenstein* was the first, but certainly not the last, novel to blend horror and futurism. The more current subgenre of techno-horror might also be called "future horror," as it challenges the optimistic futurism of science fiction, not only creating dystopias where freedom is passé, but also populating a horrifying version of our future world with out-of-control robots, menacing aliens, and murderous genetic mutations.

Cross, Michael.
After Human. New York: Kensington-Pinnacle, 2004. 304pp.

    In this post-apocalyptic, dog-eat-dog, splatterpunk world, future humans worship an iconographic media celebrity named Nikka Seven, who's sort of a kinky Egyptian priestess. Nikka travels through the night in a long black limousine, kidnapping men so she can turn them into women in her underground pyramid crypt, but when she decides to sacrifice the princess of England via the Internet, she may have gone too far.

Delaney, Matthew B. J.
Jinn. New York: St. Martin's Griffin, 2004. 560pp.

    Boston, 2007. A rescue ship that once saved the life of a young American army private, only to be shelled and sunk, is recovered from the bottom of the ocean and brought to the harbor. Only the ship wasn't empty. Now horribly mutilated bodies are strewn throughout the streets, leading Detective Will Jefferson to believe that he is up against a supernatural being.

Elkin, Richard.
Leech. Frederick, MD: PublishAmerica, 2004. 209pp.

    In 2018, war and terrorism have brought the end of the world as we know it. One particular bio-weapon, the "Wrath of God," has virtually destroyed the nation, creating horrifying genetic mutations. Those, like Rebecca Artemis, who survive the plague, fighting along crumbled streets and buildings for life on a day-to-day basis, don't feel fine. Some develop a blood lust, akin to vampirism.

Harrison, Kim.
Dead Witch Walking. New York: HarperTorch, 2004. 432pp.

"O Brave New World that has such fruits and vegetables in it." The future brings genetically modified tomatoes that make people with paranormal ability vulnerable to exposure, since they are immune from its poisonous properties, which have nearly wiped out humanity. Telekinetic Rachel Morgan hangs out in the Hallows, a sort of Las Vegas for witches, werewolves, and vampires.

Newman, Kim.
The Night Mayor. New York: Carroll and Graf, 1990. 186pp.

Who needs a getaway car when they can simply zap themselves into virtual space? In England of the future, master criminal Truro Dane has tapped into Yggdrasil and combined its data with old movies to dream his own dark universe, while taking up space in the server. Now Susan Bishopric must use her special gifts to find him—or die trying—in this science fiction crossover.

Smith, Clark Ashton, Ronald S. Hilgar, and Scott Connors, eds.
Red World of Polaris: The Adventures of Captain Volmar. San Francisco: Night Shade Books, 2003 (1930). 115pp.

Extraordinary alien beings are encountered on a planet near Polaris, and Captain Volmar makes a serious attempt to envision their biology, history, and culture. This slim volume is noteworthy for the first publication of a long-lost Smith dark science fiction tale, "The Red World of Polaris," the second Captain Volmar tale, after "Marooned in Andromeda" and before "A Captivity in Serpens."

VanderMeer, Jeff.
Veniss Underground. Newberg, OR: Nightshade Books, 2003. 192pp.

Beneath a decadent future city, subterranean "artists" create monstrous works of biology, while genetically enhanced "meerkats" decide it is time to make humanity obsolete. Nicholas, a Living Artist not quite talented enough to succeed, goes in search of the most respected mentor on the planet but makes the huge mistake of traveling beneath the city, where he finds terror.

Chapter 4

Character

Often after reading a story it is the characters who remain vivid in readers' minds—whether because they are everyday people and we can identify with them and their plights, or because they are the opposite: haunting, unusual people who are impossible to forget because we have never seen their like before. On the other hand, sometimes characters can be interesting because they are not realistic at all; rather, they are striking personifications of captivating ideas. Mainstream literature abounds with unforgettable personages. Who doesn't remember Scarlett O'Hara and Rhett Butler from *Gone with the Wind*? Or the evil Fagin and Artful Dodger from *Oliver Twist*? By the same token, horror has its "characters," such as the telekinetic (and long-suffering) Carrie White from Stephen King's first novel, *Carrie*. And then there's psychologist Hannibal Lecter, the last man whose couch anyone would ever want to grace. And don't forget (like anyone ever could) the wise-cracking Freddy Kreuger from *Nightmare on Elm Street*, a supernatural serial murderer who literally kills audiences with his sadistic musings. This chapter looks at some of the memorable characters from the horror genre—whether they be heroic, evil, or simply weird. In all cases, the characters in the books listed here drive the storyline. They are what allow readers to connect with the tale.

Ah! The Humanity!

In horror, extreme character types can be useful because they either are monsters of a sort (such as Norman Bates in *Psycho*) or make excellent fodder for monsters. Readers are probably all too familiar with the squeamish girl or the teenaged lothario, both of whom are usually the first to be "dispatched" by a knife-wielding maniac in a slasher flick. Any reader with a sense of justice probably secretly cheers when the evil CEO or mad scientist is done in by his or her own creation. These characters are useful because readers do not develop attachments to them, and because they add color to a story. They also may touch on familiar archetypes—the dark mother, the brooding male.

Common minor and often stereotypical characters in horror include the unwary librarian or antiquarian who accidentally summons a demon using an ancient text, the nagging spouse (or ex, or parent) who makes the main character's life hell, the small-town sheriff blind to the supernatural causes of various murders, and—in much recent horror fiction—the angry stripper or prostitute whose frustrations take a violent turn.

Innocent—and Not-So-Innocent—Bystanders: Monster Makers and Unwilling Victims

So often, whether someone is a monster or a victim is a matter of perspective. This is illustrated in Stephen King's *Carrie*. After the Black Prom, the people of Chamberlain, Maine revile Carrie as the misfit spawn of a religious zealot who destroyed their town, but her biographers, and the few like Sue Snell who actually knew Carrie, know that she was a victim twice over, first of horrendous child abuse and then of adults who refused to intervene on her behalf. And in Jack Ketchum's *Red*, Avery Ludlow is likewise transformed from victim to monster after a wealthy punk kills his dog for the fun of it, and Avery is unable to get justice through official channels. These books make us realize that monsters are made, not born, that no one is wholly innocent, and that all of us have the potential to become monstrous.

> **Campbell, Ramsey.**
> *The Last Voice They Hear.* New York: Forge, 1998. 384pp.
>> Geoff Davenport is getting mysterious phone calls from his brother Ben, who ran away from home when he was 18 and now claims to be the serial killer murdering happily married couples in the area. But Ben wasn't always a monster. . . . Typical of Campbell's best psychological horror, this is about character development and atmosphere.
>
> **Crowther, Peter.**
> *The Longest Single Note.* New York: Leisure, 2003. 368pp.
>> These 26 pieces range from a sly, visceral Lovecraftian tale about a young scientist who gets his arm stuck in another dimension, to a pensive, charming story of one man's realization that music is what makes life worth living, to a melancholic exploration of whether or not vampires can feel, love, and form relationships with humans. Crowther involves readers emotionally

with his carefully drawn, realistic characters who find themselves in horrifying encounters with monsters, or simply realizing some disquieting truth.

De la Mare, Walter.
The Return. Mineola, NY: Dover, 1997 (1922). 224pp.

Imagine falling asleep one night and waking to find that you are no longer yourself. This happens to Arthur Lawford when he falls asleep on the grave of an eighteenth-century pirate. When he awakens his face is no longer the one he has seen before in the mirror. He is unchanged psychologically, but small inconsistencies begin to insinuate themselves into his personality, making him wonder if he is losing his mind—or being taken over.

Du Maurier, Daphne.
Rebecca. New York: Doubleday, 1938. 357pp.

Rebecca Manderly was the beautiful and adored wife of Maxim de Winter; now she is dead. Maxim's new wife is haunted by the ghost of the first wife, Rebecca. The de Winter home is a monument to Rebecca's style and taste, and Mrs. Danvers, the malignant housekeeper, continually compares her master's new wife to the dead one, whom she adored. Although dead, Rebecca dominates the household and holds a secret that must be released.

Fowler, Christopher.
Breathe: Everyone Has to Do It. Surrey, England: Telos, 2004. 102pp.

What chance do ordinary workers have when their home away from home—the workplace—is possessed? SymaxCorp is the embodiment of the soul-less corporate entity that many swore in college they would avoid working for. It sucks the lifeblood from employees in the name of increased profits, reducing them to battery hens, while they have to minimize their own personalities, even their own bodies.

Ketchum, Jack.
Red. London: Headline, 1995. 211pp.

Regular guy Avery Allan Ludlow goes on a peaceful fishing trip in the woods, where three cruel local boys blow his dog's head off with a shotgun. The elderly Ludlow attempts to get justice, but the sheriff's office fails him, for the triggerman is a rich man's son. Left with no recourse, Ludlow transforms. He takes the dog's body, his gun, and his frustration, and pays a visit.

King, Stephen.
Carrie. New York: Signet Books, 1975. 245pp. **YA**

What teen doesn't feel like a misfit? Carrie White's mother, a religious fanatic, torments her. A high school full of the usual good kids and creeps bully and tease. Then, on the night of the prom, rage built up during 16 years of abuse unleashes Carrie's telekinetic powers, with deadly results. King's classic novel is memorable 30 years later in part because he captures the psychology of a teen on the brink, as well as the typical but cruel people who populate small towns.

King, Stephen.
Dreamcatcher. New York: Scribner, 2001. 620pp.

Four men on their annual pilgrimage to their remote cabin in the woods discover that the world is coming to an end when a strange man steps into the local watering hole sporting mole-like creatures on his body. The creatures are harbingers of aliens who are coming to take over the planet. In spite of the apocalypse/science fiction theme, this novel is more character than plot driven, with four middle-aged men, friends since childhood, having this friendship cemented by extraordinary events.

King, Stephen.
Misery. New York: New American Library, 1988. 338pp.

A famous romance writer and his obsessive, psychotic fan populate this claustrophobic novel about a man who makes his living writing bodice rippers. The tables are turned on Paul when he suddenly finds that he is the one being held as a prisoner of love. His biggest fan, who is enamored not of the writer, but of one of his characters—whom he has unfortunately decided to kill off in his next novel—takes issue with his authorial decisions and takes matters into her own hands.

Lansdale, Joe R.
The Bottoms. New York: Time Warner, 2000. 328pp.

A teenager and his sister make a gruesome discovery: They find the mutilated body of a local black woman tied up near the river bottom. Soon the children find out that the world is full of sexual deviants and killers—as well as a mysterious creature called the Goat Man, and that they may be helpless victims, for even adults cannot be trusted.

Little, Bentley.
The Policy. New York: Signet, 2003. 389pp.

When Hunt Johnson makes a claim against his renter's insurance, he discovers the Devil is in the details when his policy gives him what is specified *to the letter,* such as replacing lost CDs with items of like monetary value. Thus, Hunt's music collection is "restored" with Debbie Boone CDs. When Hunt tries to fight the vast bureaucracy, whose rules fly in the face of common sense, he discovers it has a power of nearly supernatural dimensions. Can Hunt, just a regular guy, successfully fight this entity, with its insidious power? Little is a master at rendering surreal everyday encounters with horrifying bureaucracy.

Saul, John.
Creature. New York: Bantam, 1989. 377pp. **YA**
Young Mark Tanner's family moves to an idyllic Colorado community, believing that life will be pleasant. But when Mark bows to his father's and peers' pressure to go out for football, he discovers a dark secret behind the local high school's winning record and the town's overall perfection. This Saul classic young adult crossover is original, with an emphasis on everyday characters, who find themselves victimized by extraordinary circumstances.

I Need a Hero: Psychic Detectives, Monster Killers, and Vampire Hunters

Sometimes people need a little help when it comes to exorcising demons, chasing off ghouls, and capturing wayward spirits. So who we gonna call? Since The Ghostbusters are busy with their own hell-on-earth in New York City, we have to rely on the likes of Martin Zolotow and Repairman Jack. They get the job done.

Hopkins, Brian A.
🕮 *The Licking Valley Coon Hunters Club.* Alma, AR: Yard Dog Press, 2000. 173pp.
Private Investigator Martin Zolotow is kidnapped at an airport and taken out into the desert, where he is physically coerced into working for a mobster who needs him to help save the mobster's daughter from a man who thinks he is a vampire. Martin must now travel to Oklahoma City to visit a vampire nightclub. Fortunately for him, as well as for various kidnapped women who are being systematically hunted down, Zolotow is skilled in the survival and killing arts.

Huff, Tanya.
Blood Price. Victoria Nelson Novels. New York: Daw, 1991. 272pp.
These Toronto detectives don't waste their time with petty cases like infidelity and divorce. Detective Vicki Nelson teams up with novelist Henry Fitzroy to chase down 400-year-old vampires, protect a family of werewolves from extinction, stop an ancient priest from invoking an Egyptian god, and prevent a mad scientist from bringing the dead back to life. Stock characters abound in this fun, gossipy series that is a fan favorite. This is the first title in the Victoria Nelson Novels series. Other titles include *Blood Trial, Blood Lines, Blood Pact,* and *Blood Debt.*

King, Stephen, and Peter Straub.
Black House. The Talisman series. New York: Ballantine, 2002. 672pp.
As an adolescent, Jack saved his dying mother by traveling to a parallel universe called The Territories, a world ruled by magic instead of science.

Now 31 and a police detective, he has convinced himself that this was boyish fantasy. But when the children of his small town begin to disappear and are later found dismembered, Jack must again venture into The Territories. King and Straub's series is a complex saga spanning many decades. This is the second title in the series; the first is *The Talisman*.

Masterton, Graham.
The Devil in Gray. New York: Leisure, 2004. 355pp.

Grisly murders in Richmond, Virginia, have Detective Decker baffled. He must use supernatural means, including speaking with his deceased girlfriend and consulting a voodoo priestess, to discover what is behind the murders —the Devil's Brigade, a band of special troops that committed atrocities using voodoo to demoralize Union soldiers. This complex novel is filled with easily recognizable types, such as a modern voodoo priestess and a cop whose personal life is in tatters.

Partridge, Norman.
The Ten Ounce Siesta. New York: Berkley, 1998. 254pp.

What do a sick chihuahua, gun-toting maniacs, a dragon, and a few Satanists have in common? They are all strange characters that have suddenly come into ex-prize fighter Jack Baddalach's life. Currently a mob runner, Jack is given a strange assignment: escort the dog across the Nevada desert, while fighting off various monsters that want to stop him. This is a clever and original dark fantasy/horror satire.

Wilson, F. Paul.
Legacies. Repairman Jack series. New York: Forge, 1998. 381pp.

He's not a private eye. He's just a regular Manhattanite (with no last name or official identity) who fixes "situations," and he's handy with tools. When your back is to the occult wall, Jack will do what is necessary. Call Jack to prevent certain pictures from becoming public, or to find a missing son who was last seen in a strange cult. This is the first book in Wilson's popular series, now in its eighth title, *Infernal*, published in 2005.

Hey, You Look Much Smaller on TV: Historical and Famous Characters

Most readers like the lure of the familiar, and what could be more familiar than actual historical people? The tales in this section reinvent real life legends like Harry Houdini (who was quite fond of the occult), Sir Arthur Conan Doyle (who often helped Houdini expose charlatans), and Montague Summers (a Catholic priest who was the last serious "witch hunter" in recorded history and a learned expert on the subjects of witchcraft and demonology).

Constantine, Storm.
Stalking Tender Prey. Grigori Trilogy. London: Creed, 1995. 648pp.

Historical figures such as Aleister Crowley and Joseph Campbell populate this series, which is full of mythology and religion. In this first volume, fallen angel Shemyaaza moves to Cornwall with plans to regain his power, but he will need the old magic of the Grigori brothers and sisters. They gladly oblige. With the millennium coming to a close, a newly powerful Shemyaaza calls his followers for the final battle to determine the fate of humanity. Other titles in the trilogy are *Scenting Hallowed Blood* and *Stealing Sacred Fire*.

Knight, H. R.
What Rough Beast. New York: Leisure, 2005. 374pp.

Harry Houdini and Sir Arthur Conan Doyle attend a séance, hoping to expose an occultist as a fraud, but the hot-headed magician accidentally frees the god Dionysus, who acts as a conduit for sexual decadence and violent tendencies. Soon one member of the séance party is accused of a grisly murder because he is found in a locked room with the remains of his older brother, who has literally been torn limb from limb.

Lee, Edward, and Elizabeth Steffen.
Dahmer's Not Dead. Baltimore: Cemetery Dance, 1999. 288pp.

Murderer Jeffrey Dahmer has not been in the ground two days when Columbus County, Wisconsin is terrorized by a new cannibal killer whose fingerprints, handwriting, and voiceprint match the infamous serial cannibal's. And while the press and police are convinced that Dahmer has faked his own death and is at large, Captain Helen Cross of the state police Violent Crimes Unit sees nuances in the crime scenes that suggest a clever copycat.

Michaels, Barbara.
Other Worlds. New York: HarperCollins, 1999. 217pp.

Who hasn't heard of the Blair Witch by now? Its historical predecessor is the subject of this tale set in nineteenth-century Robertson County, Tennessee (based on the true story of the Bell Witch Haunting). It follows the Bell family's first meeting with the witch and then changes pace to become a discussion with that master of illusion, Harry Houdini, witch hunter Montague Summers, and detective Sir Arthur Conan Doyle, three historical experts on the occult.

Powers, Tim.
The Stress of Her Regard. New York: Ace, 1989. 470pp.

Powers' fictionalization of the interesting lives of Byron, Shelley, and Keats tells the story of their obsession with female lamia, or shapeshifters. These beautiful "women," who haunt the dreams of the Romantic poets, are actually eons-old, unmerciful, mythological creatures whose tender embraces drain the life from their victims. Imaginative, thought-provoking, and strong on slow character development and image.

Savile, Steve.
Houdini's Last Illusion. Tolworth, Surrey, England: Telos, 2004. 74pp.

Harry Houdini was not merely an illusionist. Here he is a practitioner of magic. He breathes life into a set of gloves and turns them into two birds, which he uses to help find out why he sees dead people—more specifically, deceased fellow magicians. Could it be that Death is not happy that Houdini has cheated him so often, and has come to collect his prize?

Yarbro, Chelsea Quinn.
In the Face of Death. Dallas, TX: Benbella Books, 2004. 288pp.

One of St. Germain's many vampire lovers, Madelaine de Montilla, is sent to pre–Civil War America to document the folkways of American Indian tribes before they disappear. She ends up in San Francisco in 1855, where she meets and falls in love with the unhappily married General William Tecumseh Sherman.

The Ghouls All Came from Their Humble Abodes: Monsters and Maniacs

They're Creepy and They're Spooky: Our Favorite Monsters

Midgets, hydrocephalic hillbillies, fallen angels, Elizabeth Bathory, Lord Byron, and Lucretia Borgia—they can all be found in this rather eclectic subsection, which lists books with the most memorable monsters we've encountered recently.

Barron, Diana.
Phantom Feast. St. Petersburg, FL: Barclay Books, 2001. 269pp.

Did you hear the one about the two dwarves, twin midgets, and the morbidly obese phone sex operator? They walked into a bar—and proceeded to crush every table, stool, and person into a pulp by invoking an army of animals that they can produce from any painting or photo. At first it's personal. But then two members of the motley crew manage to transform themselves into phantom animals. Now no one is safe.

Clegg, Douglas.
The Attraction. North Webster, IN: Delerium Books, 2004. 151pp.

    A desiccated corpse, billed as an Aztec mummy and displayed for all to see in a gas station, is revealed to be the remains of a small child with fake fingernails glued on its hands. But when Griff suggests to his friend Ziggy that it would be funny to feed the pathetic "attraction," they end up awaking The Flesh Scrapper. This tale is Clegg's homage to B slasher flicks, with the requisite characters who do things such as feed the mummy against all sensible advice, with predictable and gory results.

Codrescu, Andrei.
The Blood Countess. New York: Simon & Schuster, 1995. 347pp.

    Thirty years after the fall of the Soviet Union, Drake Bathory-Kereshutur returns to his native Hungary, where he learns that history is not a dead past that can be erased but a living force that shapes his life—and that his infamous ancestor, Countess Elizabeth Bathory, can compel him to do her terrible will. Bathory, with her decadent love of cruelty and torture, is no stranger to modern readers steeped in the tradition of the serial killer who takes similar pleasure in his work. Codrescu's version of Elizabeth Bathory, ancestor of Vlad Tepes, is morbid but erudite.

Giron, Sephera.
Borrowed Flesh. New York: Leisure, 2004. 340pp.

    Sometimes Retin A and Botox just aren't enough. This is the case for a twenty-first-century Countess Elizabeth Bathory. She is an immortal witch whose eternity has but one catch—she needs regular virgin sacrifices to keep her skin fresh and healthy. Then a friend of her latest sacrifice starts sniffing around. Giron captures female stereotypes well.

Holland, Tom.
Lord of the Dead: The Secret History of Byron (Originally published as *The Vampyre: Being the True Pilgrimage of George Gordon, Sixth Lord Byron*). Lord of the Dead series. New York: Simon & Schuster, 1995. 342 pp.

    What if Dr. John Polidori was not writing fiction when he used poet Lord Byron as his model for *The Vampyre*? What if Byron were actually one of the undead? This series takes on that possibility, allowing the English poet Byron to narrate his history as the fanged progeny of his vampire creator, Lord Ruthven. As it turns out, Byron's vampirism is the main cause of his rakishness, which ultimately destroys his friendships with Polidori and Mary Shelley. This is the first title in the series; others include *Slave of My Thirst, Deliver Us from Evil*, and *The Sleeper in the Sands*.

Jefferson, Jemiah.
Voice of the Blood. New York: Leisure, 2001. 283pp.

Sometimes good girls make bad choices. Ariane falls in love with two vampires. A hopeless romantic, Ricari is averse to killing, and spends his undeath starving and brooding, while decadence and selfishness are Daniel's only qualities. Ariane begins to fall for Daniel, who makes her into a vampire. But what of Ricari? How did he become so dark and brooding? His story is told in his own words in a sequel, *Fiend* (New York: Leisure, 2005. 326pp.), in which readers learn what it means to be immortal—and evil.

Lee, Edward.
The Bighead. Woodstock, GA: Overlook Connection, 1999. 354pp.

A hydrocephalic child born in Appalachia becomes known as The Bighead, a misshapen and mentally retarded creature who only knows how to eat and mate. And when his grandfather, the only parent he knows, dies, Bighead is left to wander through the woods and terrorize hapless inhabitants of the nearby small town. Lee's novel is filled with many weird Appalachian types, such as moonshiners and crazed mountain folk.

Preston, Douglas, and Lincoln Child.
The Relic. The Relic (series). New York: Tor, 1995. 474pp.

A monster that feeds on human brain tissue is loose in the New York Museum of Natural History. Can Margo Green, graduate student/museum researcher, discover the creature's secret and destroy it before the opening reception for a new exhibit? Whereas the movie versions of this series turned the tale into an action-adventure story, this novel and its sequel (*Reliquary*) concentrate on characterization, especially of the unfortunate creature that haunts the museum and kills out of necessity.

Romkey, Michael.
I, Vampire. I, Vampire series. New York: Fawcett, 1990. 360pp.

Julius Caesar and Lucretia Borgia were vampire clan leaders? Who'd a thunk it? This action-based series follows along as vampire armies clash by night, in places as diverse as the Civil War American South, modern-day Costa Rica and the Caribbean (yes, a vampire cruise ship), and late nineteenth-century London. Historical and literary characters such as John Wilkes Booth and Abraham Van Helsing make appearances throughout. Other series titles include *The Vampire Papers*, *The Vampire Princess*, *The Vampire Virus*, and *The London Vampire Panic*.

Stableford, Brian.
The Werewolves of London. The Werewolves of London Trilogy. New York: Carroll and Graf, 1990. 467pp.

Remember the stories of the fallen angels from the Bible? Ever wondered what happened to them? Stableford uses lush, neo-Victorian prose to relate the story of werewolves in an original way, as the progeny of fallen angels who, at the dawn of the twentieth century, have been awakened during an archeological expedition and now pass among humans, having the ability to change their shapes. This is the first title of the trilogy. The others are *The Angel of Pain* and *The Carnival of Destruction.*

Yarbro, Chelsea Quinn.
A Flame in Byzantium. Atta Olivia Clements series. New York: Tor, 1987. 480pp.

Get ready to be taken to Rome in 545 C.E., after the time of Nero, with Olivia Clemens, an assertive Roman citizen, in this first volume of the series. From there the reader flees to Constantinople with Clemens, now a vampire. In the second novel in the series, *Crusader's Torch,* the reader ultimately returns (some 600 years later) to Rome, traversing deserts filled with crusaders and seas besieged by pirates. Finally, *A Candle for D'Artangan: An Historical Horror* takes place in Louis XIV's French court, where the reader will meet the famed Musketeer D'Artangan.

With Humans Like These, Who Needs the Supernatural?: Maniacs and Sociopaths

All of the monsters in this subsection are of the flesh and blood variety, yet their penchant for cruelty and ability to elude capture border on the supernatural. Robert Bloch is credited with beginning this subgenre of horror, the maniac tale, with his novel *Psycho,* which explains the sociopath as a phenomenon caused by bad mothering. Writers such as Thomas Harris, with his Hannibal Lecter Novels, take this sort of monster to new heights with a serial killer's serial killer, whose deviance cannot be explained.

Bloch, Robert.
Psycho. New York: Simon & Schuster, 1959. 185pp.

Norman Bates, a middle-aged loner, is dominated by his nagging mother and kills "loose" young women who arouse him. This novel differs from Alfred Hitchcock's 1960 film, in that it trades on the stereotypically creepy relationship between an unmarried adult man and his mother, whereas the film portrays him as someone suffering from multiple personality disorder.

Campbell, Ramsey.
The Count of Eleven. New York: Tor, 1992. 310pp.

Mild-mannered Jack Orchard, a devoted husband and father, finds a discarded chain letter and decides that it must be the cause of a recent series of unfortunate events. To turn his life around, he quickly follows the letter's instructions, which require that he send the missive to 13 others without divulging the list. But Jack suffers from obsessive compulsive disorder, so whenever anyone stands between him and his task, he goes over the edge—even as far as murder.

Campbell, Ramsey.
The Face That Must Die. New York, Tor. 1979. 351pp.

Horridge, a young loner, is haunted by faces, horrifying childhood experiences, and the voice of serial killer named Craig. Eventually "Horridge the Horror," as he was called by cruel children in his youth, loses his sanity and becomes what he fears most. Campbell provides a well-written and subtly engaging treatment of what goes on in the mind of a psychopathic killer.

Crouch, Blake.
Desert Places: A Novel of Terror. New York: Thomas Dunne Books, 2004. 280pp.

Andrew Thomas, a successful crime novelist, receives a mysterious missive directing him to the location of the body of a recently missing woman, buried on his property. The note's directions soon reunite him with his twin brother Orson, who has been missing for over a decade. Orson knows a great deal about gory crimes, since he is now a full-blown serial killer. He kidnaps his brother, hoping to "educate" his sibling.

Harris, Thomas.
The Silence of the Lambs. Hannibal Lecter Novels. New York: St. Martin's, 1988. 338pp.

Rookie FBI agent Clarice Starling, anxious to prove that her sex and humble origins won't hinder her professionalism, is sent to interview Dr. Hannibal Lecter, the infamous, cultured, and cruel serial killer, who enjoyed a census taker's liver with fava beans and a good Chianti. Can Lecter's insights help Starling stop Buffalo Bill, a serial killer who skins his victims? And can Starling stand Lecter's relentless probing of her own personality? This popular, character-driven novel was made into a movie and spawned a series, including *Red Dragon*, *Hannibal,* and *Behind the Mask*.

Ketchum, Jack.
The Lost. New York: Leisure, 2001. 394pp.

Meet Ray Pye, who suffers from Little Man Syndrome. He compensates for his shortcomings by stuffing crushed beer cans in his boots, playing the bully, and heightening his facial features with cosmetics. His animal magnetism allows him to attract willing sexual partners. But any woman who dares to reject him will suffer.

Lee, Edward, and John Pelan.
Goon. Woodstock, GA: Overlook Connection Press, 2003. 138pp.

A police officer and reporter go undercover as wrestling groupies to discover who has been murdering "ringrats," the name given to fans of the sport. The suspect, Goon, is a wrestler who has the amazing ability to take a fatal blow to the head and emerge unscathed. Pelan and Lee's fictional universe is populated with inbred hicks and equally strange fans of pro wrestling.

McCabe, Patrick.
The Butcher Boy. New York: Dell, 1994. 231pp.

Francie Brady, a young Irish lad from a working class family, is a psychopath in the making. Son of an alcoholic father and a suicidal mother, he has no one to help him manage the rage he feels. An unsympathetic neighbor pushes Francie over the edge when she doesn't want her son to associate with the likes of him. This story, told in the first person through Francie's eyes, is all the more disturbing because of its immediacy, as we witness Francie's descent into madness. It was made into a film in 1998.

McCrann, Michael.
Midnight Tableau. Ontario: Double Dragon Press, 2004. 178pp.

What is more frightening than any monster? How about a painfully shy college student who concocts a highly effective aphrodisiac; or a would-be pledge who will do absolutely anything to join Sigma Phi; or a desperate father who discovers a creature that, when fed living beings, brings good luck. Everyday characters become exceptional through fantastic situations that seem almost believable.

Nykanen, Mark.
The Bone Parade. New York: Hyperion, 2004. 324 p

Ashley Stasser is world renowned for his series of bronze sculptures, each a detailed representation of families in agonizing pain. While Stasser certainly has an eye for composition, the detail in his work does not come wholly from his imagination. Instead, he travels the country and kidnaps individual families, whom he brings back to his remote studio, where he tortures and kills them while making impressions of them during their death throes.

Straczynski, Michael J.
Othersyde. New York: Dutton, 1990. 294pp. **YA**

Sixteen-year-old Chris Martino moves to Los Angeles to live with his mother, and there he becomes friends with a misfit classmate named Roger, who is taunted by the other kids and nicknamed Horseface. One day Chris sends a note to his friend, but the message his friend receives is not the one Chris wrote. The note, from a mysterious entity named Othersyde, encourages Horseface to take revenge against his classmates.

West, Owen (pseudonym of Dean Koontz).
The Funhouse: A Novel. New York: Berkley, 1980. 333pp.

    Yes, clowns are scary. A woman is hunted by her ex-husband, a carnival barker bent on revenge after she killed their son 25 years before, because she was convinced that the child was evil. Now her ex will have his revenge, by taking her children the way she took their son. This strange thriller is filled with many off-the-wall characters from the circus.

Chapter 5

Language

Sometimes how a writer says something, that writer's style or technique, is as important as what he or she says. This is as true in the horror genre as it is in mainstream and literary fiction. Take, for example, the writing team of Stephen King and Peter Straub. King is known for straightforward prose and believable dialogue. Perhaps this is why he has sold more novels than any other author in the genre; his style appeals to the average reader. Straub, on the other hand, is extremely introspective and sometimes overly experimental with language, constructing complex, challenging sentences. Some readers relish the complexity; others do not like it. Ramsey Campbell, on the other side of the Atlantic, is the master against whom all writers in the genre are measured because of his erudite, subtle prose, while Simon Clark, an extremely imaginative writer, chooses to keep his sentences simple and concentrate more on action and realistic description. But whether readers like fast-paced and suspenseful narrative or thoughtful, even ponderous prose, they'll find some great reads in this chapter.

Description

You Can Almost Taste the Blood: Lush, Vivid Detail

There is an old saying that the devil is in the details, and this is especially appropriate in descriptive horror fiction, where authors use sensory details so readers can almost see, hear, feel, smell, or even taste what's happening. Here are stories containing vivid images and descriptions that might be called "graphic," "visceral," "sensational," "gory," or "shocking." The sheer physicality of the experience—the blood, the darkness, the shrieking, the putrid smells—intensifies the emotional charge and makes these stories more real.

Amis, Kingsley.
The Green Man. New York: Harcourt Brace, 1969. 252pp.

Before Jack Torrence stuck his head through a demolished door and said, "Heeere's Johnny," before the word REDRUM became a staple of horror lingo, there was Maurice Allington and The Green Man Inn. It seems Mr. Allington rather likes the bottle, and now he is seeing ghosts. But are they in his mind, or real? This story is subtle and well-written, played as much for wry smiles as for shivers. It showcases Amis's offbeat humor, as well as his gift for creating atmosphere and memorable writing.

Brite, Poppy Z.
Exquisite Corpse. New York: Scribner, 1996. 240pp.

More gory and disturbing than Bret Easton Ellis's controversial novel *American Psycho,* this book follows the exploits of Jay Byrne and Andrew Compton, two cannibalistic serial killers who have taken torture and killing to an epicurean art form. Their interests come together when the duo seeks to torture and devour a young Vietnamese man. Brite describes the most abominable of suffering so graphically that readers cannot turn away, no matter much the subject matter might make them want to.

Brite, Poppy Z.
Lost Souls. New York: Bantam-Dell, 1992. 355pp.

A misunderstood and isolated teenager named Nothing discovers that his father is a vampire who travels with a duo of undead goons with an insatiable desire for blood, alcohol, sugar, and violence. On his quest to find his father and understand his own odd nature, Nothing befriends Steve and Ghost, members of the band Lost Souls who are also struggling to come to terms with their sexuality. Brite creates intensely descriptive homoerotic scenes set amid the gothic splendor of tiny Missing Mile, North Carolina, and the New Orleans French Quarter. This is typical Brite, describing unspeakable violence and suffering with great lyricism.

Campbell, Ramsey.
Midnight Sun. New York: Tor, 1991. 336pp.

As a child, Ben found himself attracted to the magical yet eerie powers that seemed to inhabit the forest near his aunt's house. Twenty years later Ben, now a family man, has inherited his aunt's house—and is even more attracted to the forest's dark forces. Ben slowly loses his reason with each victim that the entity claims, succumbing to its promise of immortality in exchange for lives. The artful use of metaphor here paints a frightening portrait of one man's mental breakdown.

Gaiman, Neil.
American Gods. London: Headline, 2001. 504pp.

    Shadow, a newly released prisoner who has served time for murder, picks up a hitchhiker, Odin, and finds himself in the middle of a battle between the Old Norse god and manifestations of the new American gods—gambling, credit cards, television, and the Internet. The old gods, led by Odin, are not pleased that they are not receiving the attention they feel is their due; it is being diverted to these false idols. Lush, hallucinogenic descriptions of the old gods in their new but less spectacular forms as little old ladies and undertakers fuel a story set in a blighted American Midwest.

Hand, Elizabeth.
Waking the Moon. London: HarperCollins, 1984. 598pp.

    Everyone was in love with Angelica during freshman year at the Divine, but she disappeared after a group held a strange moonlight ritual, culminating in one of the boys castrating himself and later committing suicide. Now Angelica has resurfaced as a successful author, giving workshops about feminist spirituality. Her ex-classmates are dying mysterious deaths, and Earth is plagued by unusual natural phenomena. Could the Second Coming be at hand? If so, the coming of whom? *Waking the Moon* is related in Hand's erudite style, which demonstrates her extensive knowledge of old religious traditions and mythologies.

Newman, Kim.
Jago. New York: Caroll and Graf, 1991. 534pp.

    The tiny English village of Alder is dominated by a bizarre religious community known as the Agapemone. Now dreams—and nightmares—are beginning to come true, and at the heart of it all is the Reverend Anthony Jago, spiritual leader of the Agapemone, whose telepathic abilities can control collective reality. Newman's novel features a motley cast of violent characters described in highly literate, epic-style prose, colored by lots of gruesome and explicit sex.

Rice, Anne.
Blood Canticle. The Vampire Chronicles. New York: Alfred A. Knopf, 2003. 305pp.

    The series started with Rice's blockbuster, *Interview with a Vampire. Blood Canticle* is the ninth volume. Eighteenth-century aristocrat Lestat de Lioncourt is a vampire of his age. An iconoclast, he would break all the rules established by his undead elders, wreaking havoc among immortals. But several centuries of undeath and disillusionment ultimately lead Lestat back to the Catholic Church, vowing to do God's work on Earth. Rice's series is characterized by a lush, descriptive style that brings various historical periods and foreign places alive for the reader.

Tryon, Thomas.
The Other. New York: Knopf, 1971. 280pp.
    This eerie novel begins with a description of a how a water spot on the ceiling makes a face, and its Victorian, spellbinding quality never lets up. Preteen twins Niles and Holland disrupt the quiet lifestyle of their quaint, New England town when Niles, the evil twin, begins cleverly murdering anyone who displeases him. Is the twins' grandmother's experimentation with ESP adversely affecting the boys, or are there deeper, darker secrets in the family? Arguably a little known modern classic.

Zinger, Steve.
The Sab. Bloomington, IN: Authorhouse, 2004. 508pp.
    Vampires are haunting Montréal. A girl who has recently entered her teens, an alcoholic police officer, and an undead Blackfoot Indian must stop them from taking over. A young Blackfoot roams the wilds of New York state and is found and turned by a female vampire. Flash forward to modern-day Montréal, where he finds an insomniac Montréal Urban Community policeman and enlists his aid in stopping the exquisitely evil vampire Talissa. Zinger's descriptions of mysterious events are subtle but hypnotic, frightening, raw, and psychologically disturbing—guaranteed to make a chill run down your spine.

Say What You Mean to Say: Spare and Austere Language

Journalistic writing, spare and stark, holds the power to tell a story by using an economy of language, or a minimum number of words. Short sentences and brief paragraphs are composed of a few vigorous, action-oriented words and phrases. In the horror genre, this style is disquieting. A calm, matter-of-fact or straightforward telling of a horrible event seems unnatural, even spooky, and its effects can be more profound than a blow-by-blow description of some atrocity.

Barker, Clive.
The Hellbound Heart. New York: Harper, 1986. 164pp.
    When Frank, a playboy and thrill-seeker, decides that life holds no more pleasure for him, he experiments with Lamarchand's Box, which supposedly will summon the gods of pleasure. Frank should have known about The Pleasure Principle, which describes the relationship between pleasure and pain. He summons the demons of torture, and they want more than just him. Characteristic of Barker's simple, yet graphic style, this novella tells a story through vividly drawn images and metaphors.

Huysmans, J. K.
La-Bas (*Down There*). Translated by Brendan King. London: Dedalus, 2001 (1891). 329pp.

Huysmans's singular contribution to supernatural literature takes as its subject matter demonology, Satanism, the black arts, and the Black Mass. Interesting in itself as a novelty piece—a horror novel written by a canonized writer of literature—it is a prime example of Huysmans's love of decadent, descriptive prose. A matter-of-fact dialogue between a writer, his friend, a church bell ringer, and his wife leads to a witnessing of Satanic rites and altar sacrifices.

Jackson, Shirley.
The Lottery and Other Stories. New York: Farrar, Straus & Giroux, 1982 (1949). 306pp.

No writer has ever used the third-person objective point of view to convey scenes of unspeakable horror as masterfully as Jackson does. A case in point is "The Lottery," one of the most popular and often taught tales of terror of all time. Suppose that your town held an annual drawing, and the "lucky winner" had to be made into a human sacrifice, murdered by the entire town right before your eyes. Jackson's writing style is sparse, giving her works an aloof quality reminiscent of any encounter with the uncanny.

King, Stephen.
The Shining. New York: Plume, 1977. 690pp.

King is typically a straightforward writer, but here his mastery of telling a complex story using simple prose shines. Alcoholic ex-teacher Jack Torrance has a second chance at life when he is given the position of off-season caretaker of The Overlook Hotel. But Jack has overlooked one problem: The hotel is full of ghosts—one of whom murdered his family and would like Jack to be his new "recruit."

Koja, Kathe.
The Cipher. New York: Dell, 1991. 368pp.

It's almost like reading a newspaper report. In terse, blunt language, Koja tells about Nicholas and Nakota, two Generation X nonconformists who discover a mysterious black hole in a wall. This hole devours or changes anything that ventures into it. An adventurous Nakota tries to stick her head through; Nicholas tries to stop her and sticks his hand in instead. Now his hand has become a terrifying, weeping sore.

Matheson, Richard.
I Am Legend. New York: Tor, 1995 (1954). 320pp.

Maybe all the bats can fly in the wrong direction. At least that is what the last human on Earth realizes, when he wakes to find himself alone in a post-apocalyptic world overrun by hemophiliac, vampirelike creatures that shun daylight and want him to join their party or die. Matheson's masterpiece, which anchors this short story collection, was later made into the film *The Omega Man*. Matheson is a master stylist whose writing isn't characterized so much by a paucity of description as by his careful selection of words.

Oates, Joyce Carol.
Zombie. New York: Penguin, 1995. 192pp.

Meet Quentin P., serial killer. He wants to meet someone who will love him unconditionally, but his social skills are extremely limited, and he has difficulty dealing with his own homosexuality, so he cannot find a soul mate. His solution is simple, and is told with childlike simplicity in his diary; but it may make readers' flesh crawl.

Walpole, Horace.
The Castle of Otranto. Mineola, NY: Dover, 2004 (1764). 128pp.

Not many writers can describe giant helmets falling out of the sky while keeping a straight face, but in this novel the straightforward storytelling makes the absurd seem eerie. On the day of his wedding, Prince Conrad, the son of Otranto, is killed. When Otranto divorces so he can marry his son's fiancée, a young woman who can produce for him another son, ghosts are forced to intervene and expose a dark family secret. This classic is defined by its sparse description and to-the-point dialogue, as well as its melodramatic feel.

Think Before You Speak, and After: Reflective Horror

Seeing events through a narrator's eyes makes a story all the more real, and in the case of horror fiction, all the more frightening. These are highly personal, even confessional, stories, but more important, they are immediate, making readers feel as though they are in the story. When the stories are told as diary entries or letters, the reader gets to become the main character.

Brite, Poppy Z.
Are You Loathsome Tonight? Springfield, PA: Gauntlet, 1998. 193pp.

This collection showcases Brite's flair for morbid humor and clever self-referentiality. Included is "Mussolini and the Axeman's Jazz," about the turn-of-the-century Texas/Louisiana axe murders and a record banned because it allegedly induced suicide. Brite's writing is characterized by thoughtful descriptions of the nuances of human emotion, filling the reader's mind with vivid images of pain and beauty.

Brown, Charles Brockden.
Wieland; or The Transformation: An American Tale and Other Stories. New York: Random House, 2002 (1798). 416pp.

Step inside the mind of Wieland, a man convinced that he is speaking with God. Wieland's father was a religious fanatic, so Wieland does what God says. Now God says he must prove his loyalty by killing those he holds most dear. This early American gothic tale is loosely based on the eighteenth-century murder spree of John Yates. It is related in epistolary format in a pensive tone by a dazed young woman who survived her brother's madness.

Campbell, Ramsey.
Waking Nightmares. New York: Tor, 1991. 273pp.

Some say that we never get over our childhood fears, our recurring nightmares of monsters in the closet, faces at the window, and creatures under the bed. Many of these thoughts of peril inform the traditional ghost story. Here the reader can revisit those early fears, with a touch of self-referential cleverness, in stories about horror writers, omnibus editors, and professional booksellers. After all, even horror bibliographers were children once. Campbell's writing is creative, often humorous, balancing physical horror with psychological terror.

Charnas, Suzy McKee.
The Vampire Tapestry. New York: Tor, 1998. 247pp.

In what is arguably the most thoughtful, psychologically realistic treatment of vampirism, four vignettes tell the story of a not-quite-human anthropology professor. This mild, unassuming, middle-aged man is one of the last of his species, and to stay that way, he needs to keep his special talents under wraps. But fake psychological experiments can only go so far when thrill seekers who would love nothing more than to capture him are around every corner. Charnas relates her tale in the clinical style of the academic through whose eyes the story is told.

Hoffman, Nina Kiriki.
A Stir of Bones. New York: Viking, 2003. 208pp. **YA**

Wealthy teenager Susan appears to have everything, but she is tightly controlled by her abusive father, who punishes his daughter's transgressions by beating her mother. Then Susan meets Nathan, the ghost of a boy who committed suicide after World War I. Now more than anything, Susan wants to join her ethereal friend—in death. Hoffman's thoughtful style mimics the confusion of her adolescent protagonist, forced to deal with unspeakable domestic violence.

Jackson, Shirley.
We Have Always Lived in the Castle. New York: Penguin, 1984. 214pp.

"Poor strangers—they have so much to be afraid of." So comments Merricat, the first-person narrator of this tale about two eccentric sisters and their uncle, living in the house where the rest of their family was murdered. The voice of Merricat is both hypnotic and eerily sweet, as she matter-of-factly describes how no one visits Blackwood House any more, how she and her older sister Constance are shunned by the townspeople, and how she buries artifacts on the grounds for protection. But the safe realm she lives in is about to be shattered.

James, Henry.
Ghost Stories of Henry James. Hertfordshire, England: Wordsworth Classics, 2001. 448pp.

A nanny and two children are haunted by the spirit of a decadent ex-servant; in her determination to protect the children, will she actually harm them? A man meets his shadow self in his childhood home, an event that threatens his sanity. Or is he "not quite himself" to begin with? These late nineteenth-century ghost stories ask, is it all just in the mind? Rendered in the excruciatingly descriptive and convoluted prose style that characterizes all of James's work.

Levin, Ira.
The Stepford Wives. New York: Random House, 1972. 145pp.

Gothamites Walter and Joanna Eberhardt move from New York City to Stepford Village, a place they believe will be more conducive to properly raising their family. Walter begins to change after they move, due to the mysterious male-only men's association. Joanna discovers what she believes is the reason: the men's association is replacing its members' wives with robotic replicants. Or is Joanna just losing her mind? Levin's matter-of-fact description conveys Joanna's ambivalence about what she witnesses.

Lovecraft, H[oward]. P[ierce].
The Founding Father of Modern Horror collections.

The Call of Cthulhu and Other Weird Stories. New York: Penguin, 1999. 420pp.
The Thing on the Doorstep and Other Weird Stories. New York: Penguin, 2001. 443pp.
The Dreams in the Witch House and Other Weird Stories. New York: Penguin, 2004. 453pp.

These introspective, almost claustrophobic volumes contain some truly inspired stories, such as the fairy-tale-like "The Cats of Ulthar" and the classic "The Lurking Fear." Their strength is that editor S. T. Joshi does a good job of making sure that various types are presented together, rather than creating single-themed collections. There are tales in which the language emphasizes the uncanny or macabre; disturbing, surrealistic stories based on nightmares and fantastical visions; a couple of Victorian-style antiquarian studies; and a handful of atmospheric, truly frightening tales of the Old Gods, returned to Earth to dominate humans.

Marano, Michael.
Dawn Song. New York: Tor, 1998. 396pp.

On the eve of the Gulf War, a demon uses mass hysteria, war, and bigotry and religious oppression to increase his power. One of his demonic rivals sends a succubus, who takes up residence in a Boston apartment complex to learn about human emotions. She does this by killing her human lovers, for she must absorb into herself the souls of 20 men. But that's only the beginning. Marano's lyrical descriptions of human suffering impart a dreamlike quality to the work.

Dialogue

All You Do Is Talk Talk: Lots of Interactive Dialogue

Reading dialogue is like overhearing a conversation, and in horror stories it can entertain and amuse or provide a glimpse into the darkest of minds. Dialogue can be snappy and humorous, clipped and terse, or melancholy and lugubrious. Masters of dialogue marry it to description and character, telling the story through conversations. These titles often feature the additional appeal of character. If conversation and characters are your cup of tea, check out some of the titles in this section.

Brite, Poppy Z.
Drawing Blood. New York: Dell, 1994. 403pp.

Trevor Black discovers that Missing Mile, North Carolina, is aptly named. It is a sort of gothic Bermuda Triangle, where, among other things, his father inexplicably murdered his mother and toddler brother before committing suicide, leaving only Trevor alive. Twenty years later, Trevor is drawn to this place and the ghosts of his family. Much of the tale is related through Trevor's dialogues with his lover and with the ghosts.

Evans, Gloria.
Meh'Yam. Gainesville, FL: T. Bo Publishing, 2000. 257pp.

When an orange creature taller than the average NBA player is looking to pick up women, it had better be a shapeshifter, and a smooth talker to boot. Pomoda, of an alien race at the top of the universe's food chain, is attracted to

Earth by its abundance of dark-skinned humans, whose flesh is rich in melanin, a chemical he lacks. So he dons the shape of a tall, dark-skinned aristocrat—and hunts in Miami area nightclubs. Lots of thoughtful dialogue interspersed with raw scenes of death.

Hambly, Barbara.
Traveling with the Dead. New York: Ballantine, 1995. 343pp.

Dr. James Asher works for Her Majesty's Secret Service, and at the beginning of the twentieth century he is sent to Austria to investigate rumors that the Austrian Empire is using the undead to turn the tides of war. And what would Bond, as a vampire hunter, be without a lovely female assistant, with whom he can exchange witty repartee in Victorian English?

King, Stephen.
Insomnia. New York: Penguin-Signet, 1995. 663pp.

After his wife's death, Ralph Roberts begins seeing things: strange auras of light around people and three small, bald men in doctors' uniforms. No, they are not Rogain salesmen. These men seem to be somehow connected with the sudden violent tendencies of some of Ralph's friends and with the general mayhem that is taking over the town. This lengthy but interesting read is steadily paced and conversational, with Ralph learning about this strange phenomenon through gossip.

Koontz, Dean.
Phantoms. New York: Putnam, 1983. 352pp.

More than half of the residents of Snowfield, California, have either mysteriously disappeared or died. Dr. Jennifer Paige, her teenaged sister Lisa, and Sheriff Bryce Hammond must get to the bottom of these strange occurrences, while avoiding being gruesomely killed by It, the shapeshifting creature that seems to know each person's innermost fears. The dialogues between the humans and the demon, on computer, are priceless. One of Koontz's best.

Massie, Elizabeth.
Shadow Dreams. New York: Leisure, 2002. 337pp.

A homeless woman dares to love a beautiful man, but only from afar, as her physical appearance is something other than human. A young girl dreads snow days, when school is canceled, because she'll be subjected to "the special way" her mother and stepfather show their love. A family is under siege from some mysterious outsiders, who routinely take family members. These conversational gothic tales feature the hopelessness of Appalachian poverty, related in a version of Southern English that is realistic rather than the illiterate parody of this dialect that is so often seen.

Masterton, Graham.
A Terrible Beauty. New York: Pocket Books, 2003. 369pp.

Dateline: Cork, Ireland. Today a farmer unearthed in his field 11 skeletons dating back to the 1940s, and a local detective is on the case, looking for connections between this and grisly, recent killings of American tourists. Here Masterton conjures a richly detailed world in Cork, complete with police officers speaking Gaelic into cell phones and troubled members of a minority gypsy culture.

McCabe, Patrick.
Emerald Germs of Ireland. New York: HarperCollins, 2001. 306pp.

After killing his mother by beating her on the head with a sauce pan, a young Gullytown lad named Patrick, considered the village idiot, goes about his day-to-day life. In the process, he introduces the reader to the people who have made him a serial killer, in a witty and energetic narrative full of local color and dialogue in Irish dialect.

Rice, Anne.
The Queen of the Damned. New York: Knopf, 1988. 448pp.

Through their intimate conversations, Akasha and Enkil tell the story of all vampire beginnings. They are the mother and father of the undead, predating even ancient Egypt. But for the past two millennia, Akasha has been held prisoner as a statue by her husband. With Lestat's help she is freed, and she wants Lestat to help her unleash her wrath on humanity. And Akasha's storytelling abilities are as deft and hypnotic as those of Lestat.

Giving as Good as They Get: Witty Repartee

Back-and-forth insulting, or verbal sparring and jesting, are commonplace in these books. Whether they be humorous works, novelizations of television series, or parodies of hard-boiled detective stories, these titles show that monsters can be witty, too.

Burns, Laura J., and Melinda Metz.
Apocalypse Memories. <u>Buffy and Angel novelizations</u>. New York: Simon & Schuster, 2004. 256pp. **YA**

Okay, so it's like Willow comes back to Sunnydale, but she totally hates her magical powers, then she figures out she'd better use them or the world's gonna end. Then this friend from grad school asks Fred for help with her job at a lab, but he gets wasted, so Angel has to catch his killer, who is, like, murdering all these wizards. Buffy has to chase all these bad guys to find pieces of a soul sword, *and* Xander and Willow get a virus. Some 10 titles, written by various authors, are now included in the series.

Collins, Nancy A.
🎀 *Sunglasses After Dark*. Sonja Blue series. New York: New American Library, 1989. 253pp.

    Talk about a vamp with an attitude! Denise Thorne, heiress, is raped by a vampire, and after nine months in a coma, she is reborn as Sonja Blue, a butt-kicking, leather-clad, sarcastic female vampire who can inhabit dream worlds, and who violently kills cruel humans, ghosts, and other revenants—lipping all the way. Other titles in the series include *In the Blood*, *Midnight Blue: The Sonja Blue Collection*, *Paint It Black*, *A Dozen Black Roses*, *Darkest Heart*, and *Dead Roses for a Blue Lady*.

Elrod, P. N.
Jonathan Barrett: Gentleman Vampire (Omnibus). The Vampire Files. New York: Doubleday, 1996. 960pp.

    He could have crawled out of a novel by Dashiel Hammett or Mickey Spillane. He's hard-boiled, tough-talking journalist and private dick Jack Fleming, and he doesn't mind an all-night stake out, especially after a gangland hit that fails to kill him makes him realize that he has been made into a vampire. Think being a detective is hard? Try dealing with vampires. This omnibus edition contains all four novels in The Vampire Files: *Red Death*, *Death and the Maiden*, *Death Masque*, and *Dance of Death*.

Gorman, Ed.
The Dark Fantastic. New York: Leisure, 2001. 391pp.

    Sure, we'd all like to take revenge on people who have hurt us, allowing our baser instincts to help us get even. Interaction and dialogue shine in these 17 tales of battered women acting out their most violent fantasies. The reader will also will run into a time-traveling professor who chronicles his voyages to strange, dark realms, as well as various serial killers who murder because they enjoy inflicting pain.

Grant, Charles L.
Genesis. Black Oak series. New York: ROC, 1998. 271pp.

    Got a ghost in your attic? Werewolves howling while you try to sleep? No problem. Just call Black Oak Security, an investigative firm that handles not only fraud and missing persons' complaints, but also paranormal phenomena. Ethan Proctor heads a band of misfits with varying degrees of power and/or occult knowledge, in this marriage of horror, fantasy, and mystery. Grant uses back-and-forth, witty dialogue masterfully. Other titles in the series include *The Hush of Dark Wings*, *Winter Knight*, *Hunting Ground*, and *When the Cold Wind Blows*.

Hamilton, Laurell K.
The Midnight Café (omnibus edition). Anita Blake, Vampire Hunter series. New York: Berkeley, 1998. 825pp.

She's sassy. She's tough. She's quirky. She talks like a Mickey Spillane character, and she can kill even the oldest and most powerful of vampires. Follow the adventures (yeah, like you have a choice) of the most famous of all vampire huntresses as she deals with vampire vigilantes in a futuristic world, in which the Supreme Court protects undead rights. This omnibus edition contains *The Lunatic Cafe*, *Bloody Bones*, and *The Killing Dance*. The author has published a dozen titles in this popular series, with no signs of quitting.

Harris, Charlaine.
Dead Until Dark. The Southern Vampire Mysteries. New York: Ace, 2001. 260pp.

Four years before, vampires "came out of the coffin" and made their presence known to the world, as did a host of other supernatural creatures. Sookie Stackhouse, telepathic Southern waitress, just wants to enjoy her life, but she is often called upon by various vampire friends and lovers to use her supernatural gifts to solve crimes. Wisecracking Sookie, the series narrator, exchanges witty repartee with other creatures of the night, but she is a down-to-earth Southern girl at heart. Other titles in the series include *Living Dead in Dallas*, *Club Dead*, *Dead to the World*, and *Dead as a Doornail*.

Kihn, Greg.
Horror Show. New York: Tor, 1996. 274pp.

When *Monster Magazine* reporter Clint Stockbern sets out to interview the legendary horror movie director Landis Woodley (an Ed Wood type B movie maker), he uncovers a bizarre story of real-life horror. In 1957 Woodley shot his last zombie flick, *Cadaver*, in an actual morgue, where the available dead doubled as actors who didn't demand union scale. But then a deadly curse began to claim those involved with the production. Kihn's clever satire on the horror genre includes witty dialogue reminiscent of 1950s popular culture.

Koontz, Dean.
🅱 *Fear Nothing.* New York: Bantam, 1998. 448pp.

After the mysterious deaths of both of his parents, 28-year old Christopher Snow suspects that he is the product of military experimentation, and soon he finds himself on the lam in the surfing community of Moonlight Bay, California. His investigation into who is responsible tests his mettle. Surfer lingo adds a comical dimension.

Get This Down: First-Person Confessional

A first-person narrative is the most intimate of styles. The reader is put in the position of confessor and confidante, reading the personal diary of a stranger or "listening" to the darkest of secrets and thereby often sharing in guilt. Getting the story from the horse's mouth helps readers connect with a tale, so it is no accident that two classics of horror, Mary Shelley's *Frankenstein* and Anne Rice's *Interview with the Vampire*, are in this subsection. Selections here differ from those in the subsection on reflective horror in that they are in the form of monologue, often taking the form of confessions.

Campbell, Ramsey.
Needing Ghosts. London: Century, 1990. 80pp.
Certainly being a horror writer takes a good imagination, something that Simon Mottershead has in spades. Maybe his imagination is a bit overactive. Here he rambles about being trapped in an alternative universe, escaping only to find that he has forgotten who he is. He briefly recovers, just long enough to return home and find his wife and children slain. If he could only bring himself to wake up from what must be a nightmare.

Holland, David.
Murcheston: The Wolf's Tale. New York: Tor, 2000. 376pp.
The arrogant Edgar Lenoir, Duke of Darnley, is a member of the British aristocracy. He is also a werewolf and is almost joyous about that fact. He becomes convinced that the "primal beast" is the true essence of life, and as he tells his story, he will try to convince the readers also that the life of the werewolf is an attractive one. Blood and death are nothing compared to satisfying bestial cravings.

King, Stephen.
Rose Madder. New York: Viking, 1995. 420pp.
In this gripping, fast-paced novel that serves as a companion piece to *Dolores Claiborne*, King uses stream-of-consciousness and a female narrator to enlighten us about domestic abuse, while retaining his typical flair for horrifying violence. It's frightening what some victims are driven to do to survive. Rose Madder confesses to the police that she murdered her abusive husband, painting a picture of the hell of petty cruelties she endured at his hands.

Kupfer, Allen C.
The Journal of Professor Abraham Van Helsing. New York: Tor, 2004. 208pp.
Fragments of a recently discovered journal allow the legendary vampire hunter Van Helsing to tell his own story, about his background and early years researching in Romania, his medical training, and his discovery of the

greatest threat to humanity. Filled with well-researched data, his journal is the story of an obsession with the world of a dark evil that claimed his wife.

Langston, Alistair.
Aspects of a Psychopath. Surrey, England: Telos, 2004. 112pp.
   Saul Roberts, a psychopathic murderer, tells how he enjoys killing annoying neighbors and random strangers, and torturing and mutilating young women unfortunate enough to go home with him. But then Saul discovers mysterious notes on his door implying that its author knows about his misdeeds and intends to make him pay.

McGrath, Patrick.
Spider. New York: Simon & Schuster, 1990. 221pp.
   In this first-person confessional, Spider Clegg relates the events that led to his losing his mind. For one, he witnessed his father's infidelity and the murder of his mother—or so he believes. This intelligent and disturbing study of paranoid schizophrenia was made into a film by David Cronenberg in 2002.

Rice, Anne.
Interview with the Vampire. New York: Ballantine, 1977. 352pp.
   Louis, a man suffering during a time of unbearable grief, describes how he was forcefully made a vampire, seduced into a life of darkness by Lestat de Lioncourt. Lestat's response follows in *The Vampire Lestat* (New York: Ballantine, 1985. 560pp.). There he claims that Louis's confession amounts to slander, and he presents a much different perspective on vampirism.

Rice, Anne.
Merrick. New York, Knopf, 2000. 307pp.
   David Talbot comes to Merrick Mayfair, scion of the African American branch of the Mayfair witches, to use Merrick's powers to conjure the ghost of Claudia for the benefit of Louis, David's father in darkness. But before Merrick agrees, she first tells her own story, beginning with how she realized her own powers. For those keeping score, *Merrick* is the intersection between two series, The Vampire Chronicles and The Mayfair Witches.

Sanders, Dan.
Chelydra Serpentina: Terror in the Adirondacks. Santa Barbara, CA: Astral Publishing, 2000. 332pp.
   Scientists at a research facility create a reptilian creature that evolves in a matter of months into a humanoid. During that time, people disappear from a nearby lake, and women are attacked by a serial rapist. Biology professor Matt Goddard suspects that the experimental creature is responsible, but he is

mysteriously fired just as he begins investigating. This intriguing read is written from both the human (first-person confessional) and reptile (first-monster confessional?) points of view.

Sebold, Alice.
The Lovely Bones. Boston: Little, Brown, 2002. 328pp.
    On her way home from school, 12-year-old Susie Salmon is raped and killed by a neighborhood pedophile. The Salmons never find Susie's body, and their grief and lack of closure completely transform the family. Meanwhile, Susie can only observe, and narrate, from her otherworldly perch. Here is a horror novel with no body count or mutilation, a quiet brand of horror that is deeply disturbing.

Shelley, Mary.
Frankenstein (The Essential Frankenstein). Edited by Leonard Wolf. New York: iBooks, 2004 (1816). 368pp.
    Dr. Victor Frankenstein had one ambition—to create a living being from parts of dead humans. He achieves his goal, but soon realizes he has created a monster. This is the tragic confession of Dr. Frankenstein and his creation, as well as the story of a monster that possesses the human emotions of love and hate, but is forced into an existence of isolation, pain, and suffering.

Stoker, Bram.
Dracula. New York: Signet, 1997 (1897). 382pp.
    Five friends, concerned for the declining health of their beloved Lucy, consult Dr. Abraham van Helsing, physician and metaphysician. She has been infected by the bite of the nosferatu, who is lurking among them. Van Helsing and the five must now join forces to stop Count Dracula before he pollutes the best of English womanhood and brings about the ruin of the empire. Related from multiple points of view in diaries and recorded confessions, this is the original classic that started it all.

Pacing

Short, crisp sentences and lots of dialogue put a tale into overdrive, while complex sentence structures, lengthy sentences, and a dependence on description will slow the pace of a tale, letting the horror creep up on the reader rather than having it jump out from behind a corner.

Slam, Bam, Thank You Ma'am: Fast-Paced, Action-Packed Language

In these works, the action may not be wall-to-wall, but the writers keep up a fast pace through their clipped writing styles. This is the section in which most of the works by the master of action horror and cliff-hangers, Dean Koontz, are located.

Climer, Steven Lee.
Soul Temple. Grandview, MO: Dark Tales, 2000. 181pp.
>He wished he could sing "I Feel Good," but his mother's death had young Spencer Welles looking for answers. Then he accidentally invoked Thoth, a fallen angel who thrives on death and misery. Now as a college student, Welles must discover a way to rid himself of the demon, before Thoth kills his friends, his family, his fiancée, and his unborn child in this energetic, well-written Christian fiction crossover.

Farris, John.
The Fury. The Fury series. Chicago: Playboy Press, 1976. 341pp.
>Danger and death await at every cliff-hanging turn of the page in this first volume of the story of Gillian Bellaver and Robin Sandza, psychic twins physically separated right before birth. Both have telekinetic ability, but Gillian is too painfully aware of how much harm she can do. As the series continues, we meet second-generation psychic Eden Waring, who is called upon when the United States is besieged by terrorists. The other titles in the series are *The Fury and the Terror* and *The Fury and the Power*.

Griffiths, W. G.
Driven. Gavin Pierce Novels. New York: Warner Books, 2002. 357pp.
>Those who love cliff-hanger scenes and vivid characterization, culminating in a final, explosive chase scene will find themselves reading into the wee hours of the night to see what mayhem unfolds in this Christian fiction crossover. Detective Gavin Pierce finds himself chasing a homicidal drunk driver—only the perp is no mortal; rather, he is possessed by the demon Krogan. And then Krogan takes over the body of a professional wrestler who can kill with his bare hands. A second novel in the series, *Takedown*, was published in 2004.

Koontz, Dean.
The Bad Place. New York: Putnam, 1990. 382pp.
>Frank Pollard awakens one day in an alley, with no idea how he got there. He does know that people are chasing him and mean to do him harm. A computer hacker and a maniacal killer who believes he is a vampire are indeed after Frank, in this suspenseful tale related from multiple points of view.

Koontz, Dean.
Cold Fire. New York: Putnam, 1991. 382pp.

Jim Ironheart suffers from visions that allow him to foresee disaster just in time for him to prevent the tragedy. Holly Thorne, a jaded but determined journalist, happens to be on the spot of one of Ironheart's miraculous deeds, when he saves a child from a road accident. Their fates become intertwined, but can the two survive a showdown with evil?

Koontz, Dean.
Velocity. New York: Bantam, 2005. 416pp.

Billy lives a quite life as a bartender, until he receives a cryptic note telling him that he has six hours to choose who is to live—a young school teacher or an elderly humanitarian. Initially Billy dismisses this as a joke, but then the teacher is found strangled. So when he receives the next note, Billy takes it seriously. Worse still, the killer is leaving evidence at each crime scene that incriminates Billy.

Koontz, Dean.
Watchers. New York: Putnam, 1987. 406pp.

Two altered life forms are born from a top secret lab, and they both escape, leaving a trail of death. A super-intelligent yellow Labrador retriever; a murderous, grotesque beast; and a hit man who takes too much pleasure in his work drive this intense novel about science gone awry.

Lee, Edward.
Messenger. New York: Leisure, 2004. 337pp.

Fifty—count 'em, fifty—gruesome killings populate just the first half of this novel about an idyllic small town on the Florida beach, the kind of place with a low crime rate, affordable real estate, and no harsh winters. The peace is literally shattered when several seemingly mild-mannered residents go on bloody killing sprees because they're possessed by the Messenger, a minion of Satan.

Moore, James A.
Possessions. New York: Dorchester, 2004. 339pp.

The book begins with a fast-paced interstate chase with a flying demon, and doesn't let up much from there. Chris Corin has just celebrated his eighteenth birthday, when his mother is killed. Chris's grief is compounded when he finds a creature going through his mother's room. When a necklace that she prized is stolen from her grave, Chris decides to take matters into his own hands.

Pacing ⊃ 117

Nichols, Leigh (pseudonym of Dean Koontz).
The Servants of Twilight. Arlington Heights, IL: Dark Harvest, 1984. 327pp.

    Christine Scivello and her six-year-old son are getting into their car in a store parking lot when an old woman approaches them, insisting the boy is the Antichrist and must die. The old woman turns out to be the charismatic leader of a religious cult, and her minions are soon on a rampage, attempting to kill Christine's son.

Rhodes, Natasha.
Blade: Trinity. New York: Simon & Schuster-Games Workshop, 2004. 416pp. **YA**

    Vampires are getting closer to unlocking the secret that will allow them to dominate the world. In the midst of his race against the evil undead and the clock, the Daywalker, Blade, is driven underground. Now with the help of the vampire hunters called Nightstalkers, Blade must unleash a deadly plague that will wipe out vampire-kind.

Saul, John.
Shadows. New York: Bantam, 1992. 390pp. **YA**

    Children are disappearing from The Academy, a boarding school for the gifted. But when Josh MacCullum discovers that the administration is behind the disappearances, he knows only half the truth. The real horror is the fate of these unsuspecting teenagers, in this fast-paced and gripping young adult crossover.

Slow Agonies: Pensive, Plodding Stories

In a slow-paced novel, action takes a back seat to characterization, dialogue, psychology, philosophy, and description. This is not to say that a slow pace will not intensify suspense. Reading a slow-paced horror novel, the reader may know what's coming, but the process of how it happens is exquisitely drawn out, and the outcome is excruciatingly unavoidable. These are the stories in which the reader wants to intervene, to shake the characters and tell them to wake up, or cry "stop." The reader is helpless, an innocent bystander, and witness to the horror.

Aickman, Robert.
Sub Rosa. London: Gollanz, 1968. 256pp.
Cold Hand in Mine. New York: Scribner, 1975. 215pp.
The Wine Dark Sea. New York: Arbor House, 1988. 388pp.

    Aickman was a master of the elegant supernatural tale. In these stories, a man traveling in Europe finds himself in the home of an old crone with a pair of scissors, and a desire to use them on him. A boy just coming of age sexually witnesses a bizarre sword swallowing act at a carnival, then finds himself backstage, watching as a young girl is impaled by sword-toting, middle-aged men. These dark, pensive, plodding gothic psychological mysteries work on the psyche like surreal, imagistic nightmares.

Brontë, Emily.
Wuthering Heights. New York: Penguin, 2003 (1847). 400pp.

When Mr. Lockwood comes to stay at Wuthering Heights, an isolated cottage located near the stormy British cliffs, he doesn't believe that the place is haunted by the ghost of Catherine Earnshaw, whose soul won't rest quietly because in life she was denied her heart's desire, the mysterious Heathcliff. But when Catherine's ghost appears to him in the middle of the night, he is ready to hear the tale of these tortured lovers.

Gaiman, Neil.
Neverwhere. New York: Avon, 1997. 337pp. YA

Stockbroker Richard Mayhew and his fiancée are out for a romantic dinner, when they stumble upon Door, a woman left to bleed in the streets after a switchblade attack. Richard takes the woman home to help her but soon finds himself involved in the politics of a secret, surrealistic underground society.

Hand, Elizabeth.
Black Light. New York: HarperPrism, 2000. 380pp.

Ancient gods never really die. Instead, they are reborn—again and again—in endless cycles. One of the oldest gods is about to be reborn in a sleepy little village in the hills of New York state. Old television actors retire here to lives of decadence. While death by misadventure and suicide may be common here, the possession of a 17-year-old girl by an ancient god is bound to raise a few eyebrows. Hand's erudite writing style brings to life a world of obscure signs of the Old ones, visible to those willing to immerse themselves in her tightly crafted illusion.

Klein, T. E. D.
The Ceremonies. New York: Viking, 1984. 502pp.

A dark force is awakening in a small New Hampshire town: The Old One, Satan himself, is hatching a new scheme to bring about the world's end. However, he needs a virgin and a scholar of the occult to complete his plans, so he assumes a pleasant disguise as a harmless old man. Building slowly toward a volcanic conclusion, this is a clever and haunting novel by one of the new Lovecraftian masters of the genre.

Laymon, Richard.
B *The Traveling Vampire Show.* New York: Dorchester-Leisure, 2001. 400pp. YA

Sixteen-year-old Dwight and his friends, Slim and Rusty, come across fliers that tout the "Gorgeous" and "Lethal" vampire show. The three plot to see what is forbidden to anyone under 18, and discover to their horror that what they hoped was real all along truly does exist. Now their lives will be changed forever.

LeRoux, Gaston.
The Phantom of the Opera (The Essential Phantom of the Opera). Edited by Leonard Wolf. New York: iBooks, 2004 (1911). 352pp.

    Cursed with leprosy, Erik runs away from home and hides himself in the cellars and corridors of the Paris Opera House. He helps in the reconstruction of the cellars and incorporates many trapdoors in the building. While there he falls in love with a young singer, Christiane Daaé, and arranges a series of deaths to advance her career.

Maturin, Charles Robert.
Melmoth the Wanderer. New York: Penguin, 2001 (1820). 704pp.

    An Irish gentleman makes a deal with the devil that enables him to live for as long as he wishes. Eventually he wants to dissolve the pact, but to do so he must travel the world over, looking for someone to take on his pact with Satan—and cursed to tell stories to anyone who will listen—in this collection of vignettes (Melmoth's stories). For good measure, purple prose is interspersed in this challenging read.

Polidori, John.
The Vampyre and Other Tales of the Macabre. Edited by Chris Baldick and Robert Morrison. New York: Oxford University Press, 2001 (1819). 312pp.

    Lord Ruthven, an aristocrat, gleefully seeks the ruin of all around him. His traveling companion, Aubrey, at first cannot believe ill of his friend, whom he thinks is mysteriously aloof rather than truly depraved. Of course eventually he learns the truth, but he agrees to keep the former friend's secrets for a year and a day.

Reeve, Clara.
The Old English Barron. New York: Oxford, 1967. 164pp.

    This thoughtful, eerily slow-moving adaptation of Walpole's *The Castle of Otranto* transfers the story to medieval England. Sir Philip Harclay returns home, only to discover that his old friends, Lord Lovel and his pregnant wife, are dead. Since then the estate has twice changed hands, and there is now a mysterious set of rooms that no one dare enter, except for a fearless peasant youth whom Harclay has taken under his wing.

Rickman, Phil.
Midwinter of the Spirit. London: Macmillan-Pan Books, 1999. 537pp.

    Anglican Reverend Merrily Watkins is now in charge of a kinder, gentler version of what was once called exorcism. But strange things are happening in the Ministry's cathedral home, and Merrily is unprepared to deal with the powers of darkness while protecting the reputation of a faith becoming increasingly irrelevant in the modern world. This dense and compelling work is based on the true exorcism practices of the Church of England.

Wilde, Oscar.
The Picture of Dorian Gray. New York: Modern Library, 1998 (1891). 304pp.

Dorian Gray, a callow and lovely young man, has his portrait painted, wishing that the picture would age while he would remain unchanged. His wish is granted, and for a time Dorian does not prove the old adage that "you get the face you deserve," since his various misdeeds, including driving a young woman to suicide, do not corrupt his youthful visage. But time wounds all heels in this disturbing and atmospheric classic.

Appendix A

Horror on Film

Okay, we'll admit it. There are times when, rather than curl up with a good book, we'd prefer to fill up the popcorn popper, grab a bowl of Baked Tostitos and HOT salsa, fluff up a few throw pillows, and kick back with a scary flick. For those of you who can relate to this primal urge, and for those of you who understand why it is important to see Samara crawl out of the well, out of the television, and slither across the floor toward us on the big screen, we devote this appendix. While films do share some of the same appeals found in the written word, such as fascinating characters, intricate storylines, eerie settings, and sparkling (or howlingly funny) dialogue, they are also unique in their own way. Most obviously, films can be more visual than the written word. For example, it is one thing to read about Carrie White being drenched with a bucket of pig's blood, but quite another to actually *see* the red liquid stain her white prom gown. And in fact, visual representations of horrors in films make reality seem *un*real: Dead bodies just look pitifully dead, and actual human blood is never as red as it is in the movies. And films also have an aural appeal. Books don't come with soundtracks, or sound effects, for that matter. But the films can also leave more to the imagination. The denouements of movies such as *The Others* or *The Sixth Sense* are all the more intense since viewers are lulled into a false sense of security regarding the trajectory of the plotline, conditioned by other films to believe that one thing will happen, when in fact something entirely different transpires. And if the viewer is watching the film in a theater or does not always go back and review a key scene before moving on, miniscule visual clues about where the film is really heading can be missed.

122 ◌ Appendix A: Horror on Film

While it is true that this book is about horror *literature*, we felt that we could not adequately discuss the genre without also delving into film, as the two formats—the written word and the movie—have mutually influenced one another since the making of Murnau's *Nosferatu* in 1922 (which is actually a version of Bram Stoker's *Dracula*, adapted drastically in a failed attempt to avoid copyright infringement), and the 1931 reinterpretations of Mary Shelley's *Frankenstein* and Stoker's *Dracula*, by James Whale and Tod Browning, respectively. Here we have listed films that have been influential in the genre or those that are noteworthy for adding new dialogue to horror fiction. This list is by no means exhaustive. Instead, this is meant to be a selective sampling, which we freely admit is influenced by our own tastes and prejudices; therefore, we humbly apologize if we have left something off the list that any given reader or film connoisseur believes is important.

This segment has been broken into two basic categories, books made into movies and stories born on film. We did this for a simple reason: We felt it was important to very clearly identify those movies that are adaptations of written texts, particularly since virtually all of those books are listed somewhere in this guide. This practice makes it easier for the reader to follow up viewing of a movie by reading the book that inspired it, if inclined to do so. The second half of this chapter is devoted to noteworthy films in the genre that aren't based on any novel or short story, but instead are wholly original.

Within each of these categories, we have grouped films into various subcategories, listed below, which reflect common areas of interest among horror film fans. These categories are not mutually exclusive. A film we decided to place in cult classics, for example, could have just as easily have been placed in classics or even mainstream horror. Again, we have made judgment calls.

- **Classics**: Films in this category are mainly the black-and-white Universal Horror Studios films made between the 1930s and 1950s. To be a classic, a film must be at least 50 years old, and it must have received popular or critical acclaim. Subsequent horror films pay homage to these movies in one way or another, even if it is merely to rewrite them.

- **Modern classics**: These more modern films are often reactions to earlier stories established by Hollywood's classic era of horror. Others return more faithfully to stories previously adapted from horror literature, reinterpret old monsters, or create completely new stories.

- **Remakes**: Films in this category are remakes of earlier *films*. These new versions reinterpret the original in some significant way, either re-presenting the subject matter comically or casting the monster as a sympathetic being.

- **Slashers**: This type of horror film began with Alfred Hitchcock's 1960 film *Psycho*, in which a disturbed man hacks to death women he perceives as sexually promiscuous. *The Texas Chainsaw Massacre* was the watershed slasher film that changed the category: Now women can (and must) survive by their own devices, rather than being saved by a man. (The main appeal of this type of film is visceral—there is generally a lot of messy violence, with blood, guts, brains, and other body parts playing a big role.)

- **Mainstream horror**: Although the films in this segment are still horror films, they are also often seen as "legitimate" movies rather than genre flicks. Many of the selections here earned the actors, writers, and directors Academy Awards, most notably *Rebecca* (which won the Oscar for Best Picture in 1941), *The Green Mile*, *Shadow of the Vampire*, and *The Sixth Sense* (nominated for several Oscars). *The Silence of the Lambs* swept the Oscars in 1991 for Best Actor and Best Actress, as well as Best Film and Best Director.

- **Cult classics**: Most of these films received little critical acclaim in their time but are nevertheless well known by fans of the genre for their unusual stories or other features. Some even raised the ire of censors.

The entries in this appendix present the name of the film, the name of the director, and the date.

Books Made into Films

This section is devoted to film interpretations of novels and short stories. Note that some of the films in this section have spawned their own interpretations, which purport to either better represent the original literary work, or in their storytelling take into consideration both the literary work and any subsequent film interpretations.

Classics

The Birds. Alfred Hitchcock. 1963.
  A blonde bombshell pursues a staid widower to the island home he shares with his mother and daughter. Her presence in the community, and in the family unit, provokes an attack on all by the birds, emblems of romantic love. The script from this film was loosely based on the Daphne DuMaurier story "The Birds."

Bride of Frankenstein. James Whale. 1935.

Boris Karloff reprises his role as Frankenstein's monster in this rendition of the second half of Mary Shelley's novel *Frankenstein*. The lonely and somewhat inarticulate creature that evaded destruction in *Frankenstein* demands his creator make him a mate. This classic also stars Elsa Lancaster and Colin Clive.

Dr. Jekyll and Mr. Hyde. Victor Flemming. 1941.

This faithful adaptation of Robert Louis Stevenson's story stresses psychological horror. Excellent makeup and special effects for the time transform Spencer Tracy from the handsome Dr. Henry Jekyll into the hideous and cruel Mr. Hyde. Lana Turner and Ingrid Bergman also star.

Dracula. Tod Browning. 1931.

This adaptation of both Bram Stoker's novel and Hamilton Deane and John Balderston's stage play of the story gave Bela Lugosi his first film role. Dracula comes to London, purchases a ruined abbey, and searches for victims by night. He is presented as the suave, caped fiend first seen in Deane and Balderston's stage play rather than the aging, hooked-nosed nosferatu of Stoker's tale and Murnau's 1922 film.

Dracula's Daughter. Lambert Hillyer. 1936.

This film picks up where the 1931 version of *Dracula* ended. Dr. Van Helsing has killed Dracula and believes the world is rid of vampires. But Dracula's daughter, Countess Marya Zaleska, claims her father's body, and soon several people are found mysteriously killed. This version is loosely based on Joseph Sheridan LeFanu's classic novella, *Carmilla*.

Frankenstein. James Whale. 1931.

This adaptation of the first half of Mary Shelley's *Frankenstein* is set in the twentieth century. Dr. Frankenstein's creation isn't a monster due to his creator usurping the powers of God, but rather because he is made with inferior parts. If Dr. Frankenstein's bumbling assistant had procured a normal brain, then presumably the creature would have truly been the new Adam.

The Incredible Shrinking Man. Jack Arnold. 1957.

Based on the novella by Richard Matheson, who also wrote the script. After he is sprayed by radioactive mist, Scott Carey begins to shrink, until he is so small he can no longer be seen by his family and is forced to battle a spider to survive. The story is often seen as a metaphor for the anxieties of men in post–World War II America.

The Invisible Man. James Whale. 1933.

Relatively faithful adaptation of H. G. Wells's novel of the same name stars Claude Raines as the mad scientist who makes himself invisible and wreaks havoc on a small English village.

Nosferatu. F. W. Murnau. 1922.

This silent classic is an adaptation of Bram Stoker's *Dracula,* which changes the names of the principals due to the complexities of German copyright law. Count Orlock, Murnau's version of Dracula, is much closer to Stoker's idea of the Count than the celluloid Dracula made famous by Bela Lugosi in 1931.

Modern Classics

Blade. Stephen Norrington. 1998.

Blade is half human, half vampire, cursed to crave blood when his pregnant mother was attacked by one of the undead. Now, with the combined strength of vampires and humans, Blade seeks to eliminate all bloodsucking fiends from Earth before they turn humans into cattle. Gory and action oriented, with excellent special effects, and based on the DC Comics graphic novel series of the same name.

Carrie. Brian DePalma. 1976.

In this faithful adaptation of Stephen King's novel, Carrie White is made into a misfit by her fundamentalist mother and cruel peers, who make her the butt of everyone's jokes. So when Carrie's telekinetic powers surface, her anger toward her tormentors culminates in their destruction.

The Exorcist. William Friedkin. 1973.

A divorced mother notices disturbing changes in her previously well-behaved 12-year-old daughter, Regan. Suddenly Regan begins sleep walking, bed wetting, and later, talking back in another voice. Now her mother must ask the Catholic Church to help her with what seems to be a case of demonic possession. Enter Father Merrin, a priest who has lost his faith. This adaptation of William Peter Blatty's novel was considered graphic and shocking in its time.

The Haunting. Richard Wise, 1963.

This classic is an eerie and faithful version of Shirley Jackson's *The Haunting of Hill House*. Although it lacks the special effects found in most of today's blockbusters, fine acting and good direction make a very chilling and atmospheric ghost story.

Interview with the Vampire. Neil Jordan. 1994.

This stylish film version of Anne Rice's novel of the same name sports an all-star cast, including Tom Cruise, Brad Pitt, Christian Slater, Antonio Banderas, and Kirsten Dunst.

Misery. Rob Reiner. 1990.

Kathy Bates was the first actress to win an Oscar in a horror film, as crazed nurse Annie Wilkes, in this faithful adaptation of Stephen King's novel. Paul Sheldon wants to be known as a serious writer, so he kills off his main character in his bodice rippers, thus ending the popular series. But this doesn't sit well with his "biggest fan," who holds him hostage until he writes a novel just for her.

The Omen. Richard Donner. 1976.

When the wife of the ambassador to the United States gives birth to a stillborn child, he substitutes another baby without her knowledge. Years pass, and grisly deaths befall those in close proximity to the child. Further investigation reveals that the foundling is actually the son of Satan and can be stopped only by the seven daggers of Meggado. Based on a 1976 David Seltzer novel that won an Edgar.

Queen of the Damned. Michael Rymer. 2002.

In this second film based on Anne Rice's Vampire Chronicles, Lestat becomes a rock star and challenges all the other vampires who hide from humans to make themselves known. This angers all other vampires, whose survival depends on keeping their ways secret. His music has awakened Akasha, the bloodthirsty mother of vampires, who in Ancient Times nearly drank the human race dry before going dormant.

The Ring. Gore Verbinski. 2002.

When her teenaged niece dies a mysterious and horrible death, journalist Rachel Keller investigates a rumor that the girl had watched a strange video that promised the viewer would die within seven days. Rachel finds and watches the tape, a montage of disturbing images, and realizes that the rumor is true. Now she must decipher the riddle of the video lest she die, too. As an added incentive, her son has also seen the video, and Rachel must save him. Based on Koji Suzuki's novel *Ring* (*Ringu*) and the Japanese film *Ringu,* based on Suzuki's book.

Rosemary's Baby. Roman Polanski. 1968.

In this faithful adaptation of Ira Levin's novel, a man makes a pact with the devil. His wife will unwittingly bear Satan's child in exchange for his worldly success as an actor.

The Shining. Stanley Kubrick. 1980.

In this film version of Stephen King's novel, recovering alcoholic and abusive father and husband Jack Torrence loses his teaching position as a result of assaulting one of his pupils. He is given a second chance as the winter caretaker of the Overlook Hotel, isolated in the Rockies. But the isolation and the hotel's ghosts push Jack over the edge and make him attempt to kill his wife and son.

Sleepy Hollow. Tim Burton. 1999.

In this loose retelling of Washington Irving's story "The Legend of Sleepy Hollow," colonial criminal investigator Ichabod Crane comes to

Sleepy Hollow to solve a few mysterious murders. Crane, for all of his scientific methods of investigation, is not prepared for the Headless Horseman and the supernatural means employed to bring him to life and do the bidding of Katrina van Tassel's evil stepmother.

The Stepford Wives. Bryan Forbes. 1975.

The Stepford wives are every man's dream: beautiful, demure, with no desire beyond pleasing their husbands, caring for children, or cleaning the house. Could there be something in the water, or something far more sinister at work? One horrified newcomer attempts to find out when this strange compulsion to serve comes over her formerly independent best friend. Faithful adaptation of Ira Levin's novel of the same name.

Underworld. Len Wiseman. 2003.

The ancient war between werewolves and vampires is renewed in the twenty-first century. In the middle of the battle is Selene, a vampire who rescues Michael, a human whom the werewolves have a mysterious interest in. During the rescue, Michael is bitten by a werewolf; he will soon become one of them. This film reminds us that vampires and werewolves, now separate monsters, stem from a common source in folklore. Based on a short story by Nancy Collins.

Remakes

***Bram Stoker's* Dracula**. Francis Ford Coppola. 1992.

Coppola returns to the original source of the Dracula myth, drawing on Stoker's novel as well as the historical Vlad Tepes, taking into consideration all other versions of the tale, and adding a prequel for context. The result is not so much an immortal monster to be destroyed but a man who defied death because church and country betrayed him.

Dracula 2000. Patrick Lussier. 2000.

Abraham Van Helsing, wealthy and eccentric owner of Carfax antiques, is now the immortal keeper of the vanquished Dracula. When thieves steal what he has hidden in the vault, they unwittingly unleash the undead count. Dracula flees to New Orleans to exact his vengeance on Van Helsing's daughter and create a new army of the undead.

Slasher Films

American Psycho. Mary Harron. 2000.

Harron's faithful adaptation of the Brent Easton Elllis novel is as much a parody of the "greed is good" 1980s as it is a portrait of a serial killer. Still, it is as chilling and gory as the story on which it is based. Christian Bale,

Willem Dafoe, Jared Leto, and Reese Witherspoon star in this brilliant character study. The script is by Brent Easton Elllis.

The Butcher Boy. Neil Jordan. 1997.

Prepubescent Francie Brady has much to deal with at his tender age: a mother who commits suicide, an alcoholic father who drinks himself to death, and a town that has nothing but scorn for the boy. Francie tries to maintain some semblance of family life after his father dies by keeping his father's corpse and cleaning the house. Little wonder that he begins to have visions of the Virgin Mary, who understands his compulsion to kill anyone who has slighted him. A faithful adaptation of Patrick McCabe's novel of the same name.

Candyman. Bernard Rose. 1992.

Candyman is the embodiment of the urban legend about the Hook, an escaped lunatic with a hook for a hand who menaces young lovers in compromising positions. And when two graduate students attempt to unearth the legend of Candyman, they find the real revenant, a black man who, in the 1890s, was lynched for miscegenation and now exacts revenge on those who doubt his existence. An interesting interpretation of Clive Barker's short story "The Forbidden."

From Hell. Albert Hughes and Allen Hughes. 2001.

In his quest to find Jack the Ripper, Inspector Frederick Abberline is led through a vast conspiracy involving the royal family, Scotland Yard, and the Freemasons. Based on a graphic novel by Eddie Campbell and Alan Moore, the film does a fine job of incorporating all known theories about Jack the Ripper's identity, motivations, and victims.

Psycho. Alfred Hitchcock. 1960.

Alfred Hitchcock's classic film rendition of Robert Bloch's slasher novel of the same name is about a boy's love for his mother and the lengths he will go to, to prove that love. Loosely based on the Ed Gein murders of the 1950s, this film is the original slasher flick.

Mainstream Horror

Beloved. Jonathan Demme. 1998.

In Demme's eerie and atmospheric interpretation of Toni Morrison's novel, escaped slave Sethe does the unthinkable to keep her children from being returned to bondage: She tries to kill them all, and succeeds in killing her infant daughter in a grisly manner. But Beloved will not lie quietly and returns twenty years later in ghost form, to destroy her entire family.

Ghost Story. John Irvin, 1981.

In this loosely based adaptation of Peter Straub's novel about a vengeful ghost, four elderly men harbor a secret from their youth: their involvement in the accidental death of Eva Galli, a beautiful secretary. Now their pasts have come back to haunt them, as the ghost of Galli is out for revenge.

The Green Mile. Frank Darabont. 1999.

In this version of Stephen King's novel, prison guard Paul Edgecombe discovers that John Coffey, a death row inmate at Cold Mountain Penitentiary, has special powers—almost godlike—over living creatures. But his powers are misunderstood by society, and now he must pay with his life.

Hannibal. Ridley Scott, 2001.

In this faithful adaptation of Thomas Harris's novel, the infamous Dr. Hannibal Lecter is lured out of hiding by the evil Mason Verger, Hannibal's only victim to survive. FBI agent Clarice Starling must capture America's most-wanted serial killer, who seems to know all of her secrets.

Night of the Hunter. Charles Laughton. 1955.

A psychotic traveling evangelist marries the widow of a recently executed bank robber in the hopes of finding the stolen money that was never recovered. When he can't find the whereabouts of the money from his new bride, he kills her and tries to pry the information out of her young children, who travel across the country to elude him. Based on David Grubb's 1953 novel of the same name.

Rebecca. Alfred Hitchcock. 1940.

Hitchcock's first American film is a faithful adaptation of Daphne DuMaurier's novel of the same name, about a young woman who marries a widowed nobleman. Both fight the "ghost" of his former wife. Joan Fontaine and Lawrence Olivier star. This film was the winner of Academy Awards for Best Picture and Cinematography.

The Silence of the Lambs. Jonathan Demme. 1991.

Rookie FBI agent Clarice Starling is assigned to help find the kidnapped daughter of a U.S. senator before she becomes the next victim of a serial killer who skins women. Clarice attempts to gain insight into the twisted mind of the killer by talking to another psychopath, ex-psychiatrist Hannibal Lecter, now in maximum security prison because of his cannibalistic habits. Based on Thomas Harris's novel, this was one of the first modern horror films to win an Oscar.

Cult Classics

Fight Club. David Fincher. 1999.

Darkly comic rendition of Chuck Palahniuk's novel, in which an average, run-of-the-mill insurance claims investigator befriends an antisocial monomaniac. Together they form "Fight Club," a support group for men based on the idea that a little violence helps males get through the day and reconnect to their essential selves. But things get out of hand when Project Mayhem, the ultimate act of terrorism, is born: the obliteration of free enterprise, achieved by blowing up buildings that house major credit card companies.

Hellraiser. Clive Barker. 1987.

Barker directs this film version of his novella *The Hellbound Heart*. When Frank, a playboy and thrill-seeker, decides that life holds no more pleasure for him, he experiments with Lamarchand's Box, which supposedly will summon the gods of pleasure. Instead, Frank summons demons of torture, and they want more than just Frank.

The Hunger. Tony Scott. 1983.

Miriam and John Blaylock are forever young because they're vampires. But when John begins to age at an accelerated pace, Miriam seeks the help of an outsider, a scientist who studies aging and who will be seduced by Miriam's promise of eternal youth. This classic is a reasonably faithful adaptation of Whitley Streiber's novel of the same name.

Ringu. Hideo Nakata. 1998.

In this Japanese film, the basis of the American film *The Ring*, a reporter investigates a story about a mysterious video that kills viewers within seven days. A journalist discovers the tape, which is linked to a famous Japanese psychic from the 1940s and her daughter, who had even greater supernatural gifts. And the rumors are true: The reporter now has seven days to discover the video's mystery before she will also die. Based on Koji Suzuki's novel of the same name.

Spider. David Cronenberg. 2003.

Dennis returns to the town of his birth after his release from a mental institution. Through flashbacks we learn about his childhood, when, he believes, his father murdered his mother and then attempted to pass off his paramour as Dennis's new mother. Now in a halfway house, Dennis believes that his landlady is none other than his father's former lover. Based on Patrick McGrath's 1990 novel.

Original (and Influential) Stories

Works included in this section are not based on any novel or short story. Instead, they are either wholly original additions to the genre or are reinterpretations of classic films that are not grounded in any literary work.

Classics

Attack of the 50-Foot Woman. Nathan Juran. 1958.
    A wealthy woman marries a gold-digging playboy, later finding solace in alcohol after discovering his inability to remain faithful. Then an encounter with an alien makes her literally larger than life. As her size grows proportionately to her wrath, the 50-foot woman wreaks vengeance on her faithless spouse and his doxy before being destroyed by the military.

Godzilla: King of the Monsters. Terry Morse. 1956.
    A giant, fire-breathing lizard threatens Japan and terrifies a young reporter, played by Raymond Burr. This is the original classic that has spawned several sequels that transformed Godzilla from a monster into the protector of Japan. It has inspired several remakes, most notably, and most expensively, in 1998.

Invasion of the Body Snatchers. Don Siegel. 1956.
    Small town residents are being replaced by mindless replicants that are hatched in pods. This is a class science fiction/horror flick with a McCarthy era subtext.

King Kong. Merian C. Cooper and Ernest B. Schoedsack. 1933.
    In this subtle jab at the slave trade and racism, King Kong, a giant gorilla, is brought from the jungles of Africa to be displayed in chains to crowds of gawkers. But King Kong falls in love with a human woman, breaks free, and carries her up to the top of the Empire State Building before being shot down by airplanes.

M. Fritz Lang. 1931. (German with subtitles).
    This is an early talkie about a child murderer who is hunted down and brought to justice by the Berlin underworld. Dazzling cinematography and fine acting by Peter Lorre make this film a classic.

The Mummy. Karl Freund. 1932.
    When the mummy's tomb is desecrated by archeologists, he is reanimated and kills those responsible for disturbing his rest. He then discovers that the reincarnation of his mate is among the band of those who opened his tomb. Boris Karloff stars as the mummy. Be sure to look for the zipper in the back of the mummy costume.

Son of Frankenstein. Rowland V. Lee. 1939.

The son of Dr. Frankenstein returns to his ancestral castle 25 years after the monster's presumed death. But the creature isn't dead—he's only disabled, and is guarded by Igor, the last of the father's misshapen attendants. The doctor's scientific curiosity gets the better of him, and he reanimates the creature, believing that this time he can prevent it from going on yet another fatal rampage.

Supernatural. Victor Halperin. 1933.

A woman who is executed for murdering her lovers vows she'll return from the dead, which she does, and possesses the body of Carole Lombard, a virginal heiress, and causes her to misbehave.

Village of the Damned. Wolf Rilla. 1960.

Nine months after a bus accident, all the fertile women in an English village are suddenly pregnant. The resulting progeny are all eerily similar in appearance and can fix people with their mesmerizing stare.

White Zombie. Victor Halperin. 1932.

In this first ever zombie film, the undead are created through black magic based on traditional Haitian lore rather than through radioactivity or a mutant virus. Voodoo bokur Murder Legendre (Bela Lugosi) turns his enemies into zombies, who labor on his plantation.

The Wolf Man. George Waggner. 1941.

This Universal Studios classic stars Lon Cheney, Jr., who is bitten by a vampire in wolf form (Bela Lugosi) and turned into a werewolf. Claude Rains also stars.

Modern Classics

Alien. Ridley Scott. 1979.

A commercial exploration spacecraft unwittingly takes on an alien life form, which stalks the crew in deep space, where no one can hear them scream. The monster special effects are stunning, even some 25 years later, and the scene in which the creature is born out of a stomach has achieved cult status.

The Blair Witch Project. Daniel Myrick and Eduardo Sanhez. 1999.

In this pseudo-documentary, three students disappear while making a film about the Blair Witch legend in Burkittsville, Maryland. All that is known of their disappearance comes from their video footage, found in the woods. This low-budget film made by industry unknowns mixes documentary techniques with the horror genre.

Blair Witch 2: Book of Shadows. Joe Berlinger. 2000.

After the success of *The Blair Witch Project*, Burkittsville, Maryland, is overrun with tourists. Shops now hawk Blair Witch sticks and "genuine" soil from the haunted woods, and competing groups of residents offer Blair Witch camping tours retracing the steps of the ill-fated film crew. One of these tours discovers that the Blair Witch is no legend, but a vengeful spirit that will not be mocked.

Bones. Ernest R. Dickerson. 2001.

In this stylish blacksploitation film Jimmy Bones, a benevolent 1970s O.G. (original gangster), makes his living running numbers. When white gangsters want Jimmy to become one of the first in his neighborhood to distribute crack, he declines. This decision costs him his life. But 20 years later, when a rap group wants to open up Jimmy's abandoned building as a night club, Bones's ghost reveals his killers.

The Cell. Tarsem Singh. 2000.

A child psychologist uses virtual reality technology to communicate with comatose, emotionally disturbed children. When a serial killer is caught but falls into a coma, she must go into his deranged mind to find the whereabouts of his latest kidnap victim before it is too late. The only problem is that no one is sure if it is possible to survive in the physical world after dying in virtual reality.

The Lost Boys. Joel Schumacher. 1987.

A family moves to what they believe will be a peaceful town, Santa Carla, California, only to discover that they reside in the murder capital of the world. The local gang is a pack of teenaged vampires who, like Peter Pan, never want to grow up.

Monster. Patty Jenkins. 2003.

Charlize Theron won an Academy Award for her portrayal of female serial killer Aileen Wuornos in this film. *Monster's* representation of Wuornos is balanced; the character has sympathetic qualities, such as her horrifying childhood and her need to be loved. Wuornos is also a mentally disturbed, cold-blooded killer. Jenkins's film is notable in that her actors aren't "Hollywood pretty."

Night of the Living Dead. George Romero. 1968.

Radiation fallout from a satellite reanimates the newly dead, and they're hungry for human flesh. Once the dead bite the living, the victims are similarly turned into zombies. Seven strangers thrust together in a remote farmhouse next to a cemetery try to keep the ravenous dead at bay, while working out their generational and ethnic differences. This influential film radically redefined the concept of the zombie, and has spawned three sequels (*Day of the Dead*, *Dawn of the Dead,* and *Land of the Dead*), as well as remakes of the originals.

Poltergeist. Tobe Hopper. 1982.

    A developer and his wife discover that their brand new suburban home is haunted when their daughter is snatched by one of the poltergeists she communicates with through the television. But it's not enough to hire a medium to journey to the spirit world to retrieve their daughter; they must discover the reason for the haunting in the first place.

Scary Movie. Keenan Ivory Wayans. 2000.

    This parody of the *Scream* series of films and *I Know What You Did Last Summer* is chock-full of references to all horror flicks ever made, as well as to parodies of many well-known commercials and some of the Wayans brothers' own comedy, as well as many bawdy jokes.

Stigmata. Rupert Wainwright. 1999.

    A New York hairdresser who isn't particularly religious receives from her mother the rosary of a deceased Brazilian priest who was said to have performed miracles. Now possessed by the priest, her body manifests stigmata as it struggles to tell the story of an apostle whose words the Catholic Church silenced. This eerie film is a sort of feminist version of *The Exorcist*.

Tales from the Hood. Rusty Cundieff. 1995.

    Four gangsters go to a funeral home just before midnight to make a drug deal with the proprietor, who insists on regaling them with tales about each of his clients. The tales parody the classic style of the Universal Studios horror pics of the 1930s, as well as B-movie horror from the 1950s and 1960s, but their content is deadly serious.

The Terminator. James Cameron. 1984.

    A cyborg is sent from the future to kill a woman pregnant with a future revolutionary leader. Arnold Schwarzenegger, Linda Hamilton, Paul Winfield, and Bill Paxton star.

28 Days Later. Danny Boyle. 2002.

    Jim awakens from a coma to discover that London is deserted, for humans are infected with Rage, a disease that turns the victim into a snarling killer. Jim eventually finds a colony of survivors, who head for the supposed safety of another colony in an abandoned military base. But when the group arrives, it discovers a tiny band of soldiers who want women with whom to repopulate the world.

Willard. Daniel Mann. 1971.

    Ernest Borgnine and Elsa Lancaster star in this original classic about Willard Styles, a social misfit, and his pet rats, his only friends in the world, who assist him when he goes on a rampage against all who have done him wrong.

Remakes

Blackula. William Crain. 1972.

Manuwalde, Ambassador of Ebonia, meets with Dracula to persuade him to stop supporting slave trading. Instead, Dracula makes Manuwalde undead, an eternal slave to blood, imprisoned in a coffin to thirst forever. Manuwalde awakens 150 years later in 1970s Los Angeles, hungering for blood and his reincarnated, long-deceased wife. Blacula is the first African American vampire in horror cinema history.

The Mummy. Stephen Sommers. 1999.

This parody of the 1932 Universal Studios classic, with its emphasis on action adventure, is a cross between *Bram Stoker's* Dracula and *Raiders of the Lost Ark*. The Mummy, former high priest Imhotep, is executed for falling in love with Pharaoh's favorite concubine. Imhotep rests quietly in the Underworld until librarian and Egyptologist Evelyn Carnahan accidentally raises him from the dead by reading a particular book.

Night of the Living Dead. Tom Savini. 1990.

This remake of George Romero's classic features a woman named Barbara, who picks up a gun and quickly turns into Savini's version of Ripley from *Alien*, rather than the shrieking, hysterical Barbara of the earlier version. This version also gives the viewer a peek at the post-zombie world that will follow.

Willard. Glen Morgan. 2003.

This remake resembles a graphic novel, with its emphasis on typical mise en scenes found in this type of literature. Shy and lonely Willard lives in a crumbling mansion with his elderly mother and works at a menial job in his late father's business. But when his father's business partner wants to force Willard out of the business, he gets revenge by unleashing an army of rats.

Young Frankenstein. Mel Brooks. 1974.

Mel Brooks' parody of James Whale's 1931 film *Frankenstein* and Roland Lee's 1939 *Son of Frankenstein* has the good doctor's grandson inheriting the family castle and resuming his ancestor's experiments in reanimating the dead. Gene Wilder, Marty Feldman, Peter Boyle, Madeline Kahn, Teri Garr, and Cloris Leachman star.

Slasher Films

Halloween. John Carpenter. 1978.

Young Michael Meyers murdered his sister on Halloween night, 1963, and was promptly sent to a mental institution. Now, 15 years later, Michael has escaped and come home to kill again. This is a well-made example of the slasher film, and it has inspired several sequels.

High Tension. Alexnadre Aja. 2005 (Originally released in France as *Haute Tension* in 2003).

Alex and Marie return to Marie's family farm after a wild junket to Spain. But during the night a killer breaks in, butchers Marie's parents and brother, and rapes and kidnaps her, while Alex witnesses the horrors from her hiding place. Now she must follow the killer and rescue Marie. The surprising conclusion is not typical of this genre.

Nightmare on Elm Street. Wes Craven. 1984.

Freddy Kreuger, a school janitor who molested and brutally murdered children, is not convicted for his crimes due to a technicality, so a posse of enraged parents burn him to death. But Freddy returns in an invincible form, entering the dreams of his executioners' children and causing them to die unspeakable deaths.

Scream. Wes Craven. 1996.

It's Halloween 1996 and exactly one year to the day since Sidney's mother was raped and murdered. Now a killer cognizant of the conventions of horror film is stalking her.

The Stepfather. Joseph Ruben. 1987.

Jerry Blake is a cheerleader for the traditional American family. As a matter of fact he'd kill for it, and he did, when his family disappointed him. Now he is settling into his role as pater-familias in a new family, by wedding a widow with a teenaged daughter. But Jerry's expectations are too high, and now this family is also beginning to disappoint him.

The Texas Chainsaw Massacre. Tobe Hooper. 1974.

This is a drive-in theater classic about five teens who fall victim to a family of unemployed meat packers turned cannibals. This campy horror flick is historically important in that the only survivor of the maniac's wrath is a female who rescues herself rather than depending on a man to save her.

Mainstream Horror

Angel Heart. Alan Parker. 1987.

Private investigator Harry Angel is hired by Louis Cyphere to find a missing singer, Johnny Favorite. His investigation leads him from Times Square to the South, specifically Louisiana, where Christianity isn't the only religion practiced by locals. Harry becomes the police's number one suspect when everyone he contacts ends up killed in grisly ways. Who is Johnny Favorite, and why does Cyphere want Angel to find him?

Fallen. Gregory Hoblit. 1998.

    Before his execution, serial killer Edgar Reese speaks to Detective John Hobbes in biblical tongues. After the execution, others are murdered in imitation of Reese's style, and Hobbes's fingerprints are found at the crime scenes. Meanwhile, Hobbes discovers that another officer committed suicide after he was similarly framed. Now his daughter, a theology professor, believes the demon Azazel is responsible

Land of the Dead. George Romero. 2005.

    The fourth film in Romero's influential series, which began with *Night of the Living Dead*, stars Dennis Hopper as a greedy millionaire who re-creates a zombie-free civilization on an island. Other wealthy people live inside glass and steel condo towers , their needs being met by the hoards of desperately poor humans who keep the zombies at bay. This thought-provoking and gory flick invites us to contemplate who are the real monsters, the zombies or the greedy, idle rich.

One Hour Photo. Mark Romanek. 2002.

    Sy Parish develops the film of strangers. Outside work, his life is a sterile existence with nothing but a television set for company. But over the past decade, Sy has secretly kept copies of family photos from the Yorkin family, his regular customers, pouring over their memories, and in fantasy inserting himself in their lives as their Uncle Sy. All is fine until Sy is fired. Disturbing and thoughtful slasher film without a body count.

The Others. Alejandro Amenabar. 2001.

    After World War II, Grace and her children live in isolation in a sprawling mansion on the isle of Jersey, waiting for her husband to return, with only the help of three mysterious servants, who appeared a week after the previous help left in the middle of the night with no explanation. Then the children see strange people in the house, and Grace herself finds furniture disturbed and locked doors left open.

Shadow of the Vampire. E. Elias Merhing. 2001.

    In 1922, director F. W. Murnau finds an actual vampire to play the role of Count Orlock and add realism to his film, *Nosferatu*. But vampires aren't as easily controlled as actors and can't be prevented from snacking on the occasional camera operator or script girl. This pseudo-biographical film gives a human touch to the vampire.

Signs. M. Night Shyamalan. 2002.

    Graham Hess, a former minister who lost his faith when his wife was killed in a freak car accident, now spends his days raising his children and tending to his farm. But when Graham discovers massive and intricate crop circles in his field, his life and the lives of everyone in the world change. The circles are signs made by aliens, giving directions to their brethren, who are about to invade the earth.

The Sixth Sense. M. Night Shyamalan. 1999.

Bruce Willis stars as a child psychologist who must help a little boy come to terms with his special gift: He sees dead people. During the course of the child's therapy, Willis's character learns about his own true nature. This fine film is chilling and original.

The Village. M. Night Shyamalan. 2004.

A group founds an idyllic community in the middle of the woods by striking a bargain with the bloodthirsty creatures that live there. The villagers stay out of the woods, and the creatures will leave them alone. But when one of the villagers becomes mortally ill, the elders allow a girl to travel to the "nearest town" to get medicine. What she learns about the nature of her world will take viewers completely by surprise.

What Lies Beneath. Robert Zemeckis. 2000.

When Claire begins hearing voices and seeing strange faces in her home, her husband believes she's suffering a mental breakdown precipitated by empty nest syndrome or "the change." But Claire perseveres, and with the help of the ghost discovers the truth about her husband.

Cult Classics

Carnival of Souls. Herk Harvey, 1962.

An organist has a near-death experience when her car veers off a bridge and she nearly drowns. Later she leaves home to pursue her musical career in another city but is inexplicably drawn to a now-defunct carnival that is haunted by beings only she can see. This low budget film has rightfully developed quite a cult following; what it lacks in plot it makes up for with its eerie atmosphere.

Cronos. Guillermo Del Toro. 1992. (Spanish with subtitles).

Elderly antiques dealer Jesus Gris stumbles upon the Cronos device, an invention of a fourteenth-century alchemist, which makes the bearer immortal. In spite of several serious accidents and an attempt to embalm him, Jesus cannot die, and his discovery of the device has alerted the attention of an Anglo corporate mogul, who will stop at nothing to steal it from Gris.

Dogma. Kevin Smith. 1999.

Two fallen angels attempt to reenter heaven while God is occupied playing bocce ball with mortals. The last living descendant of Christ, Jay and Silent Bob, and the 13th Apostle must stop the duo, whose reentry will destroy the fabric of the universe as we know it. This satire is a funny and thoughtful film.

Original (and Influential) Stories ⊃ **139**

Frailty. Bill Paxton. 2001.

One day Fenton is awakened by his father, who claims to have been instructed by God to find and kill the ungodly. As Fenton matures, he realizes that his father isn't on a mission from God, but rather just murdering people and using him and his younger brother as accomplices. This is a disturbing film that doesn't lead the viewer to a pat ending.

Freaks. Tod Browning. 1932.

Sideshow freaks demonstrate their camaraderie in a deadly way when one of their own is ill used by a "normal" person. Browning, an ex-carnival performer (he would allow himself to be buried alive for days), used actual sideshow freaks for this film, giving dignity to people the world would often rather not see as human.

Ginger Snaps. John Fawcett. 2000.

Teenaged sisters Ginger and Bridget are unusual in that neither has entered menarche, but that changes for Ginger when one night "the curse" comes cascading down her legs. Unfortunately, a werewolf catches the scent, and he manages to scratch Ginger before being killed. And werewolf bites transform the recipient into a lycanthrope.

House of 1000 Corpses. Rob Zombie. 2003.

On Halloween night, a group traveling throughout the United States searching for unusual roadside attractions learns about Dr. Satan, who has never been found after committing infamous murders. On the proverbial dark and stormy night, their car breaks down near his home, and they become the unwilling guests of the good doctor and his strange family. *The Devil's Rejects* is the 2005 sequel to this original film, and both pay homage to horror flicks from the 1970s.

I Spit on Your Grave. Mark Zarchi. 1978.

This film was banned in Austria, Germany, Finland, and the United Kingdom for its graphic representation of a vicious gang rape and a woman's brutal revenge. This is not a film for the faint of heart. The lack of fancy special effects or even background music makes the rape and revenge scenes especially realistic.

J.D.'s Revenge. Arthur Marks. 1976.

The spirit of J.D., a small-time thug murdered nearly 40 years earlier, requires someone to tell his tale to bring his killers to justice, so he possesses a mild-mannered law student. This is one of the few horror films of the twentieth century with African American characters.

Nadja. Michael Almeredya.1996.

Twin brother and sister vampires, children of Count Dracula, struggle against each other and against their own desires to fight or embrace their nature.

Set in modern-day New York City, this stylistic parody of art films is also a remake of the 1936 classic *Dracula's Daughter*.

Paperhouse. Bernard Rose. 2001.

A teenager discovers she can visit another world, based on a house she has drawn herself but that is mysteriously occupied by a young disabled boy. But as she is drawn deeper into this world, an adult stalker begins invading it.

Peeping Tom. Michael Powell. 1960.

A photographer by day and a serial killer by night takes pictures of his nubile female victims before he kills them. This is a cult classic that doesn't end with a pat psychological analysis of the killer as does its more famous and obvious cousin, Alfred Hitchcock's *Psycho*.

The People Under the Stairs. Wes Craven. 1992.

Fool and his family are being evicted from their tenement by their money-hungry landlords, a brother and sister couple who pose as man and wife. The only way Fool can save his family is to brave the landlords' house and steal the gold that is kept there. But during his quest Fool discovers the people under the stairs.

The Wicker Man. Robin Hardy. 1973.

The people of Summerisle practice pagan fertility rites to ensure the success of their crops. But lately the sacrifices made to the gods haven't been sufficient, and their crops are failing. Meanwhile Sergeant Howie is dispatched from the mainland to investigate a missing girl, who might be the next sacrifice to the gods. Howie himself is tricked into participating in the yearly sacrifice; he soon discovers the residents of Summerisle have outsmarted him.

Appendix B

Series Titles

Titles in this section are arranged in chronological order. Although we tried to list every title in each series identified in this guide, we do realize that like everyone, we sometimes make mistakes, and because series are so volatile, it is difficult to keep up. So we apologize in advance if there are any omissions.

One of the problems with series is that they are not always given a proper series title. Sometimes the writer helpfully christens the series, such as Brian Lumley's Necroscope Series, and sometimes publishers give a series a title in retrospect, such as Anne Rice's The Vampire Chronicles. However, for the most part series are not given standardized titles, so we followed what we consider one of the definitive sources for horror bibliography, *Fantastic Fiction* (www.fantasticfiction.co.uk). The administrators and bibliographers of this free site are truly a godsend to fans of horror, and they do a great job not only of keeping up with just about every published writer in the genre, but also of assigning series names when none exist. They were also our source, for the most part, for determining which novels and collections belonged in a given series, although at times we deviated from their categorization when common sense dictated that we do so.

So, without further ado, here is the list of all titles in all series mentioned in this guide. (The series are listed alphabetically by author or series name, and the titles within the series are listed in order of publication.)

Andrews, V. C.
The Dolanganger Children series.

Flowers in the Attic. New York: Pocket, 1979. 412pp.

Petals on the Wind. New York: Pocket, 1980. 439pp.

If There Be Thorns. New York: Pocket Books, 1981. 374pp.

Armstrong, Kelley.
Women of the Otherworld series.

Bitten. New York: Plume, 2002. 382pp.

Stolen. New York: Plume, 2004. 480pp.

Dime Store Magic. New York: Bantam, 2004. 414pp.

Industrial Magic. New York: Bantam, 2004. 528pp.

Haunted. New York: Bantam, 2005. 495pp.

Bacon-Smith, Camille.
Daemons, Inc. series.

Eye of the Daemon. New York: Daw, 1996. 332pp.

Eyes of the Empress. New York: Daw, 1998. 304pp.

Daemons, Inc. (omnibus: 2 novels). New York: Science Fiction Book Club, 1998. 478pp.

Banks, L[eslie]. A.
Vampire Huntress Legend series.

The Minion. New York: St. Martin's, 2003. 320pp.

The Awakening. New York: St. Martin's, 2004. 320pp.

The Hunted. New York: St. Martin's, 2004. 512pp.

The Bitten. New York: St. Martin's, 2005. 434pp.

The Forbidden. New York: St. Martin's, 2005. 352pp.

Bergstrom, Elaine.
The Austra Family series.

Shattered Glass. New York: Jove, 1989 (reissued 1994). 372pp.

Blood Alone. New York: Jove, 1990. (reissued 1994). 325pp.

Blood Rites. New York: Jove, 1991. (reissued 1994). 332p.

Daughter of the Night. New York: Jove, 1992. (reissued 1994). 323pp.

Nocturne. New York: Ace, 2003. 384pp.

Borchardt, Alice.
  Legend of the Wolves series.
   The Silver Wolf. New York: Ballantine, 1998. 451pp.
   Night of the Wolf. New York: Ballantine, 1999. 454pp.
   The Wolf King. New York: Ballantine, 2001. 384pp.

Boyd, Donna.
  The Devoncroix Dynasty series.
   The Passion. New York: Avon Books, 1998. 387pp.
   The Promise. New York: Avon Books, 1999. 340pp.

Bray, Libba.
  The Great and Terrible Beauty series.
   A Great and Terrible Beauty. New York: Delacorte, 2003. 403pp.
   Rebel Angels. New York: Delacorte, 2005. 560pp.

***Buffy* and *Angel* novelizations.**
   Golden, Christopher. *Pretty Maids All in a Row.* New York: Pocket Books, 2000. 305pp.
   Passarella, Jack. *Ghoul Trouble.* New York: Pocket, 2000. 239pp.
   Holder, Nancy. *The Book of Fours.* New York: Pocket, 2001. 352pp.
   Navarro, Yvonne, Mel Odom, and Nancy Holder. *Buffy the Vampire Slayer: Tales of the Slayer.* New York: Simon & Schuster, 2001. 288pp.
   Ciencin, Denise, and Scott Ciencin. *Mortal Fear.* New York: Simon & Schuster, 2003. 496pp.
   Holder, Nancy. *Blood and Fog.* Minneapolis, MN: Sagebrush, 2003. 304pp.
   Odom, Mel. *Cursed.* New York: Simon & Schuster, 2003. 488pp.
   Burns, Laura J., and Melinda Metz. *Apocalypse Memories.* New York: Simon & Schuster, 2004. 256pp.
   Ciencin, Denise, and Scott Ciencin. *Nemesis.* New York: Simon & Schuster, 2004. 400pp.
   Passarella, John. *Monolith.* New York: Simon & Schuster, 2004. 336pp.

Clegg, Douglas.
  Harrow Academy series.
   Mischief. New York: Leisure, 2000. 359pp.
   The Infinite. New York: Leisure, 2001. 377pp.
   The Nightmare House. Baltimore: Cemetery Dance, 2002. 207pp.
   The Abandoned. New York: Leisure, 2005. 370pp.

Collins, Nancy A.
 Sonja Blue series.

Sunglasses After Dark. New York: New American Library, 1989. 253pp.

In the Blood. New York: Penguin, 1992. 302pp.

Midnight Blue: The Sonja Blue Collection. Clarkston, GA: White Wolf, 1995. 560pp.

Paint It Black. Clarkston, GA: White Wolf, 1995. 253pp.

A Dozen Black Roses. Clarkston, GA: White Wolf, 1996. 237pp.

Darkest Heart. Clarkston, GA: White Wolf, 2002. 183pp.

Dead Roses for a Blue Lady. Holyoke, MA: Crossroads, 2002. 207pp.

Constantine, Storm.
 Grigori Trilogy.

Stalking Tender Prey. London: Creed, 1995. 648pp.

Scenting Hallowed Blood. London: Signet, 1996. 356pp.

Stealing Sacred Fire. London: Penguin, 1997. 356pp.

Cook, Robin.
Not a series, but all medical thrillers.

The Year of the Intern. New York: Signet, 1972. 211p.

Coma. Boston, MA: Little, Brown, 1977. 280pp.

Brain. New York: Putnam, 1981. 283pp.

Fever. New York: Putnam, 1982. 365pp.

Outbreak. New York: Putnam, 1987. 366pp.

Mutation. New York: Putnam, 1989. 367pp.

Harmful Intent. New York: Putnam, 1990. 400pp.

Vital Signs. New York: Putnam, 1991. 394pp.

Blindsight. New York: Putnam, 1992. 429pp.

Fatal Cure. New York: Berkley, 1993. 464pp.

Terminal. New York: Putnam, 1993. 445pp.

Acceptable Risk. New York: Putnam, 1994. 404pp.

Contagion. New York: Penguin, 1995. 434pp.

Chromosome 6. New York: Putnam, 1997. 461pp.

Invasion. New York: Berkley, 1997. 337pp.

Mortal Fear. New York: Putnam, 1998. 364pp.

Toxin. New York: Putnam, 1998. 357pp.

Vector. New York: Putnam, 1999. 404pp.

Shock. New York: Putnam, 2001. 370pp.

Seizure. New York: Putnam, 2003. 464pp.

Marker. New York: Putnam, 2005. 533pp.

Davidson, Mary Janice.
Undead and . . . series.

Undead and Unwed. New York: Berkley Sensation, 2004. 277pp.

Undead and Unemployed. New York, Berkley Sensation, 2004. 294pp.

Undead and Unappreciated. New York, Berkley Sensation, 2005. 352pp.

Due, Tananarive.
The Living Blood series.

My Soul to Keep. New York: HarperPrism, 1997. 346pp.

The Living Blood. New York: Pocket, 2001. 515pp.

Elrod, P. N.
Jonathan Barrett series.

Red Death. New York: Ace, 1993. 288pp.

Death and the Maiden. New York: Ace, 1994. 244pp.

Death Masque. New York: Ace, 1995. 261pp.

Dance of Death. New York: Ace, 1996. 340pp.

Jonathan Barrett: Gentleman Vampire (omnibus: all 4 novels). New York: Doubleday, 1996. 960pp.

Elrod, P. N.
The Vampire Files.

Bloodlist. New York: Ace, 1990. 200pp.

Lifeblood. New York: Ace, 1990. 208pp.

Bloodcircle. New York: Ace, 1990. 202pp.

Art in the Blood. New York: Ace, 1991. 208pp.

Fire in the Blood. New York: Ace, 1991. 208pp.

Blood in the Water. New York: Ace, 1992. 199pp.

Chill in the Blood. New York: Ace, 1998. 327pp.

The Dark Sleep. New York: Ace, 1999. 359pp.

Lady Crymsyn. New York: Ace, 2000. 410pp.

Cold Streets. New York: Ace, 2003. 380pp.

The Vampire Files (omnibus: *Bloodlist, Lifeblood, Bloodcircle*). New York: Ace, 2003. 452pp.

A Song in the Dark. New York: Ace, 2005. 352pp.

Farren, Mick.
The Victor Renquist Novels.

The Time of Feasting. New York: Tor, 1996. 394pp.

Dark Lost. New York: Tom Doherty, 2000. 470pp.

More than Mortal. New York: Tor, 2001. 383pp.

Underland. New York: Tor, 2002. 448pp.

Farris, John.
The Fury series.

The Fury. Chicago: Playboy Press, 1976. 341pp.

The Fury and the Terror. New York: Tom Doherty, 2001. 384pp.

The Fury and the Power. New York: Forge, 2003. 348pp.

Grant, Charles L.
Black Oak series.

Genesis. New York: ROC, 1998. 271pp.

The Hush of Dark Wings. New York: ROC, 1999. 236pp.

Winter Knight. New York: ROC, 1999. 240pp.

Hunting Ground. New York: Penguin, 2000. 246pp.

When the Cold Wind Blows. New York: Penguin, 2001. 241pp.

Grant, Charles L.
The Millennium Quartet.

Symphony. New York: Tor, 1997. 332pp.

In the Mood. New York: Forge, 1998. 304pp.

Chariot. New York: Tor, 1998. 309pp.

Riders in the Sky. New York: Forge, 1999. 304pp.

Griffiths, W. G.
Gavin Pierce Novels.

Driven. New York: Warner Books, 2002. 357pp.

Takedown. New York: Warner Books, 2004. 325pp.

Hamilton, Laurell K.
Anita Blake, Vampire Hunter.

> *Guilty Pleasures.* New York: Ace, 1993. 266pp.
>
> *The Laughing Corpse.* New York: Ace, 1994. 293pp.
>
> *Circus of the Damned.* New York: Ace, 1995. 329pp.
>
> *The Lunatic Café.* New York: Ace, 1996. 369pp.
>
> *Bloody Bones.* New York: Ace, 1996. 370pp.
>
> *The Killing Dance.* New York: Ace, 1997. 397pp.
>
> *Burnt Offerings.* New York: Ace, 1998. 392pp.
>
> *Blue Moon.* New York: Ace, 1998. 418pp.
>
> *Obsidian Butterfly.* New York: Ace, 2000. 386pp.
>
> *Narcissus in Chains.* New York: Berkeley, 2001. 404pp.
>
> *Cerulean Sins.* New York: Berkley, 2003. 560pp.
>
> *Incubus Dreams.* New York: Berkeley, 2004. 658pp.

Harris, Charlaine.
The Southern Vampire Mysteries.

> *Dead Until Dark.* New York: Ace, 2001. 260pp.
>
> *Living Dead in Dallas.* New York: Ace, 2002. 262pp.
>
> *Club Dead.* New York, Ace, 2003. 258pp.
>
> *Dead to the World.* New York: Ace, 2004. 291pp.
>
> *Dead as a Doornail.* New York: Ace, 2005. 204pp.

Harris, Thomas.
Hannibal Lecter Novels.

> *Red Dragon.* New York: Putnam, 1981. 348pp.
>
> *The Silence of the Lambs.* New York: St. Martin's, 1988. 338pp.
>
> *Hannibal.* New York: Dell, 2000. 544pp.
>
> *Behind the Mask.* New York: Delacorte, 2005. 480pp.

Holland, Tom.
Lord of the Dead series.

> *Lord of the Dead: The Secret History of Byron.* (Originally published as *The Vampyre: Being the True Pilgrimage of George Gordon, Sixth Lord Byron*). New York: Simon & Schuster, 1995. 342pp.
>
> *Slave of My Thirst.* (Originally published as *Supping with Panthers*). New York: Simon & Schuster, 1996. 421pp.

Deliver Us from Evil. New York: Warner, 1998. 578pp.

The Sleeper in the Sands. London: Little, Brown, 1999. 428pp.

Houarner, Gerard Daniel.
Max novels.

Painfreak. Orlando: Necro Publications, 1996. 116pp.

The Beast That Was Max. New York: Leisure, 2001. 392pp.

Road to Hell. New York: Dorchester, 2003. 342pp.

Huff, Tanya.
Victoria Nelson Novels.

Blood Price. New York: Daw, 1991. 272pp.

Blood Trial. New York: Daw, 1992. 304pp.

Blood Lines. New York: Daw, 1992. 271pp.

Blood Pact. New York: Daw, 1993. 332pp.

Blood Debt. New York: Daw, 1997. 330pp.

Johnstone, William W.
The Devil series.

The Devil's Kiss. New York: Kensington, 1980. 400pp.

The Devil's Heart. New York: Zebra, 1983. 382pp.

The Devil's Touch. New York: Kensington, 1984. 350pp.

The Devil's Cat. New York: Kensington, 1987. 380pp.

Kalogridis, Jeanne.
Diaries of the Family Dracul.

Covenant with the Vampire. New York: Delacorte, 1994. 324pp.

Children of the Vampire. New York: Delacorte, 1995. 300pp.

Lord of the Vampires. New York: Delacorte, 1996. 347pp.

Kemske, Floyd.
Corporate Nightmares series.

Lifetime Employment. Highland Park, NJ: Catbird Press, 1992. 236pp.

The Virtual Boss: A Novel. New Haven, CT: Catbird Press, 1993. 237pp.

Human Resources. New Haven, CT: Catbird Press, 1995. 223pp.

Labor Day: A Corporate Nightmare. New Haven, CT: Catbird Press, 2000. 203pp.

Kilpatrick, Nancy (writing as Amarantha Knight).
  The Darker Passions Books.

> *The Darker Passions: Dracula.* Cambridge, MA: Circlet Press, 2002. 256pp.
>
> *The Darker Passions: Dr. Jekyll and Mr. Hyde.* Cambridge, MA: Circlet Press, 2002. 190pp.
>
> *The Darker Passions: Frankenstein.* Cambridge, MA: Circlet Press, 2002. 300pp.
>
> *The Darker Passions: Carmilla.* Cambridge, MA: Circlet Press, 2004. 256pp.

Knight, Amarantha. *See* **Kilpatrick, Nancy.**

Lee, Edward.
  City Infernal series.

> *City Infernal.* New York: Leisure, 2001. 366pp.
>
> *Infernal Angel.* New York: Dorchester, 2003. 302pp.

Lee, Tanith.
  Secret Books of Venus series.

> *Faces Under Water.* Woodstock, NY: Overlook Press, 1999. 335pp.
>
> *Saint Fire.* Woodstock, NY: Overlook Press, 1999. 335pp.
>
> *A Bed of Earth (The Gravedigger's Tale).* Woodstock, NY: Overlook Press, 2002. 345pp.
>
> *Venus Preserved.* Woodstock, NY: Overlook Press, 2003. 316pp.

Lumley, Brian.
  Necroscope series.

> *Necroscope.* New York: Doherty, 1986. 505pp.
>
> *Necroscope II: Vamphyri!* New York: Doherty, 1988. 470pp.
>
> *The Source: Necroscope III.* New York: Doherty, 1989. 505pp.
>
> *Deadspeak: Necroscope IV.* New York: Doherty, 1990. 487pp.
>
> *Deadspawn: Necroscope V.* New York: Doherty, 1991. 602pp.
>
> *Necroscope The Lost Years.* New York: Doherty, 1995. 593pp.
>
> *Necroscope: The Lost Years II (Resurgence).* New York: Tor, 1996. 414pp.
>
> *Invaders.* New York: Tor, 1999. 416pp.
>
> *Defilers: Necroscope.* New York: Tor, 2000. 446pp.
>
> *Avengers: Necroscope.* New York: Tor, 2001. 445pp.
>
> *Harry Keogh: Necroscope and Other Weird Heroes.* New York: Tor, 2003. 319pp.

Necroscope also has a "subseries," Vampire World.

    Blood Brothers. New York: Roc, 1992. 740pp.

    The Last Aerie. New York: Tor, 1993. 479pp.

    Bloodwars. New York: Tor, 1994. 509pp.

McCammon, Robert.
Speaks the Nightbird series.

    Speaks the Nightbird (2 novels). Montgomery, AL: River City Publishing, 2002. 726pp.

    Judgement of the Witch. New York: Pocket, 2003. 483pp.

    Evil Unveiled. New York: Pocket, 2003. 418pp.

Mitchell, Mary Ann.
Marquis de Sade novels.

    Sips of Blood. New York: Leisure, 1999. 358pp.

    Quenched. New York: Leisure, 2000. 363pp.

    Cathedral of Vampires. New York: Leisure, 2002. 355pp.

    Tainted Blood. New York: Leisure, 2003. 334pp.

    The Vampire de Sade. New York: Leisure, 2004. 337pp.

Monahan, Brent.
Book of Common Dread.

    The Book of Common Dread. New York: St. Martin's, 1993. 328pp.

    The Blood of the Covenant: A Novel of the Vampiric. New York: St. Martin's. 1997. 320pp.

Monteleone, Thomas F.
The Blood of the Lamb Series.

    The Blood of the Lamb. New York: Tom Doherty, 1992. 419pp.

    The Reckoning. New York: Tor, 2001. 432pp.

Moore, Elaine.
The Dark Madonna Trilogy.

    Dark Desire. (Originally published as *Madonna of the Dark*). New York: iBooks, 1999. 269pp.

    Eternal Embrace. (Originally published as *Retribution: A Vampire Novel*). New York: iBooks, 2002. 253pp.

Newman, Kim.
  Anno Dracula series.

  Anno Dracula. New York: Avon, 1992. 409pp.

  Bloody Red Baron. New York: Avon, 1995. 370pp.

  Judgment of Tears. (Originally published as *Dracula, Cha Cha Cha*). New York: Carroll & Graf, 1998. 288pp.

Palmer, Michael.
 More medical thrillers.

  Side Effects. New York: Bantam, 1985. 344pp.

  Flashback. New York: Bantam, 1988. 385pp.

  Extreme Measures. New York: Bantam, 1991. 390pp.

  The Sisterhood. New York: Bantam, 1991. 343pp.

  Natural Causes. New York: Bantam, 1994. 389pp.

  Silent Treatment. New York: Bantam, 1995. 404pp.

  Critical Judgment. New York: Bantam, 1996. 450pp.

  Miracle Cure. New York: Bantam, 1998. 399pp.

  Patient. New York: Bantam, 2000. 324pp.

  Fatal. New York: Bantam, 2002. 387pp.

  The Society. New York: Bantam, 2004. 351pp.

Poltergeist and Poltergeist, The Legacy.

  Kahn, James. *Poltergeist.* New York: Warner, 1982. 301pp.

  Kahn, James. *Poltergeist II.* New York: Ballantine, 1986. 179pp.

  Hautala, Rick. *Poltergeist, The Legacy: The Hidden Saint.* New York: Ace, 1999. 230pp.

  Costello, Matthew J. *Poltergeist, The Legacy: Maelstrom.* New York: Ace, 2000. 229pp.

Preston, Douglas, and Lincoln Child.
 The Relic series.

  The Relic. New York: Tor, 1995. 474pp.

  Reliquary. New York: Tom Doherty, 1997. 382pp.

Randisi, Robert J.
 Joe Keough novels.

  Alone with the Dead. New York: St. Martin's, 1995. 262pp.

In the Shadow of the Arch. New York: St. Martin's, 1998. 355pp.

Blood on the Arch. New York, Leisure, 2001. 394pp.

East of the Arch. New York: Thomas Dunne, 2002. 370pp.

Arch Angels. New York: Thomas Dunne, 2004. 355pp.

Rice, Anne.
The Mayfair Witches series.

The Witching Hour. New York: Ballantine, 1990. 965pp.

Lasher. New York: Ballantine, 1994. 577pp.

Taltos: Lives of the Mayfair Witches. New York: Ballantine, 1994. 467pp.

Rice, Anne.
New Tales of the Vampires.

Pandora. New York: Ballantine, 1998. 368pp.

Vittorio, the Vampire. New York: Ballantine, 1999. 304pp.

Rice, Anne.
The Vampire Chronicles.

Interview with the Vampire. New York: Ballantine, 1977. 346pp.

The Vampire Lestat. New York: New York: Ballantine, 1985. 550pp.

The Queen of the Damned. New York: Ballantine, 1989. 491pp.

The Tale of the Body Thief. New York: Ballantine, 1992. 435pp.

Memnoch the Devil. New York: Alfred A. Knopf, 1995. 354pp.

The Vampire Armand. New York: Alfred A. Knopf, 1998. 384pp.

Blood and Gold. New York: Alfred A. Knopf, 2001. 470pp.

Blackwood Farm. New York: Alfred A. Knopf, 2002. 527pp.

Blood Canticle. New York: Alfred A. Knopf, 2003. 305pp.

Romkey, Michael.
I, Vampire series.

I, Vampire. New York: Fawcett, 1990. 360pp.

The Vampire Papers. New York: Fawcett, 1994. 433pp.

The Vampire Princess. New York: Fawcett, 1996. 339pp.

The Vampire Virus. New York: Ballantine, 1997. 295pp.

The London Vampire Panic. New York: Ballantine, 2001. 295pp.

Saberhagen, Fred.
  Vlad Tepes series.

  The Dracula Tape. New York: Warner, 1975. 206pp.
  The Holmes-Dracula File. New York: Ace, 1978. 249pp.
  An Old Friend of the Family. New York: Ace, 1979. 247pp.
  Thorn. New York: Ace, 1980. 347pp.
  Dominion. New York: Pinnacle, 1982. 320pp.
  A Matter of Taste. New York: Doherty, 1990. 284pp.
  A Question of Time. New York: Doherty, 1993. 278pp.
  Séance for a Vampire. New York: Tor, 1994. 285pp.
  A Sharpness on the Neck. New York: Tor, 1996. 349pp.
  The Vlad Tapes. New York: Simon & Schuster, 2000. 537pp.

Scotch, Cheri.
  Hunter's Moon series.

  The Werewolf's Kiss. New York: Berkley, 1992. 262pp.
  Werewolf's Touch. New York: Diamond Books, 1993. 260p.
  The Werewolf's Sin. New York: Diamond Books, 1994. 239pp.

Slade, Michael.
  Special X series.

  Headhunter. New York: Onyx Books, 1984. 422pp.
  Ghoul. New York: New American Library, 1989. 386pp.
  Cut Throat. New York: Signet, 1992. 397pp.
  Ripper. New York: Penguin, 1994. 416pp.
  Evil Eye. New York: Signet, 1997. 417pp.
  Primal Scream. New York: Signet, 1998. 432pp.
  Burnt Bones. New York: Signet, 2000. 408pp.

Stableford, Brian.
  The Werewolves of London Trilogy.

  The Werewolves of London. New York: Carroll and Graf, 1990. 467pp.
  The Angel of Pain. New York: Carroll and Graf, 1991. 395pp.
  The Carnival of Destruction. New York: Carroll and Graf, 1994. 433pp.

Straub, Peter.
The Blue Rose Trilogy.
Koko. New York: Dutton, 1988. 562pp.
Mystery. New York: Dutton, 1990. 548pp.
The Throat. New York: Dutton, 1993. 689pp.

Straub, Peter, and Stephen King.
The Talisman Series.
The Talisman. New York: Viking Adult, 1984. 672pp.
Black House. New York: Ballantine, 2002. 672pp.

Taylor, Karen E.
The Vampire Legacy series.
Blood Secrets. New York: Kensington, 1993. 303pp.
Bitter Blood. New York: Kensington, 1994. 351pp.
Blood Ties. New York: Kensington, 1995. 347pp.
Blood of My Blood. New York: Kensington, 2000. 318pp.
The Vampire Vivienne. New York: Kensington, 2001. 303pp.
Resurrection. New York: Kensington, 2002. 302pp.
Blood Red Dawn. New York: Kensington, 2004. 284pp.

The Universal Monsters.
Not a series, but all medical thrillers, in which same characters reappear.
Rovin, Jeff. *Return of the Wolf Man*. New York: Penguin, 1998. 339pp.
Jacobs, David. *The Devil's Brood*. New York: Berkley Boulevard, 2000. 316pp.
Jacobs, David. *The Devil's Night*. New York: Berkley Boulevard, 2001. 252pp.
Schildt, Christopher. *Night of Dracula*. New York: Pocket, 2001. 272pp.

Wilson, F. Paul.
Repairman Jack series.
Legacies. New York: Forge, 1998. 381pp.
Conspiracies. New York: Forge, 2000. 317pp.
All the Rage. New York: Forge, 2000. 383pp.
Hosts. New York: Forge, 2001. 383pp.
The Haunted Air. New York: Forge, 2002. 415pp.
Gateways. New York: Forge, 2003. 366pp.

Crisscross. Colorado Springs, CO: Gauntlet, 2004. 404pp.

Infernal. New York: Forge, 2005. 352pp.

Yarbro, Chelsea Quinn.
  Atta Olivia Clements series.

A Flame in Byzantium. New York: Tor, 1987. 480pp.

Crusader's Torch. New York: Tor, 1988. 459pp.

A Candle for D'Artangan: An Historical Horror. New York: Tor, 1989. 485pp.

Yarbro, Chelsea Quinn.
  The Saint-Germain Chronicles.

Hotel Transylvania: A Novel of Forbidden Love. New York: St.Martin's, 1978. 279pp.

The Palace: An Historical Horror. New York: St. Martin's, 1978. 408pp.

Blood Games: A Novel of Historical Horror. New York: St. Martin's, 1979. 458pp.

The Path of the Eclipse: A Historical Horror Novel. New York: St. Martin's, 1981. 447pp.

Tempting Fate. New York: St. Martin's, 1982. 662pp.

Saint Germain Chronicles. New York: Pocket, 1983. 206pp.

Out of the House of Life. New York: Tor, 1990. 446pp.

Darker Jewels. New York: Tor, 1993. 398pp.

Better in the Dark. New York: Tor, 1993. 412pp.

Mansions of Darkness: A Novel of Saint-Germain. New York: Tor, 1996. 430pp.

Writ in Blood: A Novel of Saint-Germain. New York: Tor, 1997. 544pp.

Blood Roses: A Novel of Saint-Germain. New York: Tor, 1998. 382pp.

Communion Blood: A Novel of Saint-Germain. New York: Tor, 1999. 477pp.

Come Twilight: A Novel of Saint-Germain. New York: Tor, 2000. 479pp.

A Feast in Exile: A Novel of Saint-Germain. New York: Tor, 2001. 496pp.

Night Blooming. New York: Aspect, 2002. 429pp.

Midnight Harvest. New York: Aspect, 2003. 448pp.

Dark of the Sun: A Novel of Saint-Germain. New York: Tor, 2004. 460pp.

Yarbro, Chelsea Quinn.
  Sisters of the Night series.

The Angry Angel. New York: William Morrow, 1998. 368pp.

The Soul of An Angel. New York: William Morrow, 1999. 384pp.

# Appendix C

Genreblends

Horror with a tinge of . . . . This appendix contains lists of titles in this book that either are crossovers from other genres or contain significant elements of that particular type of genre. Readers will find this resource helpful when attempting to locate a book whose themes are broader than what was used to classify them in the various chapters.

Christian Fiction

Cisco, Michael. *The Divinity Student*
Climer, Stephen Lee. *Soul Temple*
Griffiths, W. G. Gavin Pierce Novels

Classics

Austen, Jane. *Northanger Abbey*
Brontë, Emily. *Wuthering Heights*
Brown, Charles Brockden. *Wieland*
Chambers, Robert W. Collections
De la Mare, Walter. *The Return*
Doyle, Arthur Conan. *The Captain of the 'Pole-Star'*
Du Maurier, Daphne. *Rebecca*

Hawthorne, Nathaniel. *The House of Seven Gables*

Hodgson, William Hope. *Boats of the "Glen Carrig"*

Huysmanns, J. K. *La-bas*

Jackson, Shirley. *The Haunting of Hill House*

James, Henry. *Ghost Stories of Henry James*

James, M. R. *Casting the Runes*

Le Fanu, Joseph Sheridan. *Green Tea and Other Ghost Stories*

Le Fanu, Joseph Sheridan. *In a Glass Darkly*

LeRoux, Gaston. *The Phantom of the Opera*

Lewis, Matthew ("Monk") G. *The Monk*

Lovecraft, H. P. Collections

Machen, Arthur. Collections

Onions, Oliver. *The Beckoning Fair One*

Poe, Edgar Allan. *The Fall of the House of Usher and Other Writings*

Polidori, John. *The Vampyre and Other Tales of the Macabre*

Shelley, Mary. *Frankenstein*

Smith, Clark Ashton. *Red World of Polaris: The Adventures of Captain Volmar*

Stevenson, Robert Louis. *Doctor Jekyll and Mr. Hyde and Other Stories*

Stoker, Bram. *Dracula*

Stoker, Bram. *The Jewel of Seven Stars*

Walpole, Horace. *The Castle of Otranto*

Wilde, Oscar. *The Canterville Ghost*

Wilde, Oscar. *The Picture of Dorian Gray*

Detective Fiction

Bacon-Smith, Camille. Daemons, Inc.

Delaney, Matthew B. J. *Jinn.*

Elrod, P. N. The Vampire Files

Grant, Charles L. Black Oak

Hamilton, Laurell K. Anita Blake, Vampire Hunter

Harper, Andrew. *Red Angel*

Harris, Charlaine. The Southern Vampire Mysteries

Harris, Thomas. <u>Hannibal Lecter Novels</u>

Hooper, Kay. *Touching Evil*

Hopkins, Brian A. *The Licking Valley Coon Hunters Club*

Huff, Tanya. <u>Victoria Nelson Novels</u>

King, Stephen and Peter Straub. *Black House*

Koontz, Dean. *Fear Nothing*

Lee, Edward, and Elizabeth Steffen. *Dahmer's Not Dead*

Masterton, Graham. *The Devil in Gray*

Masterton, Graham. *A Terrible Beauty*

Mitchell, Mary Ann. *Siren's Call*

Randisi, Robert J. <u>Joe Keough Novels</u>

Reaves, Michael, and John Pelan, eds. *Shadows Over Baker Street*

Slade, Michael. <u>Special X</u>

Straub, Peter. <u>The Blue Rose Trilogy</u>

Taylor, Karen E. <u>The Vampire Legacy</u>

Waggoner, Tim. *Necropolis*

Wright, T. M. *Laughing Man*

Fantasy

Barker, Clive. *Abarat*

Bedwell-Grime, Stephanie. *Guardian Angel*

Bishop, K. J., *The Etched City*

Braunbeck, Gary A. *In Silent Graves*

Bray, Libba. *A Great and Terrible Beauty*

Clegg, Douglas. *Naomi*

Constantine, Storm. <u>Grigori Trilogy</u>

Cross, Michael. *After Human*

Devereaux, Robert. *Santa Steps Out: A Fairy Tale for Grown-ups*

Gaiman, Neil. *American Gods*

Gaiman, Neil. *Coraline*

Gaiman, Neil. *Neverwhere*

Golden, Christopher. *Strangewood*

Grant, Charles. <u>The Millennium Quartet</u>

Hand, Elizabeth. *Black Light*
Hand, Elizabeth. *Waking the Moon*
Holder, Nancy. *Dead in the Water*
Kiernan, Caitlin R. *Threshold: A Novel of Deep Time*
King, Stephen. *Insomnia*
King, Stephen, and Peter Straub. <u>The Talisman series</u>
Koja, Kathe. *The Cipher*
Lee, Edward. <u>City Infernal</u>
Lee, Tanith. <u>Secret Books of Venus</u>
Marano, Michael. *Dawn Song*
Masterton, Graham. *The Doorkeepers*
Masterton, Graham. *The Hidden World*
Moore, Christopher. *Practical Demonkeeping*
Moore, Christopher. *The Stupidest Angel*
Koontz, Dean. *Lightning*
Pike, Christopher. *Alosha*
Powers, Tim. *Declare*
Sabastian, Stephen. *Solomon's Brood*
Sarrantonio, Al. *Hallows Eve*
Stableford, Brian. <u>The Werewolves of London Trilogy</u>
Straub, Peter. *Mr. X.*
Thorne, Tamara. *Thunder Road*
VanderMeer, Jeff. *Veniss Underground*
Waggoner, Tim. *Necropolis*

Historical

Barker, Clive. *Galilee: A Romance*
Bleys, Olivier. *The Ghost in the Eiffel Tower*
Bloch, Robert. *American Gothic*
Borchardt, Alice. <u>Legend of the Wolves</u>
Bray, Libba. *A Great and Terrible Beauty*
Codrescu, Andrei. *The Blood Countess*
Earhart, Rose. *Dorcas Good: The Diary of a Salem Witch*

Elrod, P. N. <u>Jonathan Barrett</u>
Elrod, P. N., ed. *Dracula in London*
Holland, David. *Murcheston: The Wolf's Tale*
Holland, Tom. <u>Lord of the Dead</u>
Knight, H. R. *What Rough Beast*
Lumley, Brian. *Khai of Ancient Khem*
Martin, George R. R. *Fevre Dream*
McCammon, Robert. <u>Speaks the Nightbird</u>
Michaels, Barbara. *Other Worlds*
Morrison, Toni. *Beloved*
Newman, Kim. <u>Anno Dracula (series)</u>
Rice, Anne. *Interview with the Vampire*
Rice, Anne. *Servant of the Bones*
Rice, Anne. <u>New Tales of the Vampires</u>
Rice, Anne. *The Queen of the Damned*
Rice, Anne. *The Vampire Lestat*
Scotch, Cheri. <u>Hunter's Moon</u>
Yarbro, Chelsea Quinn. <u>Atta Olivia Clements</u>
Yarbro, Chelsea Quinn. *In the Face of Death*
Yarbro, Chelsea Quinn. <u>The Saint-Germain Chronicles</u>

Mainstream/Literary

Arensberg, Ann. *Incubus*
Bailey, Michael. *Palindrone Hannah*
Bradbury, Ray. *From the Dust Returned*
Brite, Poppy Z. *Are You Loathsome Tonight?*
Brite, Poppy Z. *The Devil You Know*
Brooks, Susan M. *Collecting Candace*
Charnas, Suzy McKee. *The Vampire Tapestry*
Codrescu, Andrei. *The Blood Countess*
Cullen, Mitch. *Tideland*
Dobyns, Stephen. *The Church of Dead Girls*
Harris, Thomas. <u>Hannibal Lecter Novels</u>

Huysmanns, J. K. *La-bas*
Kimball, Michael. *The Way the Family Got Away*
McCabe, Patrick. *Emerald Germs of Ireland*
McGrath, Patrick. *Spider*
Morrison, Toni. *Beloved*
Naylor, Gloria. *Linden Hills*
Oates, Joyce Carol. *Zombie*
Palahniuk, Chuck. *Haunted*
Palahniuk, Chuck. *Lullaby*
Radyshevsky, Dmitrv. *The Mantra*
Sebold, Alice. *The Lovely Bones*
Searcy, David. *Ordinary Horror*
Yarbro, Chelsea Quinn. Atta Olivia Clements
Yarbro, Chelsea Quinn. The Saint-Germain Chronicles

Medical Thriller

Cook, Robin. *Coma*
Ford, Steven. *Mortality*
Palmer, Michael. *The Society*

Romance

Armstrong, Kelley. Women of the Otherworld
Barker, Clive. *Galilee: A Romance*
Borchardt, Alice. Legend of the Wolves
Brass, Perry. *Warlock: A Novel of Possession*
Brite, Poppy Z. *Exquisite Corpse*
Brontë, Emily. *Wuthering Heights*
Brooks, Susan M. *Collecting Candace*
Campbell, Ramsey. *Scared Stiff: Tales of Sex and Death*
Davidson, Mary Janice. Undead and . . .
Hamilton, Laurell K. Anita Blake, Vampire Hunter
Harbaugh, Karen. *Night Fires*

Harris, Charlaine. <u>The Southern Vampire Mysteries</u>
Jefferson, Jemiah. *Fiend*
Jefferson, Jemiah. *Voice of the Blood*
Jefferson, Jemiah. *Wounds*
Kilpatrick, Nancy. *Dracul: An Eternal Love Story*
Knight, Amarantha (Nancy Kilpatrick). <u>Darker Passions</u>
Moore, Christopher. *Bloodsucking Fiends: A Love Story*
Moore, Elaine. <u>The Dark Madonna Trilogy</u>
Taylor, Karen E. <u>The Vampire Legacy</u>
Yarbro, Chelsea Quinn. <u>Atta Olivia Clements</u>
Yarbro, Chelsea Quinn. *In the Face of Death*
Yarbro, Chelsea Quinn. <u>The Saint-Germain Chronicles</u>

Science Fiction

Alten, Steve. *Goliath*
Crichton, Michael. *Jurassic Park: A Novel*
Cross, Michael. *After Human*
Elkin, Richard. *Leech*
Gustainis, Justin. *The Hades Project*
Harrison, Kim. *Dead Witch Walking*
Herbert, James. *Portent*
King, Stephen. *Dreamcatcher*
King, Stephen. *The Stand*
Koontz, Dean. *Demon Seed*
Koontz, Dean. *Fear Nothing*
Koontz, Dean. *Midnight*
Koontz, Dean. *Mr. Murder*
Koontz, Dean. *Strangers*
Koontz, Dean. *Night Chills*
Koontz, Dean. *The Taking*
Koontz, Dean. *Watchers*
Matheson, Richard. *I Am Legend*
Matheson, Richard. *Offbeat: Uncollected Stories*

Sanders, Dan. *Chelydra Serpentina: Terror in the Adirondacks*
Saul, John. *The God Project*
Shirley, John. *Crawlers*
Siodmak, Curt. *Donovan's Brain*
Smith, Clark Ashton. *Red World of Polaris*
Straub, Peter. *Floating Dragon*
Strieber, Whitley, et al. *The Day After Tomorrow*
VanderMeer, Jeff. *Veniss Underground*
Wyndham, John. *The Day of the Triffids*

Splatterpunk

Arnzen, Michael. *Grave Markings*
Brite, Poppy Z. *Drawing Blood*
Brite, Poppy Z. *Exquisite Corpse*
Brite, Poppy Z. *Lost Souls*
Brite, Poppy Z. *Love in Vein* and *Love in Vein Two*
Clark, Simon. *Blood Crazy*
Clegg, Douglas. *The Attraction*
Cross, Michael. *After Human*
Devereaux, Robert. *Santa Steps Out: A Fairy Tale for Grown-ups*
Gelb, Jeff, and Michael Garrett, eds. *Hotter Blood* and *Hottest Blood*
Gonzales, J. F., and Mark Williams. *Clickers*
Gustainis, Justin. *The Hades Project*
Harper, Andrew. *Red Angel*
Heck, Victor. *A Darkness Inbred*
Houarner, Gerard. Max Novels
Jacob, Charlee. *Haunter*
Jacob, Charlee. *This Symbiotic Fascination*
Johnstone, William W. The Devil
Koontz, Dean. *Odd Thomas*
Lee, Edward. *The Bighead*
Nykanen, Mark. *The Bone Parade*
Palahniuk, Chuck. *Haunted*

Shirley, John. *Black Butterflies*

Shirley, John. *Crawlers*

Shirley, John. *Wetbones*

Skipp, John, and Craig Spector. *The Light at the End*

Slade, Michael. Special X

Straub, Peter. *Floating Dragon*

Taylor, Lucy. *The Safety of Unknown Cities*

Young Adult

Andrews, V. C. The Dolanganger Children

Bray, Libba. *A Great and Terrible Beauty*

Clark, Simon. *Blood Crazy*

Earhart, Rose. *Dorcas Good: The Diary of a Salem Witch*

Gaiman, Neil. *Coraline*

Gaiman, Neil. *Neverwhere*

Gallagher, Diana G., and Constance Burge. *Mist and Stone: An Original Novel*

Hand, Stephen, et al. *Freddy vs. Jason*

Hoffman, Nina Kiriki. *A Stir of Bones*

King, Stephen. *Carrie*

Laymon, Richard. *Darkness, Tell Us*

Laymon, Richard. *The Lake*

Laymon, Richard. *The Traveling Vampire Show*

Massie, Elizabeth. *Sineater*

Rhodes, Natasha. *Blade: Trinity*

Saul, John. *Creature*

Saul, John. *The God Project*

Saul, John. *Midnight Voices*

Saul, John. *Shadows*

Saul, John. *Sleep Walk*

Simmons, Dan. *Summer of Night*

Straczynski, Michael J. *Othersyde*

Various authors. Buffy and Angel novelizations

Index

Abarat, 78
Acquired Taste$, 70
Adaptations, 10–13
After Human, 83
Agyar, 44
Aickman, Robert, 117–18
Alien (film), 133
Aliens, 18–19, 32, 84, 88, 107–8
Alosha, 80
Alten, Steve, 18
Alternate fictions, 10–13
Alternate universes, 77–80, 90, 112
American Gods, 101
American Gothic (Bloch), 81
American Gothic (Romkey), 21–22
American Haunting, An, 65
American Psycho (film), 127–28
Amis, Kingsley, 100
Amityville Horror, The, 69
Ancient Images, 40
Andrews, V. C., 39
Angel Heart (film), 136
Angry Angel, The, 13
Animals, 73, 92
    abnormal, 30, 73, 74, 113, 116
    as agents of evil, 22
<u>Anita Blake, Vampire Hunter series,</u> 111
Anno Dracula, 12
<u>Anno Dracula series, The ,</u> 12
Anson, Jay, 69
Apocalypse Memories, 109
Apostate, The, 71

Appeal factors
  characters
    famous, 90–92
    historical, 90–92
    monster killers, 89–90
    monster makers, 86–89
    monsters, 92–95
    psychic detectives, 89–90
    psychopaths and sociopaths, 92–98
    vampire hunters, 89–90
    victims, 86–89
  language
    austere, 102–4
    confessional/reflective, 104–7
    dialogue, 107–9
    first-person, 112–14
    pacing, 115–20
    vivid detail, 99–102
    wit, 109–11
  mood/atmosphere, 27
    comic, 27–30
    erotic, 33–35
    frightening/disturbing/disgusting, 38–52
    gory, 30–32
    holiday-related, 52–57
    intellectual, 36–38
    travel-related, 59–61
    uncertainty, 58–59
  setting
    alternate universes, 77–80
    cities, 71–72
    exotic locales, 75–77

Appeal factors (*Cont.*)
    haunted houses, 63–66
    other worlds, 77–80
    small towns, 66–69
    suburbs, 69–70
    time, 80–84
    wilderness, 72–75
  story, 1
    endings, 15–25
    plot types, 2–15
Are You Loathsome Tonight?, 104
Armstrong, Kelley, 33
Arensberg, Ann, 40
Arnzen, Michael, 31
Aspects of a Psychopath, 113
Association, The, 70
Atmosphere. *See* Mood/atmosphere
<u>Atta Olivia Clements series</u>, 95
Attack of the, 50–Foot Woman (film), 131
Attraction, The, 93
Austen, Jane, 28
<u>Austra Family series, The</u>, 2
Awakening, The, 36
Awash in Blood, 10

Bacon-Smith, Camille, 60
Bad Place, The, 115–16
Bag of Bones, 50
Bailey, Dale, 40
Bailey, Michael, 13
Baker, Trisha, 44
Banks, L[eslie]. A., 71
Barker, Clive, 2, 78, 102
Barron, Diana, 92
Bear, Greg, 42
Beckoning Fair One, The, 41
Bed of Nails, 32
Bedwell-Grime, Stephanie, 78
Beloved, 37
Beloved (film), 128
Benchley, Peter, 73

Bergantino, David, 75
Bergstrom, Elaine, 2
<u>Best Weird Tales series</u>, 43
Between, The, 3
Bierce, Ambrose, 36
Bighead, The, 94
Birds, The (film), 123
Bishop, K. J., 78
Bitten, 33
Black Butterflies, 48
Black House, 89–90
Black Light, 67, 118
Black Lightning, 7
Black magic, 17, 22, 81, 103. *See also* Witchcraft
<u>Black Oak Series, The</u>, 110
Blackula (film), 135
Blade (film), 125
Blade: Trinity, 117
Blair Witch Project, The (film), 132
Blair Witch 2: Book of Shadows (film), 133
Blatty, William Peter, 49
Bless the Child, 19
Bleys, Olivier, 80–81
Bloch, Robert, 81, 95
Blood Canticle, 101
Blood Countess, The, 93
Blood Crazy, 14
Blood of the Lamb, The, 12
<u>Blood of the Lamb series, The</u>, 12
Blood Price, 89
Blood Secrets, 35
Bloodsucking Fiends: A Love Story, 29–30
Blue November Storms, 73
<u>Blue Rose Trilogy, The</u>, 9
Boats of the "Glen Carrig" and Other Nautical Adventures, 59
Book of Renfield: The Gospel of Dracula, The, 11
Bone Parade, The, 97

Bones (film), 133
Book of Common Dread, The, 37
Book of Common Dread series, The, 37
Borchardt, Alice, 2–3
Borrowed Flesh, 93
Bottoms, The, 88
Boyd, Donna, 3, 36
Bradbury, Ray, 28
Bram Stoker's Dracula (film), 127
Brass, 14
Brass, Perry, 33
Braunbeck, Gary A., 13, 52
Bray, Libba, 81
Breathe: Everyone Has to Do It, 87
Bride of Frankenstein (film), 124
Brite, Poppy Z. , 33–34, 71, 100, 104, 107
Broadstone, Christopher Alan, 8
Brontë, Emily, 118
Brooks, Susan M., 56
Brown, Charles Brockden, 105
Brust, Steven, 44
Buffy and *Angel* novelizations, 109
Bumper Crop, 29
Burge, Constance, 17
Burns, Laura J., 109
Butcher Boy, The, 97
Butcher Boy, The (film), 128

Cacek, P. D., 31
Call of Cthulhu and Other Weird Stories, The, 106–7
Campbell, Ramsey, 8, 14, 34, 36, 40, 42, 49, 56, 58, 75, 86, 95–96, 96, 100, 105, 112
Candlenight, 77
Candyman (film), 128
Canterville Ghost, The, 30
Captain of the "Pole-Star": Weird and Imaginative Fiction, The, 58

Card, Orson Scott, 49–50
Carnival of Souls (film), 138
Carrie, 87–88
Carrie (film), 125
Carrion Comfort, 4–5
Casting the Runes, and Other Ghost Stories, 40
Castle of Otranto, The, 104
Cave, Hugh B., 22
Cavelos, Jeanne, ed, 10
Cell, The (film), 133
Ceremonies, The, 118
Chambers, Robert W., 42
Chancers, 38
Characters
 famous, 90–92
 historical, 90–92
 monster killers, 89–90
 monster makers, 86–89
 monsters, 92–95
 psychic detectives, 89–90, 110
 psychopaths and sociopaths, 92–98
 vampire hunters, 89–90, 108, 111, 113, 114, 117
 victims, 86–89
Charnas, Suzy McKee, 105
Chelydra Serpentina: Terror in the Adirondacks, 113–14
Child, Lincoln, 94
Children of the Night, 76
Chosen, The, 65
Christian crossovers, 157
Christmas-related, 55
Church of Dead Girls, The, 69
Cipher, The, 103
Cisco, Michael, 16, 42
Cities, 71–72
City Infernal, 79
City Infernal Series, The, 79
Clark, Alan M., 13
Clark, Simon, 3, 14, 44, 64

Classic crossovers, 157–58
Cleanup, The, 72
Clegg, Douglas, 8, 50, 52, 53, 58, 78, 93
Clickers, 31
Climer, Steven Lee, 115
Codrescu, Andrei, 93
Coffey, Brian (pseud. of Dean Koontz), 16
Cold Fire, 116
Cold Hand in Mine, 117–18
Collecting Candace, 56
Collins, Nancy A., 110
Coma, 5
Come Fygures, Come Shadowes, 45
Comedy, 27–30
Conley, Robert J., 14
Connors, Scott, 84
Constantine, Storm, 91
Cook, Robin , 5
Coraline, 78–79
Corporate Nightmare Series, 29
Couch, J. D., 22
Count of Eleven, The, 95–96
Crawlers, 32
Creature, 89
Crichton, Michael, 16
Crimson Kiss, 44
Cronos, 138
Cross, Michael, 83
Crota, 66–67
Crouch, Blake, 96
Crowther, Peter, 86–87
Cullen, Mitch, 44–45
Cults, 20, 24, 77, 90, 101, 117
Curses, 7, 29, 59, 73

Daemons, Inc, 60
Dahmer's Not Dead, 91
Dark Corner, 68
Dark Desire, 35
Dark Fantastic, The, 110

Dark Madonna Trilogy, The, 35
Dark Rivers of the Heart, 17
Darker, 14
Darker Passions: Carmilla, 11
Darker Passions Series, The, 11
Darker Than Night, 58
Darkest Part of the Woods, The, 42
Darkfall, 17
Darkness, Tell Us, 74
Darkness Demands, 44
Darkness Inbred, A, 46
Darrah, Royal C., 60
Davidson, Mary Janice, 28–29
Dawn Song, 107
Day After Tomorrow, The, 19–20
Day of the Triffids, The, 22
De la Mare, Walter, 87
de Lint, Charles, 75
Dead Heat, 19
Dead in the Water, 47
Dead Lines, 42
Dead Until Dark, 111
Dead Witch Walking, 84
Dead Zone, 6
Death's Door, 38
Declare, 61
Deep in the Darkness, 73–74
Delaney, Matthew B. J., 83
Demon Seed, 56
Demonized, 45
Demons, 19
Desert Places: A Novel of Terror, 96
Detective story crossovers, 158–59
Devereaux, Robert, 55
Devoncroix Dynasty series, The, 3
Devil in Gray, The, 90
Devil You Know, The, 71
Devil's Brood, The, 10–11
Devil's Kiss, The, 47
Dial Your Dreams, 38
Diaries of the Family Dracul series, 11

Divinity Student, The, 42
Dobyns, Stephen, 69
Doctor Jekyll and Mr. Hyde and Other Stories, 9
Dogma (film), 138
Dokey, Cameron, 55
<u>Dolanganger Children Series, The,</u> 39
Donovan's Brain, 46
Doorkeepers, The, 79
Dorcas Good: The Diary of a Salem Witch, 81
Down There. See La-Bas
Doyle, Arthur Conan, 58
Dr. Jekyll and Mr. Hyde (film), 124
Dr. Jekyll and Mr. Hyde and Other Stories, 9
Dracul: An Eternal Love Story, 15
Dracula, 114
Dracula (film), 124
Dracula in London, 10
Dracula 2000 (film), 127
Dracula's Daughter (film), 124
Drawing Blood, 107
Drawn to the Grave, 15
Dreamcatcher, 88
Dreams in the Witch House and Other Weird Stories, The, 106–7
Driven, 115
Du Maurier, Daphne, 87
Due, Tananarive, 3, 20, 75

Earhart, Rose, 81
Elkin, Richard, 83
Elrod, P. N., 10, 81, 110
Emerald Germs of Ireland, 109
Emerick, Roland, 19–20
Endings, 22–25
　ambiguous, 20–22
　climactic, 16–17
　foreboding, 18–20

Epperson, S. K., 69
Eroticism, 33–35
Escaping Purgatory: Fables in Words and Pictures, 13
Etched City, The, 78
Evans, Gloria, 107–08
Evil Returns, The, 22
Evil Unveiled, 82
Exorcist, The, 49
Exorcist, The (film), 125
Exotic locales, 75–77
Exquisite Corpse, 100

Face of Fear, The, 16
Face That Must Die, The, 96
Faces Under Water, 79
Fall of the House of Usher and Other Writings, The: Poems, Tales, Essays and Reviews, 46
Fallen (film), 137
Family Inheritance, 68
Famous characters, 90–92
Fantasy crossovers, 159–60
Farren, Mick, 3
Farris, John, 115
Father Exorcist, 19
Fear
　disturbing, 42–44
　gruesome/disgusting, 46–49
　haunting, 39–41
　morbid, 44–46
　terrifying, 49–51
Fear Nothing, 111
Fevre Dream, 82
Fiend, 94
Fight Club (film), 130
Films, 121–22
　from books
　　classic, 123–25
　　cult classics, 130
　　mainstream, 128–30
　　modern, 125–27

Films (*Cont.*)
    remakes, 127
        slasher, 127–28
    original
        classics, 131–32
        cult classics, 138–40
        mainstream, 136–38
        modern, 132–34
        remakes, 135
        slasher, 135–36
Fires of Eden, The, 76
Flame in Byzantium, A, 95
Flesh Gothic, 32
Floating Dragon, 5
Flowers in the Attic, 39
Ford, Steven, 5
Founding Father of Modern Horror collections, The, 106–7
Four Dark Nights, 51
Fowler, Christopher, 8, 45, 87
Frailty (film), 139
Frankenstein, 114
Frankenstein (film), 124
Franz, Darren, 66
Fraternity, 82
Freaks (film), 139
Freddy vs. Jason, 53
Freeman, Brian, 73
From Hell (film), 128
From the Dust Returned, 28
Funhouse, The: A Novel, 97
Furnace, 14–15
Fury, The, 115
Fury series, The, 115
Futuristic tales, 19, 22, 83–84, 103–4

Gaiman, Neil, 78–79, 101, 118
Galilee: A Romance, 2
Gallagher, Diana G., 17
Garrett, Michael, 34
Garton, Ray, 70
Gates, R. Patrick, 64
Gavin Pierce Novels, 115
Gelb, Jeff, 34
Genesis, 110
Genetic manipulation, 7
Gerald's Game, 73
Ghost in the Eiffel Tower, The, 80–81
Ghost Stories of Henry James, The, 106
Ghost Story, 51
Ghost Story (film), 129
Ghost Train, 66
Ghost Writer, The, 5–6
Ghosts, 6, 7, 24–25, 30, 36, 58, 64, 76, 100, 105, 106, 107, 113. *See also* Haunted houses
Ghosts and Grisly Things, 58
Ginger Snaps (film), 139
Giron, Sephera, 64, 93
God Project, 7
Godzilla: King of the Monsters (film), 131
Goingback, Owl, 58, 66–67
Golden, Christopher, 23, 53
Goliath, 18
Gonzales, J. F., 31
Good House, The: A Novel, 20
Goon, 96–97
Gore, 30–33
Gorman, Ed, 110
Gothique: A Vampire Novel, 72
Grant, Charles L., 18, 110
Grave Markings, 31
Gray, Muriel, 14–15
Great and Terrible Beauty, A, 81
Great and Terrible Beauty series, The, 81
Green Man, The, 100
Green Mile, The (film), 129
Green Mile, The: A Novel in Six Parts, 21

Index ⊃ 173

Green Tea and Other Ghost Stories, 40–41
Greenberg, Martin H., 53
Gresham, Stephen, 82
Griffiths, W. G., 115
<u>Grigori Trilogy,</u> 91
Gruber, Michael, 17
Guardian Angel, 78
Gursick, Sara, 58–59
Gustainis, Justin, 31

Hades Project, The, 31
Haining, Peter, ed, 64
Halloween (film), 135–36
Halloween Man, The, 52
Halloween-related, 52–54
Hallows Eve, 54
Hambly, Barbara, 108
Hamilton, Laurell K., 111
Hamlet II: Ophelia's Revenge, 75
Hand, Elizabeth, 67, 101, 118
Hand, Stephen, 53
Hannibal, 50, 96
Hannibal (film), 129
<u>Hannibal Lector Novels, The,</u> 50, 96
Harbaugh, Karen, 34
Hardy, Robin, 76
Harper, Andrew, 32
Harper, M. A., 64
Harris, Charlaine, 111
Harris, Thomas, 50, 96
Harrison, Kim, 84
<u>Harrow Academy Series, The,</u> 53
Harvest Home, 25
Harwood, John, 5–6
Haunted, 45–46
Haunted houses, 63–66, 69, 106, 118. *See also* Ghosts
Haunter, 47
Haunting, The (film), 125
Haunting of Hill House, The, 65
Hautala, Rick, 66

Hawthorne, Nathaniel, 59
Headhunter, 48
Heck, Victor, 46
Hell House, 65–66
Hellbound Heart, The, 102
Hellraiser (film), 130
Herbert, James, 18
Hidden World, The, 79–80
High Tension (film), 136
Hilgar, Ronald S., 84
Historical characters, 90–92
Historical crossovers, 160–61
Historical tales, 80–83
Hodgson, William Hope, 59
Hoffman, Nina Kiriki, 105
Holder, Nancy, 47
Holland, David, 112
Holland, Tom, 93
Hooper, Kay, 56
Hopkins, Brian A., 89
Horror Show, 111
Hotel California, The, 60
Hotel Transylvania: A Novel of Forbidden Love, 77
Hotter Blood, 34
Hottest Blood, 34
Houarner, Gerard, 32
Houdini's Last Illusion, 92
House of Bones, 40
House of 1000 Corpses (film), 139
House of Pain, 64
House of Seven Gables, The, 59
House of Thunder, The, 6
House on Orchid Street, The, 59
Huff, Tanya, 89
Hunger, The (film), 130
Hunted Past Reason, 74
<u>Hunter's Moon series,</u> 4
Huysmans, J. K., 103

I, Vampire, 94
<u>I, Vampire Series, The,</u> 94

I Am Legend, 103–04
I Spit On Your Grave (film), 139
Ignored, The, 21
Immortals, 5, 28, 83, 93. *See* also Vampires
In a Glass Darkly, 41
In Dark Places, 57
In Silent Graves, 52
In the Face of Death, 92
In the Shadow of the Arch, 72
In This Skin, 64
Incredible Shrinking Man, The (film), 124
Incubus, 40
Indifference of Heaven, The (see *In Silent Graves,* 52)
Insomnia, 108
Intensity, 57
Interview with the Vampire, 113
Interview with the Vampire (film), 125
Invasion of the Body Snatchers (film), 131
Invisible Man, The (film), 124–25
It, 50

J. D.'s Revenge (film), 139
Jackson, Shirley, 65, 103, 106
Jacob, Charlee, 47
Jacobs, David, 10–11
Jago, 101
James, Henry, 106
James, M. R., 40
Jaws, 73
Jefferson, Jemiah, 34, 94
Jewel of Seven Stars, The, 41
Jinn, 83
Joe Keough Novels, 72
Johnson, Adam, 29
Johnson, Scott A., 65
Johnstone, William W., 47

Jonathan Barrett: Gentleman Vampire, 81, 110
Jonathan Barrett: Gentleman Vampire series, 81, 110
Journal of Professor Abraham Van Helsing, The, 11, 112–13
Judgement of the Witch, 82
Jurassic Park: A Novel, 16

Kahn, James, 65
Kalogridis, Jeanne, 11
Karamesines, P. G., 67
Kemske, Floyd, 29
Ketchum, Jack, 76, 87, 96
Khai of Ancient Khem, 82
Kiernan, Caitlin R., 73
Kihn, Greg, 111
Kilpatrick, Nancy, 15
Kimball, Michael, 45
King, Stephen, 4, 6, 21, 50, 67, 73, 87–88, 89–90, 103, 108, 112
King Kong (film), 131
Klavan, Andrew, 76
Klein, T. E. D., 118
Knight, Amarantha (pseud. of Nancy Kilpatrick), 11
Knight, H. R., 91
Koja, Kathe, 103
Koko, 9
Koontz, Dean, 6, 9, 16, 17, 18–19, 23, 29, 47, 55, 56, 57, 60, 67–68, 79, 108, 111, 115–16, 116
Korn, M. F., 9
Kupfer, Allen C., 11, 112–13

La-Bas (*Down There*), 103
Laidlaw, Marc, 4
Laimo, Michael, 73–74
Lake, The, 60–61
Land of the Dead (film), 137
Langston, Alistair, 113

Lansdale, Joe R., 29, 88
Last Motel, The, 54
Last Voice They Hear, The, 86
Laughing Man, 7
Laws, Stephen, 23
Laymon, Richard, 54, 60–61, 74, 118–19
Le Fanu, Joseph Sheridan, 40–41
LeBlanc, Deborah, 68
Lee, Edward , 32, 65, 79, 91, 94, 96–97, 116
Lee, Tanith, 79
Leech, 83
Legacies, 90
Legend of the Wolf series, The, 2–3
LeRoux, Gaston, 119
Levin, Ira, 71, 106
Lewis, Matthew ("Monk"), 34–35
Licking Valley Coon Hunters Club, The, 89
Lifetime Employment, 29
Light at the End, The, 48
Lightning, 79
Ligotti, Thomas, 36–37
Lilith's Dream: A Tale of the Vampire Life, 17
Linden Hills, 37–38
Literary crossovers, 161–62
Little, Bentley, 21, 37, 45, 51, 70, 88
Living Blood, The, 75
Living Blood Series, The, 20, 75
Lonardo, Paul, 71
Long Lost, The, 14
Longest Single Note, The, 86–87
Looking Glass, 66
Lord of the Dead: The Secret History of Byron, 93
Lord of the Dead series, 93
Lord of the Vampires, 11
Lortz, Richard, 6
Lost, The, 96
Lost Boys, 49–50

Lost Boys, The (film), 133
Lost Souls, 100
Lottery and Other Stories, The, 103
Love in Vein: Twenty Original Tales of Vampire Erotica, 33–34
Lovecraft, H[oward] P[ierce], 106–7
Lovely Bones, 114
Lovers Living, Lovers Dead, 6
Lucas, Tim, 11
Lullaby, 24
Lumley, Brian , 21, 82
Lust Lizard of Melancholy Cove, The, 30
Lycanthropes and Leeches, 72

M. (film), 131
Machen, Arthur, 43
Madonna of the Dark. See Dark Desire
Mailman, The, 45
Mammoth Book of Haunted House Stories, The, 64
Maniacs. *See* Psychopaths
Manitou, The, 24
Manor, The, 66
Mantra, The, 77
Many Faces of Van Helsing, The, 10
Marano, Michael, 107
Marffin, Kyle, 72
Marquis de Sade series, 35
Martin, George R. R., 82
Massey, Brandon, 68
Massie, Elizabeth, 74, 108
Masters, Paul, 24
Masterton, Graham , 24, 41, 79, 79–80, 90, 109
Matheson, Richard, 43, 45, 65–66, 74, 103–4
Matthews, A. J. (pseud. of Rick Hautala), 66
Maturin, Charles Robert, 119

Mayfair Witch Series, The, 54
McBean, Brett, 54
McCabe, Patrick, 97, 109
McCammon, Robert R., 4, 15, 82
McCrann, Michael, 97
McGrath, Patrick, 113
Meca and the Black Oracle, 24
Medical thrillers, 5, 24, 162
Meh'Yam, 107–08
Melmoth the Wanderer, 119
Memnoch the Devil, 21
Merrick, 113
Messenger, 116
Metz, Melinda, 109
Michaels, Barbara, 91
Midnight, 23
Midnight Café, The, 111
Midnight Sun, 100
Midnight Tableau, 97
Midnight Voices, 24–25
Midwinter of the Spirit, 119–20
Millennium Quartet, The, 18
Mine, 15
Minion, The, 71
Mischief, 53
Misery, 88
Misery (film), 125–26
Mist and Stone: An Original Novel, 17
Mitchell, Mary Ann, 15, 35
Monahan, Brent, 37
Monk, The, 34–35
Monster (film), 133
Monster killers, 89–90
Monster makers, 86–89, 114
Monsters, 92–95
    classic, 10–11, 93
Monteleone, Thomas, 12
Mood/atmosphere, 27
    comic, 27–30
    erotic, 33–35
    frightening/disturbing/disgusting, 38–52
    gory, 30–32
    holiday-related, 52–57
    intellectual, 36–38
    travel-related, 59–61
    uncertainty, 58–59
Moonlit Road and Other Ghost and Horror Stories, The, 36
Moore, Christopher, 29–30, 30, 55
Moore, Elaine, 35
Moore, James A., 116
Moran, Tom, 70
Morrison, Toni, 37
Mortality, 5
Mr. Murder, 9
Mr. X, 43–44
Mulengro, 75
Mummy, The (film, 1931), 131
Mummy, The (film, 1999), 135
Murcheston: The Wolf's Tale, 112
My Soul to Keep, 20
My Work Is Not Yet Done: Three Tales of Corporate Horror, 36–37

Nachmanoff, Jeffrey, 19–20
Nadja (film), 139–40
Naomi, 78
Nassie, Joseph M., 51
Natural disasters, 19–20
Nature on a rampage, 31
Naylor, Gloria, 37–38
Nazareth Hill, 49
Necromancer, The, 53
Necropolis, 80
Necroscope, 21
Necroscope series, The, 21
Needful Things, 67
Needing Ghosts, 112
Neiderman, Andrew, 70
Neighborhood, The, 69

Index ⊃ 177

Neighborhood Watch, 70
Neverwhere, 118
New Neighbor, The, 70
<u>New Tales of the Vampire series</u>, 82
Newman, Kim, 12, 55–56, 84, 101
Nichols, Leigh (pseud. of Dean Koontz), 117
Nicholson, Scott, 15, 66
Night Chills, 23
Night Class, The, 43
Night Fires, 34
Night of the Hunter (film), 129
Night of the Living Dead (film, 1968), 133
Night of the Living Dead (film, 1990), 135
Night Mayor, The, 84
Night Witch, 7
Nightmare Chronicles, The, 50
Nightmare Factory, The, 36
Nightmare on Elm Street (film), 136
No Sanctuary, 74
Northanger Abbey, 28
Nosferatu (film), 125
Nykanen, Mark, 97

Oates, Joyce Carol, 104
Obsession, 8
Odd Thomas, 47
Offbeat: Uncollected Stories, 43
Old English Barron, The, 119
Omen, The (film), 126
Once Upon a Halloween, 54
One Against the World: A Ghost Story, 58–59
One Dark Night, 22
One Hour Photo (film), 137
100 Hair-Raising Little Horror Stories, 53
One Safe Place, The, 75
Onions, Oliver, 41
Ordinary Horror, 70

Other, The, 102
Other worlds, 77–80
Other Worlds, 91
Others, The (film), 137
Othersyde, 97
Out of the Dark: Diversions, 42
Out of the Dark: Origins, 42
Overnight, The, 36

Pacing
  fast, 115–17
  plodding, 117–20
Painfreak, 32
Palahniuk, Chuck, 24, 45–46
Palindrome Hannah, 13
Palmer, Michael, 24
Pandora, 82
Paperhouse (film), 140
Paranormal, 21, 23, 84, 102. *See also* Visions/ESP
Parasites Like Us, 29
Partridge, Norman, 90
Passion, The, 3
Peeping Tom (film), 140
Pelan, John, 12, 96–97
People Under the Stairs, The, (film), 140
Phantom Feast, 92
Phantom of the Opera, The, 119
Phantoms, 108
Piccirilli, Tom, 43
Pictograph Murders, The, 67
Picture of Dorian Gray, The, 120
Pike, Christopher, 80
Plot types
  adaptations, 10–13
  complex, 2–5
  dark human emotions/possession, 8–10, 33, 34
  twists, 5–7
  unique storylines, 13–15
Poe, Edgar Allan, 46

Policy, The, 88
Polidori, John, 119
Poltergeist, 65
Poltergeist (film), 134
<u>Polgergeist, the Legacy Series</u>, 65
<u>Poltergeist Series, The</u>, 65
Portent, The, 18
Possession, 8–10, 33, 87, 103, 120
Possessions, 116
Powers, Tim, 61, 91–92
Practical Demonkeeping, 30
Prescott, Michael, 57
Presence, The, 74
Preston, Douglas, 94
Prey, 41
Priest, Jack, 7
Prison, The, 64
Psychic detectives, 89–90, 110
Psychopaths, 7, 12, 18, 31, 32, 74, 92–98, 105, 113. *See also* Serial killers
Punish the Sinners, 68
Purity, 8
Puzzleman, 8
Psycho, 95
Psycho (film), 128

Queen of the Damned (film), 126
Queen of the Damned, The, 109
Quorum, The, 55–56

Rachmaninoff's Ghost, 9
Radyshevsky, Dmitrv, 77
Randisi, Robert J., 72
Reaves, Michael, 12
Rebecca, 87
Rebecca (film), 129
Red, 87
Red Angel, 32
Red Dragon, 50

Red World of Polaris: The Adventures of Captain Volmar, 84
Relic, The, 94
<u>Relic Series, The</u>, 94
<u>Repairman Jack series</u>, 90
Resume with Monsters, 30
Return, The (de la Mare), 87
Return, The (Little), 37
Reutter, R., 72
Reeve, Clara, 119
Rhodes, Natasha, 117
Rice, Anne, 7, 21, 41, 54, 82, 83, 101, 109, 113
Rickman, Phil, 68, 77, 119–20
Riders in the Sky, 18
Ring, The (film), 126
Ringu (film), 130
Riverwatch, 51
Romance crossovers, 2, 28, 163
Romkey, Michael, 21–22, 94
Rose Madder, 112
Rosemary's Baby (film), 126
Rubie, Peter, 43
Ryan, Kevin, 12

Sab, The, 102
Sabastian, Stephen, 9
Saberhagen, Fred, 12–13
Safety of Unknown Cities, The, 49
<u>Saint-Germain Chronicles, The</u>, 77
'Salem's Lot, 67
Sanders, Dan, 113–14
Santa Steps Out: A Fairy Tale for Grown-ups, 55
Sarrantonio, Al, 53, 54
Saul, John, 7, 24–25, 68, 68–69, 74, 89, 117
Savile, Steve, 92
Scared Stiff: Tales of Sex and Death, 34

Scary Movie (film), 134
Science fiction crossovers, 163–64
Scotch, Cheri, 4
Scream (film), 136
Searcy, David, 70
Sebold, Alice, 114
Secret Books of Venus, 79
Serial killers, 7, 32, 81, 86, 96, 97, 100, 109. *See also* Psychopaths
Series, 141–55
Servant of the Bones, 83
Servants of Twilight, The, 117
Setting
    alternate universes, 77–80, 112
    cities, 71–72
    exotic locales, 75–77
    haunted houses, 63–66
    other worlds, 77–80
    small towns, 66–69
    suburbs, 69–70
    time, 80–84
    wilderness, 72–75
Shadow Dreams, 108
Shadow Fires, 6
Shadow of the Vampire (film), 137
Shadowland, 59
Shadows, 117
Shadows over Baker Street, 12
Shaffer, Anthony, 76
Shannon, Damian, 53
Shattered, 60
Shattered Glass, 2
She Wakes, 76
Sheehan, K., 19
Shelley, Mary, 114
Shining, The, 103
Shining, The (film), 126
Shirley, John., 19, 32, 48
Signs (film), 137–38
Silence of the Lambs, The, 96

Silence of the Lambs, The (film), 129
Silent Children, 56
Silver Wolf, The, 2–3
Simmons, Dan, 4–5, 51, 76, 77
Sineater, 74
Siodmak, Curt, 46
Sips of Blood, 35
Siren's Call, 35
Sisters of the Night Series, 13
Sixth Sense, The (film), 138
Skipp, John, 48, 72
Slade, Michael, 32, 48
Slain in the Spirit, 57
Sleep Walk, 68–69
Sleepy Hollow (film), 126–27
Sliver, 71
Small towns, 66–69
Smith, Clark Ashton, 84
Smith, James Russell, 22
Society, The, 24
Solomon's Brood, 9
Son of Frankenstein (film), 132
Song of Kali, 77
Sonja Blue series, 110
Soul Temple, 115
Southern Vampire Series, The, 111
Spanky, 8
Speaks the Nightbird, 82
Speaks the Nightbird series, 82
Special X series, 48
Spector, Craig, 48, 72
Spellman, Cathy Cash, 19
Spencer, William Browning, 30
Spider, 113
Spider (film), 130
Splatterpunk, 164–65
Stableford, Brian, 94–95
Stalking Tender Prey, 91
Stand, The, 4
Steffan, Elizabeth, 91
Stepfather, The (film), 136

Stepford Wives, The, 106
Stepford Wives, The (film), 127
Stevenson, Robert Louis, 9
Stigmata (film), 134
Stir of Bones, A, 105
Stoker, Bram, 41, 114
Stone, Del, Jr, 19
Straczynski, Michael J., 97
Strangers, 60
Strangewood, 23
Straub, Peter, 5, 9, 43–44, 51, 59, 89–90
Stress of Her Regard, The, 91–92
Strieber, Whitley, 17, 19–20
Stupidest Angel: A Heartwarming Tale of Christmas Terror, The, 55
Sub Rosa, 117–18
Suburbs, 69–70
Summer of Night, 51
Sunglasses after Dark, 110
Supernatural (film), 132
Swan Song, 4
Swift, Mark, 53

Taking, The, 18–19
Tale of the Body Thief, The, 7
Tales from the Hood (film), 134
Talisman Series, The, 89–90
Taylor, Karen E., 35
Taylor, Lucy, 49
Technology/science misused/gone wrong, 4, 5, 7, 16, 18, 23, 38, 83, 113, 116
Tem, Melanie, 57
Ten Ounce Siesta, The, 90
Terminator, The (film), 134
Terrible Beauty, A, 109
Terror and Other Stories, The, 43
Texas Chainsaw Massacre, The (film), 136
Thank You for the Flowers, 15

Thing on the Doorstep and Other Weird Stories, The, 106–7
37th Mandala, The, 4
This Symbiotic Fascination, 47
Thorne, Tamara, 20
Three Imposters and Other Stories, The, 43
Threshold: A Novel of Deep Time, 73
Thunder Road, 20
Ticktock, 29
Tideland, 44–45
Time, 80–84
Touching Evil, 56
Travel Many Roads, 38
Travel-related tales, 59–61
Traveling Vampire Show, The, 118–19
Traveling with the Dead, 108
Tropic of Night, 17
Truth and Consequences, 55
Tryon, Thomas, 25, 102
Tulpa, 22
28 Days Later (film), 134
Twilight Eyes, 23
Tyrant, The, 16

Uncanny, The, 76
Undead and Unwed, 28–29
Undead Series, The, 28–29
Underland, 3
Underworld (film), 127
Universal Monsters Series, The, 10–11

Valentine's Day–related, 55–56
Vampire Chronicles, The, 21, 101
Vampire Files, The, 110
Vampire hunters, 71, 89–90, 108, 111, 113, 114, 117
Vampire Huntress Legend series, 71
Vampire Legacy, The, 35

Vampire Tapestry, The, 105
Vampires, 2, 3, 4, 7, 10, 11, 12, 12, 15, 16, 17, 19, 20, 21–22, 28–29, 29–30, 33, 34, 35, 68, 71, 72, 76, 77, 82, 89, 93, 94, 95, 100, 101, 102, 103–4, 109, 110, 111, 113, 114, 119
Vampyre. See *Lord of the Dead: The Secret History of Byron*
Vampyre and Other Tales of the Macabre, The, 119
Vampyrrhic, 3
Van Helsing, 12
VanderMeer, Jeff, 84
Velocity, 116
Veniss Underground, 84
Victims, 86–89
Victor Renquist Novels, The, 3
Victoria Nelson Novels, 89
Village, The (film), 138
Village of the Damned (film), 132
Violin, 41
Vision, The, 55
Visions/ESP, 16, 17, 115, 116. See *also* Paranormal
Vizenore, Gerald, 38
Vlad Tapes, The, 12–13
Vlad Tepes series, 12–13
Voice of the Blood, 94

Waggoner, Tim, 80
Waking Nightmares, 105
Waking the Moon, 101
Walpole, Horace, 104
Warlock: A Novel of Possession, 33
Watchers, 116
Way the Family Got Away, The, 45
We Have Always Lived in the Castle, 106
Weinberg, Robert, 38
Werewolf, 43
Werewolf's Kiss, The, 4

Werewolves, 2–3, 4, 33 ,72, 112
Werewolves of London, The, 94–95
Werewolves of London Trilogy, The, 94–95
West, Owen (pseud. of Dean Koontz), 97
Wetbones, 48
What Lies Beneath (film), 138
What Rough Beast, 91
Wheeler, Robert E., 38
Whispers, 57
White People and Other Tales, The, 43
White Zombie (film), 1932
Wicker Man, The, 76
Wicker Man, The (film), 140
Wieland: or The Transformation: An American Tale and Other Stories, 105
Wildwood Road, 53
Wilde, Oscar, 30, 120
Wilderness, 72–75
Willard (film, 1971), 134
Willard (film, 2003), 135
Williams, Mark, 31
Wilson, F. Paul, 90
Wind Caller, The, 31
Wine Dark Sea, The, 117–18
Wine of Angels, The, 68
Winter Moon, 67–68
Witchcraft, 82. See *also* Black magic
Witching Hour, The, 54
Wolf Man, The (film), 132
Wolfe, Ron, 38
Women of the Otherworld series, 33
Wooley, John, 10, 38
Wounds, 34
Wright, T. M., 7, 59
Wuthering Heights, 118
Wyndham, John, 22
Wyrm, The, 23

Yarbro, Chelsea Quinn, 13, 77, 92, 95
Year of Past Things: A New Orleans Ghost Story, The, 64
You Come When I Call You, 58

Young adult crossovers, 165–66
Young Frankenstein (film), 135

Zinger, Steve, 102
Zombie, 104

About the Authors

JUNE MICHELE PULLIAM and **ANTHONY J. FONSECA** are authors of the award-winning *Hooked on Horror* (Libraries Unlimited, 1999) and *Hooked on Horror II* (Libraries Unlimited, 2003). June is Instructor of English and Women's and Gender Studies, Louisiana State University, Baton Rogue, where she also teaches a class on horror fiction. Tony is Head of Serials/Electronic Resources Librarian at Nicholls State University in Louisiana. Both have contributed entries to *Supernatural Literature of the World: An Encyclopedia* and *The Dictionary of Literary Biography: Asian American Writers*. In addition, they co-edit the online quarterly journal *Necropsy: The Review of Horror Fiction* (www.lsu.edu/necrofile).